real perfect
An Unscripted Hearts Novel

lyr gray

crow haven publishing

To opposites who attract, enemies who become lovers, and anyone who's ever fallen for the absolute wrong person who turned out to be exactly right.

one

. . .

Esme

Esme tugged at the scratchy paint-splattered apron tied around her neck. The paint instructor chirped into her microphone like a deranged songbird; her demonstration canvas flawless. Esme loaded her paintbrush with what was supposed to be poppy red, but it looked more akin to crime-scene crimson. In fact, her whole field of poppies looked like flower murder victims and none of it resembled the instructor's poppy perfection.

Around her, date-night couples giggled and painted matching landscapes. A woman at the next easel flashed an engagement ring the size of a small planet while her friends squealed and took seventeen photos for Instagram. Three months ago, she'd been engaged too. Now she was single and jobless. Surrounded by love and an overly enthusiastic art instructor who praised the 'unique artistic vision of her Friday night lovebirds'. The universe had an unruly sense of humor. At least her murder poppies were authentic.

Girls' night out was supposed to be fun. Light. Something Esme needed.

But nope. Girls' night out was torture.

"You know what you need, Esme? Revenge sex." Alex's voice echoed and she may as well have shouted to the entire art studio, because now all eyes turned their way.

Choking on the sip of cabernet sauvignon she had just swallowed, Esme ignored the suggestion and took another stab at her canvas. Paint continued to drip haphazardly down the floral massacre like blood.

"I'm serious." Alex stared earnestly at Esme from her perch

on the adjacent stool. "I read the suggestion in a magazine article about moving on from relationships with cheaters."

Summer, sitting on Esme's other side, sniffed. "Ew. Alex, that is the grossest and worst idea I've ever heard. I thought prima ballerinas were supposed to be classy. You're the crassest one I've ever met."

Alex laughed and her paintbrush swept past Esme's nose as she pointed it at Summer. "I'm the only ballerina you've ever met."

Summer narrowed her eyes. "Point taken. Oh, I know!"

Esme jumped and bit back a squeak as Summer clapped her hands and bounced on her stool as though she suddenly believed in fairies. "Esme, what you need is a vacation somewhere beautiful, like Hawaii or New Zealand, where you can meet a handsome stranger on the beach and have a summer fling. That would be so romantic." Sighing dreamily, she dabbed more paint on her stunning, gallery perfect, field of poppies.

Alex coughed. "Only it's winter in New Zealand, but whatever. A winter ski fling would work too."

A sharp glance and a shush from the instructor had Alex's attention back on her canvas. Esme set her paintbrush down in defeat and looked around at the sea of canvases surrounding them. Nothing would rescue her tableau, which she was going to call *Field of Death*. Just like her career. Funny, art did imitate life.

She didn't blame her friends for trying to cheer her up. Alex had taken leave from the New York City Ballet and flown all the way to California to support her on the night when they should have been in New York City dancing on tables, a fake veil pinned to her head and a light-up penis necklace around her neck. Instead, Esme sat in front of an easel in a paint-splattered apron, breathing in the charming scent of turpentine.

Ever since Esme had arrived back in California over a month ago, Summer had been glued to her side, ever vigilant and supportive. Esme's lifelong friend was a quirky new-age superstar who dished out advice on everything from home décor to fashion on a local morning radio show. Summer also owned a popular local boutique, where she designed and sold one-of-a-kind, handmade clothing pieces. But instead of suggesting retail therapy to take Esme's mind off the bachelorette-party-not-meant-to-be, she'd made reservations at a BYOW—bring your own wine—paint studio. Too bad it wasn't working.

Esme took another deep drink from her wineglass, the warm liquid pooling in her belly. It swirled around in a bubbly dance. "What if I said I had the opportunity to spend the summer in a private beach house competing to find a match for the country's absolute most single bachelor?"

Alex turned sharply on her stool and examined Esme's face. "I'd ask 'what's the catch,' because that pitch sounded utterly miserable and you look like you might throw up."

Summer squealed, cutting Alex off. "That's amazing, Esme!"

Fighting her first smile of the evening, Esme drained the wineglass. "I got a call earlier this week offering me the opportunity to spend six weeks over the summer as a contestant on a new reality show. The catch"—Esme reached for her bag and pulled out a book, setting it face down on the art cart next to her easel—"is him." She resisted the urge to pick up her brush, dip it in black paint, and give the author's photo a childish makeover sporting bushy eyebrows and a villainous mustache.

"Now that guy is perfect for revenge sex." Alex peered at the photo. "Are his eyes green or blue? It's hard to tell, but they are seriously stunning. Sun-kissed hair, perfect lips, and amazing teeth. Sorry, Esme, I don't understand the problem."

Summer took a more tactful approach. Gently clearing her throat, she reached for the book and turned it over to read the cover. "Ah, I see the problem. Catchy title though. *Players: How to Mingle and Stay Single.*" One side of her mouth tilted up in a sympathetic smile. "He's the eligible bachelor?"

"Yep. Zack MacKenzie, the stupid mind behind that fantastic piece of literature." She seethed at the author's photo on the back of the book Summer held and poured herself another glass of wine.

Zack MacKenzie had done nothing but make a mockery of Esme's field of work. As a professional matchmaker and dating coach, her mission was to help people fall in love forever, and Zack was out there spreading a message of how great one-night hookups are and holding workshops teaching other guys the secrets of being a pickup artist. If she could tame that man and set him up with the love of his life, it could resurrect her career. Which would land differently if her own life weren't a cautionary tale and New York's favorite matchmaker didn't look like a fraud online.

Three months ago, her ex-fiancé, Clayton, had been photographed kissing her personal assistant, Luke. Not only had the story broken on Page Six of the *New York Post*, but soon Tik-Tok was aflame with gossip and meanness. Her reputation as New York's go-to girl for love and relationship advice was irreparably tarnished. Speaking engagements dried up, and clients stopped returning calls and booking appointments. With no other choice, she'd moved back to Pasadena, California. Her mother and grandmother's offer of a place to stay was helping stretch her savings while she figured out what to do. Esme avoided social media at all costs to keep her sane.

"So, what's in it for you?" Alex stood and stretched, feet in perfect first position. You could take the ballerina out of the ballet, but you couldn't take the ballet out of the ballerina. "You said you'd be a contestant, which means there is a contest."

"The contest is a reality TV show about dating. A half million-dollar prize is at stake. I could use the money to relaunch myself on the West Coast. Mimsy, the tea-leaf reading wonder grandmother, offered me a chance to buy into her matchmaking business, and that money would go a long way toward marketing and adding online systems." Esme grabbed the book from Summer's hands and stuffed it back into her bag. "The show is scheduled to start Monday, which only gives me one day to prepare."

Summer aimed a glare at Alex, then threw her arms around Esme's neck. "Seriously, what a fantabulous opportunity. You can show the whole country, no, you can show whole world how great you are at what you do!" Holding Esme out at arm's length, Summer eyed her apron and plain black T-shirt and jeans. "I can help you pack. I will pull some pieces from the store for you to wear! We'll spiff up your wardrobe and get your hair done. Everyone is going to love you!"

She untangled herself from Summer's embrace and stood up, her stool making a loud screech as it scooted across the floor. She shot the instructor, who was wrapping up class, an apologetic smile and picked up her paint supplies to take them over to the sink area.

"But that's just it," said Esme. "What if I'm a complete failure? I hate having the spotlight on me and I'm positive my career will not recover from another public disaster." Washing her hands in the paint-splattered sink, she shook her head. "But I don't see any other options. It's either that or live with Mom and Mimsy for the rest of my life. Oh, I know! I could set up shop reading tarot cards and making love charms for people, like I did in college."

Alex pumped soap into her hands and frowned at Esme. "Now you're just being silly. I'm sure Summer could get you some guest spots on her show, and you could work with some of Mimsy's clients, since it sounds like she's willing. Build your business back up slowly." She tore off a paper towel from the automatic dispenser. "Besides, you still haven't said what you have to do for the contest." Her tone dripped with accusation.

Esme slipped the apron provided by the studio off over her head and went to the hooks on the wall to hang it up. She met Alex's glare. "Zack and I each have to coach other contestants on their dating techniques as they work to identify their perfect match among the people living in the house. We propose matches each week to see who's right. She grabbed her tote bag from the floor. So basically, I help people find real love while Zack teaches them manipulation tactics. Whoever figures out the matches first proves their technique works. No pressure."

"Esmeralda Adams!" Alex hung her apron up with a huff and spun back to her. "I don't know, this thing sounds sketchy. Part of me is standing here cheering because the best thing you could do is put yourself out there and get a bit wild, putting stupid Cluke behind you. But I'm worried about you. If you lose, this could be no different from New York. I will fly back out here and pick you up and feed you ice cream and cookies, but I'd rather not have to do that again."

Summer slipped an arm through hers. "So, don't lose! You've got this. For as long as I've known you, all you have ever done is watch, observe, and find the perfect dates for everyone. Your former clients all tell stories of success. Plus, you come from a long line of matchmakers who spread good love juju. And, if you lose, you could always sell those love charms you used to make."

"Love juju? Is that a technical term?" She squeezed Summer back, her tone as light as the tinkling bell on the door as they exited the building. "I didn't realize there is a market for love charms."

Summer giggled. "It's called Etsy."

"Which reminds me…" Alex dug around in her handbag and hooted in triumph. She held up a silver necklace with a heart charm dangling from her fingers. "Look what I found. I thought maybe you could use a little extra help."

Alex poured the necklace into Esme's hand. The chain pooled and rolled as she shifted it in her palm. "Wow, I haven't seen this for years."

Alex grinned and executed a pirouette. Esme smiled. She'd missed the random dance moves Alex busted out when she couldn't contain her excitement.

"Here, help me put it on?" Esme held up her hair, and

Summer fastened the necklace around her neck, where it settled with a comforting weight. In college, Esme had gone through a phase of embracing her roots, practicing love spells of the Romany people. Descended from a long line of matchmakers—the talent only skipping over her mother—the drive to champion love was in her blood. Now she used a combination of gut instinct and a series of data points refined over the years to work her particular brand of magic. The idea of going on national television and essentially winging it based on random dates among strangers was terrifying. But all she had to do was play along and do her best to avoid Zack at all costs.

She held her painting up in the streetlight and tilted her head. Swallowing hard, she pushed the fear of failure back down from where it crept up from her stomach. "So, girls, my only choice is to say yes. Because I'm confident my future as an artist began and ended right here tonight at the Paint and Sip studio."

two

. . .

Zack

SURFING. Lingerie shopping with his sister. Being eaten alive by one thousand zombie squirrels. Zack ran through a mental list of everything he'd rather be doing than walking into the shiny chrome and glass lobby of Marcum/Tidwell Productions. The network offices smelled too corporate, dominated by the scents of new carpet, old coffee, and greed. A month ago, when reality TV's sharkiest producer, Olivia Marcum, had offered him the chance of competing in a reality television show that could propel his career forward as a life coach and make him recognizable to a young, hip audience with little effort on his part, saying yes had been a no-brainer.

A production assistant stumbled up to the elevators, arms loaded with equipment cases stacked to her chin. She tried to hit the call button but couldn't reach it. "Hey, let me get that for you." He punched the button.

"Oh my god, thank you!" She blinked up at him, clearly not expecting help. "Olivia's already fired three people this week and I'm pretty sure dropping a ten-thousand-dollar camera would make me number four." The top case teetered when she spoke.

He steadied the stack and grabbed the top two cases. "Where are you headed?"

"Second floor. But you don't have to—"

"I'm going up anyway." He held the elevator door with his shoulder. "After you."

Two minutes later, he'd helped her unload on the second

floor. The elevator climbed to eight and he stepped out, alone with his thoughts again.

The network's glass-walled conference room held a table for eight, the window wall to his right pouring in the day's glare. Zack studied the array of pastries and beverages artfully laid out across the granite countertop that spanned the back of the room and took a chair halfway down the long side of the table closest to the windows. He angled it a notch toward the view. People thought his profession was strange, but life as a pickup artist and self-help author was nothing compared to the life of television producers. But they did have one thing in common: proficiency in the Art of Wooing.

He swiveled his leather chair back and forth as he slipped a pocket-worn journal from his jacket and thumbed through pages of his father's neat, square handwriting.

'07: Let Z borrow the BMW for Heat #1. ROI: 1 broken mirror. 3 proud texts.

'15: Flew to Kona after the knee. ROI: tacos, stubborn hope.

'19: Co-signed Z's stake in Jake's club. ROI: he'll find his lane.

Buzz.

Buzz.

Buzzzzzz.

His phone lit up.

Dad: *Dr. Chen patient portal update is available*

He flipped the phone face down so it would stop judging him.

Olivia breezed through the door. Her shoulder-length brown hair and bluntly cut bangs gave her a sophisticated edge and helped shave a few years off the approach to fifty. She wore tailored black pants and a sleeveless white blouse. Olivia circled the far end, skimmed a fingertip along the chairbacks and dropped into the chair next to his. Closer than across. The kind of distance that sells a yes. She ran a bold hand up his thigh. So that's how they were going to play it. Wicked and flirty. Game on.

"Zack, I wasn't expecting to see you in here today. Did you get the package I had couriered over to you? You could have just sent the contracts back; there was no need to bring them yourself." Her expression shifted into practiced unpleasantness, and she tilted her head at the manila file folder on the table in front of him. "Although I'm not going to complain; it is nice to see you."

He cleared his throat and, doing his best not to shudder at the squeeze she gave his leg, Zack opened the folder. Notched up his own smile. Gently grasped her forearm, giving it a little squeeze. "Olivia, when you pitched the idea of the show to me, I thought the premise was that I'd be competing against one or more of my peers. You know, other PUAs." At her blank look, he explained, "Pickup artists?"

"Ah." She stood and walked to the counter to pour a glass of fruit-infused water from a sweating pitcher. He shook his head when she offered it to him. With a shrug, she sat down across from him and took a long drink from the glass. "I never said you would be competing against other pickup artists, Zacky. I said it was someone from your industry."

Triumph blazed through his veins. He had her now. He pulled out a headshot from the folder and slapped it down on the center of the table. "Esmeralda Adams is not from my industry. Hell, I don't even have an industry, what I have is a following. I teach other dudes how to do what I do. Guys want to be me." He ran a hand through his hair.

When he'd shown the picture to his workout buddy and longtime friend, Jake Preston, at the gym, Jake had immediately hit up Google. Zack's competition not only wasn't one of his fellow PUAs, but she was an experienced matchmaker and dating coach—whatever that was—from the East Coast. Dozens of keynote speech videos depicted her easy, approachable manner. She'd not only written books but had glowing reviews from what looked like most of Manhattan. Esme Adams had graced talk shows and even hosted a podcast called *Heart Talk*.

Viewers were going to love her. Women were going to identify with her relationship advice, and men were going to drool over her exotic looks.

Her kick-ass hair that tumbled to her shoulders, the sultry green eyes beneath thick lashes, and a generous, kissable mouth captivated Zack the minute he'd seen her picture. Esmeralda Adams was hot. She was a goddess and her features hinted at Middle Eastern roots.

Zack needed to guarantee she couldn't win. He'd spent his life disappointing his critically ill father. Winning this show would provide Zack the ability to show his father he wasn't a total loser in life. So he'd come up with a plan. And now it was time to turn on the Zoom charm. Zoom the Pickup Artist was his alter ego. Some days Zack couldn't determine where Zoom ended and he began anymore.

Shooting Olivia his most winning smile, he let his gaze drift down her arms briefly then float back up to meet her eyes. "Your blouse is really flattering on you. It shows off the definition in your arms. Have you been working out? It's really starting to show. Keep it up." A textbook neg. Just enough compliment given to seem sincere, wrapped around the implication that she needed improvement. "Because you are looking great, Liv."

Olivia raised an eyebrow and ran a hand up her other arm. Zack doubted she even realized she'd done it. "Yes, actually I've been taking a Pilates class at a new studio here in Glendale."

"Nice. Maybe I should check those classes out, get in shape myself." Zack stretched an arm behind his head, absolutely aware the bicep ripple would catch her eye.

Olivia laughed. "Right, like you need to get in shape. You're already the perfect specimen. Our viewers are going to go wild over you."

Bingo. Olivia had just offered him the perfect segue. "About the show, Liv, the reason I'm here today is because I have a business proposition for you." Zack pushed his chair back and crossed the few steps to the glass. The city lay stacked under his reflection. Sun glinted off the rows of parked cars below. He faced her and leaned against the windowsill, oozing casual. "What if we made a little wager? I take actions on the show, make your ratings soar, and in exchange"—he crossed his arms —"you guarantee I win the money and you help me get my own talk show."

He stood still and held his breath. Olivia was either going to love the deviousness of his plan, or she'd throw him out and fire him from the show. If he'd read her right, though, Olivia Marcum would not turn down a chance for manipulation and drama, especially if it meant high viewership.

"Zack! You bad boy. What exactly did you have in mind?" Olivia clapped her hands and brought her fingertips to her lips, watching him with interest.

What did he have in mind? Jake said he'd be crazy to suggest it, but Zack was confident it could work, and it was simple. He'd just get Esmeralda Adams to fall hopelessly in love with him before the end of the show. Although things would get messy when he had to break it off with her after filming ended. The fact that he'd possibly humiliate his costar flickered briefly across his thoughts, but who cared? In his experience, even bad publicity was good. The attention brought opportunities.

"Your whole premise for this show is for Ms. Adams and me to set all the contestants up with the people of their dreams. Perfect matches." Zack returned to his original chair and angled it a fraction toward her and leaned in catching Olivia's eye. "What if I seduce the matchmaker? I'll deliver you the show-mance of your dreams."

Olivias hands hit the table. "Yes! I love this idea. Let's sweeten the deal, shall we? If you don't manage to seduce the matchmaker and you lose, then you'll appear on any reality tele-vision show I choose to cast you in for the next ten years. *Bach-elor in Paradise* knockoffs, dating your ex's mom, whatever I want. And you'll smile doing it."

A chill ran up Zack's spine at the thought of being trapped

with Olivia Marcum calling the shots over his life for the next ten years. But his dad's diagnosis had put things in perspective. How many more years did they have? Zack wanted—no, needed —to show his father he wasn't just a washed-up surfer playing pickup artist. The talk show, the legitimacy, proving he could build something real—could change everything. His dad would finally see him as more than a disappointment. Zoom refused to give in to the fear. He shook her hand and smiled.

"Deal. And Olivia? I never lose."

three

· · ·

Esme

ESME STOOD at the curb on Seaview Drive. The asphalt wore a dusting of the day's sand and the ocean breathed loud enough to count as a neighbor. She picked at the pleats on the front of the red, A-line dress Summer had insisted she wear. From far away, the pattern looked like innocent polka dots, but up close, whimsical, fluffy white sheep danced across the fabric. Sheep-printed dresses and reality television—what had her life become? Her driver plopped her suitcase down on the ground next to her. She eyed it with suspicion. Visions of menagerie-patterned fabrics danced in her head. Her luggage was stuffed full of Summer's favorites, and it was too late to change or repack now.

She took in the crowd of people hovered around the firepit burning in the streetside courtyard of a spectacular-looking beachfront property. Sunset bathed the house in a rosy glow. Raising a brow, she said to the television host, who had accompanied her on the hour-long car ride from LA to Laguna Beach, "Nice house. Now what, Ferris? I thought filming would have already started. I've heard reality shows like to get as many hours of footage as possible so the producers can catch any exciting bits and cut the boring stuff."

Ferris Jenkins fumbled trying to pull his phone from the pocket of his skinny jeans and checked his text messages. With his curly hair and hipster glasses, he oozed a self-deprecating charm, and she found it hard to picture him as a reality television show host.

"Zack's car should be arriving in a few minutes, then I'll

introduce you to the cast. Later, I'll give you a tour of the house and explain the shooting schedule and plan for the next few days." Ferris poked at the phone's screen and put it up to his ear. "Hey, Ben, you need to get your ass down here to the driveway with some cameras before Zack arrives. Olivia is going to want this scene on film for sure."

When he hung up, he jutted a hip out and huffed. "And by the way," he said to her, "we don't manipulate exciting versus boring for ratings or anything. Our editing process simply omits nonessential scenes and focuses on the important events."

An unspoken "duh" hovered so vividly in the air Esme could practically touch it. The amount of frenetic energy that had spilled from the host in the short time she'd known him told her that spending time with Ferris was going to be super fun.

Esme shielded her eyes as the headlights from an approaching car shined in her face. The car pulled up and the driver cut the engine. Ferris danced from foot to foot as he brought his phone to his ear again.

"Where are the cameras? Olivia is going to kill us if we don't get footage from tonight."

Esme spun around at the sound of running footsteps behind her and an out-of-breath, "Here! Cameras are here!" One of the camera-lugging runners was Ben. Turning back to the party scene, she let out a squeak when she almost bumped right into a T-shirt-clad chest. Stepping away, she smoothed a hand down her skirt, while her other hand involuntarily floated up to her hair. She'd practically fallen right into the arms of Zack MacKenzie.

Standing there in a tee that hugged his broad chest and shoulders, board shorts, and flip-flops, he could have been any California surfer off the street. He had sun-streaked brown hair and his twinkling eyes morphed from green to blue, just like in his photo. In person, his model-handsome face and boyish smile gave her the impression of the guy next door, not America's most famous pickup artist. And this facade, it dawned on her, was what was so dangerous about Zack. He looked safe. Boy-next-door packaging layered over pickup-artist intent. He'd tune himself to your frequency, remember your coffee order and your dog's name. Make it feel like a promise, label it "no strings," ghost the second you leaned in, and swear he'd been clear all along. You didn't know what he was like until it was too late.

"Hi, I'm Zack MacKenzie. You must be Esme." Zack held out a hand, and she clasped it. "Nice dress! The sheep really bring out your eyes, not to mention what it does for those legs, girl. Damn."

He did not just say that to her! What did he even mean? The sheep bring out her eyes? Was he leveraging some tool of his trade? Narrowing said eyes at him, she rallied herself up to her full height—which was an entire foot shorter than Zack—and reclaimed her hand back. "Thanks. How observant of you."

Zack grinned at her hand, which was now back to smoothing over her skirt. "Observation is one of my best qualities, or so I've been told. And I'm observing how amazing that firepit looks and wondering why we're all standing out here on the curb when we could be meeting everyone else."

She watched him saunter off toward the firepit, pulling his suitcase behind him over the decorative cobblestoned patio, and couldn't help but wonder about his other ... qualities. Zack was a well-built man, perfectly proportioned. She stared as the muscles in his arm rippled. Shaking her head, she took hold of her bag and followed, not wanting to be standing alone at the curb with the cameras. The unscripted format was already making her anxious. She needed to get her head in the game and pay attention to what was going on around her. She needed to find a way to keep Zack front and center and the attention off of herself.

Ferris walked with her up the drive, gathered everyone around the firepit, and beamed at the cameras. "Okay, everyone, welcome to the Heart House! What a game we have in store for you! Here's how it's going to roll. Joining us are two experts in the game of love, who will be challenged together each week to match couples up. I'd like to introduce you to your Most Marvelous Matchmaker, Esme Adams, and your Pickup Artist Extraordinaire, Zack MacKenzie." He paused, a cocky grin taking over his face.

"But what is reality TV without a twist? Esme and Zack aren't just experts. They're contestants too. An anonymous matchmaker pre-selected all ten of you into five perfect couples before you ever arrived at this house. And yes, that includes our two experts."

Esme's stomach took a swan dive to the ground. "Wait—we're—"

"Contestants!" Ferris clapped his hands together to get their attention. "That's right. You thought you were running this show? Surprise! You're *in* it. Which means, Esme and Zack, one of you might be matched with someone in this house. Maybe each other … maybe not. But here's where it gets interesting. You two still control the Matching Ceremonies. You'll propose the matches every week, including your own.

"Here's the loop: Tuesdays, the audience votes—one couple to the Love Shack and this week's date locations. Saturdays, we have the Love Shack Ceremony. Sundays, we run the Matching Ceremony. The mystery matchmaker's selections are key and locked into our show's system. When a couple enters the Love Shack, the system checks if they're one of the five true matches. If yes, they're a confirmed Match and must be paired together at Sunday's ceremony. If no, they're a No Match and cannot be paired together."

He paused at the murmurs from the group before continuing. "At the Matching Ceremony on Sundays, Esme locks in five couples first. Then Zack gets one chance to swap up to two her choices and that's it. No backsies. Once Zack's done, the matches are locked for the week. Then we check your proposals against the mystery matchmaker's true matches. Each Heart that lights up means you got one correct couple. Get all five right, you win. Zero hearts? That's a blackout and dings the pot fifty-thousand dollars. Prize is two million dollars total—a million for the experts together, another million for the cast.

"Throughout the week, dates happen. The audience picks who goes out with whom, and what you'll do. Everyone will go on multiple dates over the next six weeks, Esme and Zack included. Think of these as your chance to figure out chemistry, compatibility, who clicks with whom." He shot Esme and Zack a pointed look. "Though there is one rule for our experts: you two can't date each other unless the audience specifically votes you together. Gotta keep some objectivity, right?"

Ferris waited for the clapping and cheering to die down. "Now, Zack, some of these faces may look familiar to you, because the guys are all alumni of the Zack MacKenzie Pickup Artist Academy. We thought it would be fun to see what they've learned."

Esme's heart pounded and her blood pressure started rising. Not only did she have to share a house with Zack but also with five of his protégés? And she had to go on dates with them? Worse, she was a contestant now. One of them could be her match. She fought an urge to look at Zack.

Ferris surveyed his reality show kingdom and continued. "Oh, and one more juicy detail. When a couple gets confirmed as a Match in the Love Shack? Boom! They're whisked away to our romantic honeymoon site for the rest of the show. Which means fewer people in this house, fewer options on the board, and higher stakes every single week. Any questions?"

After several head-shakes and a silent pause, Ferris rubbed his hands together. "All right, now the crew is going to get you all set with microphones, and after a quick round of introductions, we'll let you into the house."

Once everyone was outfitted with a microphone and receiver, Ferris directed the women to stand on one side of the firepit and the men on the other. "Ladies first. Give your name and a quick detail about yourself." He motioned to a slight woman with pigtail braids.

Stepping forward, she waved shyly. "Hi, my name is Molly Wilson and funnily enough, I work as a production assistant on a reality television show. I'll try not to take over!"

She seemed sweet and Esme made a note to remember she worked in reality television in case there were any tips and tricks to be gleaned from her, like how to avoid the cameras and find privacy.

Next, a buxom woman with blonde hair literally bounced to the front. "Hey, I'm Madison Parks. You can call me Maddie if you want, although nobody really does. I am the life of the party and down for anything. I'm a mixologist at a hot nightspot and love being around people."

A lean brunette sidled up beside Madison. "I'm Joy Radcliff. I'm a personal trainer and love extreme sports. I never say no to a challenge!"

Esme could see her adventurous spirit being a good match to Zack's athleticism, if she didn't eat him alive.

The final female contestant was a fiery redhead with a musical laugh. "I'm Isla Murphy! I come from a large, tight-knit Irish family. Every week we have family dinners together and my brothers all try to drink each other under the table. They're everything to me, and I'm going to miss them terribly while we're filming!"

A suitor stepped up on the guys' side of the firepit. Wearing a button-down with the sleeves rolled halfway up his arms, he had dark hair styled just shy of too much hair gel. "Yeah. Hey. I'm Kent Blackstone, sales executive by day and your number one fantasy by night."

Esme fought the urge to roll her eyes and gag. Was he serious? And Madison was already making googly eyes at him.

Next up was a tall, lanky guy with brown hair that flopped into his eyes. "My name is Wesley Ellington. You can call me

Wes. I'm pretty boring and no one's fantasy, just your average computer engineer."

Jumping forward came an energetic guy with shaggy blond locks who looked like he had stolen Zack's surfer look. "Heyyyyyy. Joel McKee. I'm a graphic novel artist and part-time Uber driver and a true believer that art captures the best parts of life. Ladies, I look forward to bringing you to life on the page."

Wait. Had he just said he wanted to draw the women? Yikes.

Madison and Isla were giggling together. "You want to draw us like one of your French girls?"

Joel smirked. "Oh yeah. Anytime, ladies."

A tall, well-muscled guy cleared his throat. "I guess that leaves me. I'm Trey Lewis. Former army paratrooper turned private skydiving instructor. Who wants to take a jump with me?"

Zack clapped Trey on the shoulder. "It's really great to see you guys again." He tilted his chin down in a nod to the women. "Ladies, I'm Zack MacKenzie, and the pleasure of meeting you is all mine."

Ben swung the camera her way. "Hello, I'm Esmeralda Adams, but most people actually call me Esme. I look forward to getting to know each of you better over the next several weeks as we work together."

After the introductions were done, Ferris excused the group to go explore the house. Whooping and cheering, the cast made a beeline for the front door. Esme let the pack go and realized she wasn't alone.

With a wry grin, Zack shrugged and waved her on. "After you, ladies first."

She grabbed the handle of her suitcase with another eye roll and followed everyone, her luggage bouncing over the paver tiles.

Catching up with her, Zack continued. "Seriously, I like your dress. Red is eye-catching. And then you realize the pattern is sheep, which provides a lot of subject matter for discussion. If I ran into you out on the town, it's one of the first things I'd think of to talk to you about."

Esme stopped so fast, Zack almost tripped right over her. Hopping out of his way, she pointed a finger at him. "Is this one of your PUA things? Picking out some feature that stands out and then bothering your prey about it all night long?" Aware of the cameras in her face, she took a deep breath and smiled at Zack. "I like your T-shirt and board shorts. If beach bum was the look you were going for, then you nailed it."

"Whoa, hey, I think we're getting off to a bad start here. And really, prey? It's not like that at all." Zack gently took her arm, shifting so he blocked her path into the house. "You looked so uncomfortable standing there, smoothing down your skirt, I just thought it might make you feel better to know it looked really awesome on you. And we're supposed to be swapping and sharing techniques, right? I was just pointing out that if you wanted to get attention, then that dress would do the trick."

A zing of electricity shot through where Zack held her arm. She looked up into those sparkling, smiling eyes and wondered how many women fell for his goofy grin night after night. Zack was definitely charming; there was no doubt. One of those guys who oozed charisma and self-confidence, and everyone fluttered to them like moths to a flame. Not to mention he smelled really good, all cedar and sea salt.

But not this moth, Esme thought.

Forcing a smile, she nodded to Zack. "Thank you. My friend Summer picked it out. She owns a boutique in LA, and let's just say her tastes run to the quirky side of the spectrum. Eclectic." Esme laughed. "And none of that is really important." Untangling her arm from Zack's grasp, she nodded to the front door. "I'm sure Ferris is anxious to get the house tour filming over with."

"Right." Zack stepped aside and let Esme pass through the front door.

Zack

DAMN. Esme was so cute. And tiny. A powerhouse of snark and humor in a little package. He followed her through the front door, watching the swish-swish of her silly sheep skirt as she walked. Mesmerized, he barely registered Ferris pointing out the layout—Esme and the other girls' bedroom suites upstairs, the guys' bedrooms down the hallway that branched off past the kitchen, communal spaces on the main floor, and some production sets tucked into the lower level.

Dorky Ferris led them through floor-to-ceiling sliding glass doors onto a sprawling patio that wrapped around the back of the house. Another firepit flickered in the corner, outdoor seating faced the ocean, and a hot tub bubbled invitingly on the far side. Stairs cut down through native grasses to the beach below. Twilight-kissed waves lapped against the sand, and Zack felt right at home. He stretched out on a chaise lounge, arms behind his head.

"All right, lay it on us, Ferris. Anything else you need from us tonight?"

"Right." Ferris fished his phone out of his pocket. If the dude's jeans were any skinnier, his phone would get stuck in there, Zack was positive. "Here's how the next week breaks down. Tomorrow—Monday—is a free day so the cast can hang out and get to know one another and settle into the house. We've planned a boat outing for those who want some adventure."

Esme raised her hand. "Question."

Zack had to stop himself from laughing out loud. She was just so innocent and funny. Who raised their hand and said *question* at the same time? Didn't raising your hand qualify as wanting to ask a question?

Esme continued, and he tried to focus on what she was saying. "Will we spend any time interviewing or screening the cast? My process is part interview and part organic. I want to make sure I have enough time to do a thorough job figuring out all the matches."

"Right. Uh…" Ferris poked at his phone again, as if it contained all the answers in the world. "The show is structured to be fairly organic; we just want engaging footage, so in free time knock yourself out. Might be a fun thing for the boat outing, since you'd have a captive audience?"

"All right then, I'll do my best." Esme quirked a brow at Zack. "I hope you're ready, because one of those women is going to be your future bride. I can feel it."

He smiled. He could feel it too, but the *it* wasn't an impending proposal to some lucky lady in the house. Winning Esme over was going to be so easy, he almost felt sorry for her. Not that he wanted to put her matchmaking skills to shame, but he had a bet to win, and like he'd told Olivia, he never lost.

"I might suggest you spend some time on technique and strategy together, because Tuesday night we're taking the cast out to a local hot spot the production crew has reserved. You'll all get the chance for more fun and bonding, and you both can check out the casts' social game. The audience will also start voting. They'll pick which couples go on dates the rest of the week, what activities you do, and who goes to the Love Shack. Wednesday through Friday, dates happen. Saturday, we have the Love Shack verdict ceremony. Sunday, you'll have your first Matching Ceremony. Then the whole cycle starts allllll over. Make sense?"

At the mention of fun and bonding, Esme's smile dropped, and she fidgeted. Yeah, Zack didn't figure her for much of a nightspot kind of girl.

"Don't worry, Esme, I make a good wingman. I could have you picking up any guy you want anywhere, anytime." Zack kicked his feet up onto the table and crossed them at the ankles.

"Well, I am a lucky girl. With you as my wingman, whatever could go wrong?" Esme stood and pegged them both with a cool stare. "I'm going to help the others get dinner on the table, unless the two of you have anything else to go over right now?"

Swish-swish. He watched the skirt as she stomped back into the house. Oh yeah. He could definitely make her one hell of a lucky girl.

four

. . .

Esme

MUCH MORE COMFORTABLE in the yoga pants and T-shirt she had changed into before dinner, Esme balanced a plate on her lap and watched Zack over the flames of the gaslit fire in the center of the patio table. The hot tub bubbled and burbled under a contemporary wooden pergola to her left. Near the stairs leading down to the beach, some cast members had gathered on the outdoor furniture, deep in conversation.

Despite the rhythm of the waves and the bubbles, she couldn't relax. Zack enthusiastically ate the roasted fish and vegetables the production crew had delivered from a local restaurant down the street, while she picked at her dinner. She could practically feel Alex hovering over her shoulder, whispering, "Get on with it! Ask him questions and get down to business." If she was going to play this game and match him up with some lucky girl, then she did need to get to know him.

She eyed the camera mounted atop the pergola. Cameras were placed in obvious spots all over the house, and the microphones they wore picked up every word they said. Resigned to the fact that her life was no longer her own for the next six weeks, she set her plate down on the table and reached for her glass of wine.

Deciding to deliver something spicy for the cameras, she leaned forward. "So, Zack. What do you look for sexually in a mate?" Immediately, she felt heat flush her face. Maybe she should leave spicy to Madison.

Zack choked on the bite of food he had just taken and

grabbed his glass of water to wash it down. Coughing, he looked at her. "Are you serious?"

She laughed. "No. Well, sort of, I guess. I need to get to know you so I can have any hope of matching you with a woman who is compatible."

Zack set his plate down on the table and sat cross-legged on the edge of the chaise across from her. "Okay, what do you want to know?"

God, he was so cocky and self-assured. She changed tactics.

"What's your life dream?" She sat back and watched for any emotion to play across his face.

Zack smirked. "Oh sweetheart, that kind of juvenile fantasy was shattered years ago. I'm surprised you don't know the whole sad story. Pro surfer injures his knee in a major competition, ending his career and endorsements. Sinks life savings into a crazy investment with his buddies and buys a male strip club, learns all he ever wanted to know from women patrons, and turns to a life of educating poor, nerdy guys on how to pick up the women of their choice." Zack shot her his goofy smile again. "Now I'm living the dream."

His goofy grin was stiff, his shoulders hunched slightly with tension. She thought, *If you're living the dream, then why are you participating in a reality television contest? And women, plural? Ugh.* Out loud, she just said, "I see. Do you still surf?"

"As often as I can get out into the water. Man, after a long day, there's nothing better than being one with the waves. I can't do crazy tricks anymore, but my knee holds out enough to catch some more sedate water."

She nodded. "What's your favorite childhood memory?" She expected him to come up with a surfing answer.

Zack stood up, picked up her wineglass, and walked over to the outdoor kitchen area. After retrieving a bottle of beer from the refrigerator and topping her glass off from the wine bottle, he padded back to the firepit on bare feet. He handed her the glass, sat down next to her on the couch, and stared into the fire's blue flames. She set the wine on the table; she needed to stop sucking the stuff down or she'd get drunk.

"Hmmm. I can't think of a favorite, but I can think of lots of memorable moments." Zack took a long draw on the beer. "One time, my dad took me to the mall for school clothes. I was probably around nine years old. He kept getting interrupted by his pager going off. Finally, he sat me down on a bench so he could use the pay phone." Zack laughed. "He said, 'don't move from this spot,' so I sat there for probably two hours. When he didn't come back, it was clear he had forgotten me."

"Oh my God, what did you do?" Her hand flew to touch his knee, and her throat squeezed at the thought of him as a little boy, alone on that bench, not sure if anyone was coming back.

Zack paused, staring at her hand, then cleared his throat.

"Well, I walked around the mall for a while. I needed bus fare to get home. So I went sticking my head in the fountains and scrounged up enough change to catch a bus home."

Esme's heart dropped to her stomach with a silent thud. The day her dad had left was one of the worst of her life. She spent years avoiding him, always busy with dance classes and other activities so she wouldn't have to see him on their scheduled weekends. So he couldn't disappoint her ever again. And Zack's dad forgot him at the mall while buying school clothes.

Her hand was still gripping his knee. She let go and grabbed her glass of wine. "That must have been scary."

"I lived." Zack smiled and raised his beer bottle in a toast and clinked it against her glass. "To challenging childhoods."

"What else was challenging about your childhood?"

"What wasn't? How about you? Your parents ever forget you in the mall?"

"No. Is that why you like so much attention? Because your dad left you behind while shopping?"

Zack chuckled. "Wow, you don't give up, do you? You're getting pretty serious with this interview. And how do you know I like attention? Maybe I just love impressing women."

She rolled her eyes. "Oh, so that's what you call strutting around bars, wearing goofy hats, and mesmerizing women with magic tricks and slick pickup lines. And as if it's not enough, you feel the need to have a band of protégés follow you around and mimic your every move."

"Why does what I do bother you so much, Esme?"

She was getting fired up. "Seriously? *How to Mingle and Stay Single*? Your book makes a mockery of everything I work for. Which is bringing people together in loving and committed relationships."

"Ah, so you are trying to save the world through love?"

She scowled into her wineglass. "Something like that." Not wanting Zack to get the upper hand, and not wanting to answer questions about herself, she kept him talking.

"Why a male strip club?" she asked. "Wouldn't it make more sense for men to invest in a female strip club?"

Zack ran a hand through his hair. "You are persistent, I'll give you that." He stood and stretched, then sat back down even closer to her on the couch. "Have you ever been to a male revue show? Women show up in groups and let loose. It's almost … animalistic. What better place to study what women want, what turns them on? I spent nights simply listening to their conversations and taking notes. And seriously, some things women talk about together is downright freaky."

Heat rushed to her face. His scent—a mix of ocean air, sunshine, and sunscreen—washed over her. Somewhere between the words *male revue show* and *letting loose*, her mind had wandered to images of Zack on a stage, muscles rippling as his shirt hit the floor. What was wrong with her? The last thing she needed was to imagine this man she was stuck with for the next two months sans clothes.

"So, what about the *New York Post* story? Did it change your mind any on the whole save-the-world-through-love thing?"

She was so not talking about her downfall on camera. "It was nice to meet you tonight, Zack. I'm exhausted and think it's time for me to head up to bed. I have a big day tomorrow, and you've given me a lot to think about."

Zack raised his beer bottle. "Cheers. See you tomorrow."

Her cheeks burned with heat again, and she fled as fast as she could without looking like she was running away from him.

Zack

IF YOU ASKED him to rate his conversation with Esme on a scale of that-was-interesting to what-the-fuck-just-happened, he would go with this-girl-is-a-mystery-I-must-solve. How had she managed to weasel so much information out of him? Telling her about his dad leaving him at the mall? She must have some matchmaker juju going on that cast a truth spell over everyone she met. As soon as he realized how much information he was on the verge of divulging, he'd had to get up to grab another beer and refill her drink while he regrouped.

Ping.

Calendar reminder: Dad chemo appt.

He swiped it away so the cameras couldn't get a shot. "Client check-ins." He tossed the words toward the empty porch like a joke. "My pack howls at dusk."

He shoved his feet into flip-flops and walked over to the glass wall that separated the patio from the beach, thinking about the information his friend Jake had drummed up on Esmeralda Adams.

How did you handle a woman who obviously had abandonment issues from her parents' divorce, which were driving her to match the entire world up? And then, not only did her fiancé cheat on her, but he did it with another dude. A giant wave of realization knocked him back. So far, she was gun-shy and jumpy, and he'd been coming on strong to see how she'd react.

Normally, he wouldn't consider spending any time in the dreaded friend zone, but that was exactly what this case called for. He snapped his fingers. Esme needed to see him as a friend or ally.

Running up the stairs, he knocked quietly on her bedroom door. "Hey, Es? You still awake?"

She cracked the door open. She wore a tank top that left little to the imagination, paired with very short sleep shorts emblazoned with slumbering sheep. He resisted the urge to point out how those particular sheep enhanced her very fine ass … ets.

To his disappointment, she frowned and crossed her arms over her chest. "What are you doing up here?"

Zack raised his hands in the air and took a step back. "I just wanted to see, since we have tomorrow free, if you wanted to go hang out on the beach with me? Before it gets dark I could, like, give you a surfing lesson. I've been told I'm a pretty great teacher. And then maybe we can light a bonfire?"

Esme arched a brow. "Okay, sure. Um, that sounds great. I was planning on doing the boat outing, but we can meet up after. Good night, Zack."

Satisfied, he ran back down the stairs to make a list of everything he needed the production crew to get for him tomorrow, since he hadn't exactly packed surfboards. Step one, invite her to a friendly surfing lesson—complete. Now he just needed to get her to loosen up and see that he was a dependable and trustworthy kind of guy.

five

. . .

Esme

ESME STARED up at the stars in the night sky, twinkling and wavering, as the boat floated on the gentle ocean waves. Shifting her head, she smiled up at Zack, braced on his forearms and hovering above her. Heat from where their bodies touched burned a delicious path through her core.

"God. You are so beautiful." Zack brushed a stray hair out of her face, his eyes turning from blue to gray in the shadows of night. That amazing mouth peppered kisses down her neck, moving lower. Electricity pooled in her belly.

She awoke and sat up with a start, blinking at the morning sun's rays shining through unfamiliar windows. Monday morning—their first free day at the house. With a groan, she threw herself back down on the bed and pulled a pillow over her face. Why was she dreaming about him? She sat up again and hurled the pillow across the room at the door, as if to erase the vision of him standing there last night, shirtless, board shorts hanging dangerously low on his hips. Her eyes couldn't help but follow his flat, sculpted abs down... No! Dangerous thoughts. Her traitorous body could still feel the imaginary kisses trailing down her body.

Noticing the time on the alarm clock, she scrambled out of bed. She was going to be late. She threw open the door to the large walk-in closet and examined the clothes hanging there with a critical eye. What was she thinking when she'd agreed to let Summer, the style enthusiast, help pack her bags? Romantic dress after romantic dress hung haphazardly from the hangers she had shoved them onto last night. Ruffles and silly patterns said, "Hey, everyone! I'm so much fun!" The last thing she wanted was a wardrobe that screamed, "Look at me!"

She also did not want to spend the day on a boat with the cast in a dress. She picked out a navy-blue cotton romper and examined the flirty flare at the bottom of the shorts and white eyelet trim at the top along the collar. Sighing, she slipped it off the hanger and reached for a pair of white sandals.

Stepping out of the closet, she surveyed the bedroom that was hers for the next six weeks. Airy and spacious with white-washed wood floors and a vaulted ceiling. Floor-to-ceiling windows on two walls offered panoramic ocean views, and French doors opened onto a small private balcony. A king-size bed dressed in white linens dominated the space, flanked by driftwood nightstands. Rustic beach décor—woven baskets, sea glass accents, a jute rug—made it a pleasant enough hideaway. The attached bathroom was equally luxurious with a soaking tub, rain shower, and double vanity. At least she'd be comfortable while her career imploded on reality TV.

She laid the romper on the bed. Opening a dresser drawer, she winced at the selection of swimsuits Summer had thrown in and by no surprise, the modest one-piece Esme had wanted to bring was nowhere to be found. She pulled out a navy bikini with white trim and held it up.

The top was generous enough, and the bottom would be flat-tering. It would work for a day on the boat, followed by a surf lesson and a night on the beach. Wait. Why was she even enter-taining the idea of meeting him later for surf lessons and bonfires of all things? Because, she told herself, it was a really good way to get to know him and learn his collaboration style, which could be important in matching him with a partner. And it had absolutely nothing to do with the prospect of seeing him shirtless with water dripping down his amazing chest. Ugh. Esme shook her head, picked up her clothes, and headed for the shower.

Zack

ZACK WHISTLED a tune as he headed to the kitchen and helped himself to a cup of coffee. Shirtless and comfortable, he took a seat at the kitchen table across from Ferris. Sipping his post-run coffee, he attempted to figure the kid out. Ferris sat dressed in what appeared to be his uniform: skinny jeans, a tight button-down shirt, and glasses. The host leveled a sullen stare at Zack.

"You know, now and then I give workshops. Maybe you'd be interested in signing up?" Zack casually threw out the invitation so he could gauge the kid's response.

Ferris snickered and folded his arms across his lean frame. "I don't think that would be of much benefit to me. I don't need a reality show to get a date."

Ouch, burn. Zack set down his coffee and sat back, eyes still trained on Ferris. "I see. Well, man, you're lucky."

Ferris shook his head, puffed a little laugh. "I date men. Now I know which of our love experts is the intuitive one. Speaking of —" He walked over to the stairs to yell up at Esme. "Hey, Esme, are you ready to go? We're running behind schedule."

Zack stood as Esme came trotting down the stairs. Dressed in a one-piece outfit, little of her figure was left to the imagination. Thin straps held the top in place over her slim shoulders, and the shorts were short enough to show plenty of well-toned leg. He swallowed hard. Yeah, that totally worked for him. Much better than the sheep dress. Her hair was pulled up off her graceful neck, and he could just imagine feeling her soft skin under his lips.

"Wowza. You are just full of wardrobe surprises. Glad to see you've graduated from infant patterns to onesies." Zack smirked at the blush in her cheeks. He was a pro at the neg.

Esme rolled her eyes at him and hefted her tote higher on her shoulder. "And you are just as juvenile as you were twelve hours ago." She gave him a once-over and let out a huff. "Did you forget to pack shirts, or do you just not wear any?"

A thrill shot through him; she was still willing to play the verbal warfare game, which meant she was engaged in the chase. The flush deepened in her cheeks and across her chest. He didn't want to let her exit the house without closing a deal with her, so he eased the bag from her shoulder. "Let me help you out to the car."

He opened the front door and let Esme and Ferris pass through before him. Closing the door behind him, he jogged to catch up. He opened the back door of one of the cars that had pulled up to the curb in front of the firepit, set her bag on the floorboard, and held the door open for her. The flash of leg as she slid in was almost too much for him to bear. But slow and steady was needed to win this race. Esme was like a rabbit who needed luring with carrots, or she'd run away. With a hand on the roof of the car, he leaned in so she couldn't close the door without giving him an answer.

"We're still on for tonight, right? Dinner and a surf lesson on the beach?"

Sighing, she held up her hands. "Yes. Yeah. I'll be there after we get back from filming on the boat." She pulled at a white shoulder strap. "See? I even wore my bathing suit."

Yes. Esme was going to spend the evening with him on the beach, and she was wearing a bathing suit. From the look of the strap, it was a bikini. The gods were smiling down on him today.

Glancing up at the group of giggling girls making their way to the cars, he gave them a wave then refocused on Esme. "Awesome. Looking forward to a good day out on the boat and then seeing you tonight." He stepped back to let Madison and Molly pile in the car, gently closed the door, then knocked on the roof for the driver to go. He silently high-fived himself before asking one of the other drivers to wait for him. Zack trotted back into the house to finish his list for the production assistants of every-thing he needed for a romantic night on the beach. Esme didn't know it yet, but she'd already lost this game. Zack almost felt bad for about two-point-five seconds before the thrill of winning took back over. Maybe he'd look like a schmuck, but he was the schmuck who'd win the girl.

His phone buzzed with a call from Jake. His business part-ner's face filled the screen. In the background, strobe lights flashed over the Untamed stage, and a costumer shrieked about a pair of missing tear-away pants.

"Investor boy," Jake yelled over the bass. "Answer your texts like you answer DMs."

Zack grinned for the accidental B-roll. "Brand synergy, baby. How's rehearsal going today? Sounds like someone lost their pants."

Jake scowled over his shoulder and turned back to the camera. "May be losing more than that. You got time to talk shop?"

They went over a few business points and the call ended. Zack opened the journal to a creased page.

'19: Co-signed Z.'s stake in Jake's club. ROI: he'll find his lane.

He rubbed the ink with his thumb. The male revue club in West Hollywood had been a gamble, but it paid off. Jake ran the show. Zack handled marketing and business development. If only his dad could believe in him.

six

. . .

Esme

ESME TRIED to settle into the back seat of the car. "Ugh. What is wrong with that man?"

Madison laughed. Esme had totally forgotten the others were in the car, or that cameras were stuck to the inside of the car windows, filming everything. Her cheeks heated again. The real question was, what was wrong with her? She should focus on getting to know the other girls, but all she could think was how much she wanted to lick Zack's bare chest.

She studied Madison and Molly, who were engrossed in a conversation about which reality stars each of them had met, worked with, or in Madison's case, made out with in various bars. She sank back in the seat and considered how to get to know the other cast members better so she could start figuring out who was meant for whom.

"What do you girls think about the guys?" Madison leaned forward, fully ready to dish out what she thought. "I think Kent is seriously hot."

Molly giggled. "Really? I thought Wesley was pretty cute. That skydiving guy, Trey? He's really intense. Which probably means he's my match, since the whole point of this show is to find the one person who is the opposite of the bad relationships we normally pursue."

"Pffft. Match Smatch, I say we just have fun." Madison puckered her lips. "Hey, Esme, how's my makeup look? It's so hot today, I feel like my face is melting."

Esme glanced at Madison's makeup, which of course wasn't messed up at all. "You look great, nothing amiss."

"Sweet!" Madison bounced in her seat. "I'm so ready. Let's go take advantage of the show's hospitality, girls!"

Rolling to a stop a few minutes later, the driver opened Esme's door. She stepped out, centered and ready to celebrate the day away with her new best friends aboard what she discovered was the largest luxury yacht she'd ever seen.

ESME SHOT what she hoped was a laser-beam glare at Ferris. The man sat moaning in the corner of the stateroom she had sneaked into for a break from the cameras and producers, with their endless prompts for contestants' point-of-view B-roll. She peeked out the door to make sure nobody had followed her down the hallway, then slid it shut.

Looking at Ferris, she put her hands on her hips. "What is the matter with you? Are you seasick?" He did look slightly green.

"No. I just can't listen to any more interview questions up on deck. And sailing for hours is exhausting." Ferris threw a hand dramatically against his forehead and reclined on the couch. "Why does Olivia hate me so much? And whose idea was it to give a boatload of people an unlimited supply of wine? If I have to listen to one more sad relationship story about why people suck, I'm going to jump overboard. Honey, I don't know how you do this day in and day out for a living. You must be a glutton for cruel and unusual punishment."

She stifled a giggle at his dramatics and felt a little bad that Ferris was so miserable. She'd let him moan and groan a while longer while the boat finished docking. Satisfied that she had gotten a good read on the other cast members and identified the women who could be a perfect match for her wayward clients—thinking of Zack as a client helped Esme draw a boundary between drooling over his incredible body and professionalism—she prepared to make her way above deck and join the excited and bubbly group of women for the return car ride.

"Come on, drama queen. Ben informed me that the camera crew will be waiting for us on the docks to do the final girl interviews before heading back to the house." She held out a hand and helped pull Ferris to his feet.

"Fine, fine. Let's go make some television." Ferris opened the door and followed Esme up to the deck. He stopped at the gangplank, surveying the group of women and men horsing around on the dock.

"Hey, Ben," he called out to the cameraman standing at the bottom of the plank. "Let's wrap up the interviews and cut everyone loose."

Ben nodded and gave a thumbs-up. "Heard."

After the crew spun everyone through interviews about their day on the boat and announced their evening was free to do with as they pleased, there was cheering and clapping and then Ben shouted for the cameras to cut.

On the drive back, Esme observed the sun's slow, lingering decent on the horizon and was suddenly nervous to meet Zack on the beach. What she needed was a shield. After the car had left her standing alone at the curb, Esme sat on one of the benches near the front firepit, debating what to do.

How was she going to survive six weeks of this reality television madness? Although they technically had the night off, cameras still followed her every move. Cameras would follow her out onto the beach, and frolicking around in a bikini with Zack was the exact opposite of lying low in the background.

Spotting the other girls at the curb, she jumped up. So what if the game wasn't supposed to start yet? She had the perfect idea to keep attention off her and on Zack.

"Hey, ladies!" She jogged over to where the women were standing, Molly among them. "I was just about to go find Zack down on the beach for a surf lesson and some dinner. How about we all go?" Shooting Molly a smile, she kept talking before the shy girl could say no. "It will be fun, Molly! And surprising Zack should be great for the cameras."

Taking red-headed Isla by the hand, Esme started dragging the woman with her around the back of the house to the stairs that led to the beach. Chatting enthusiastically, the other women followed Esme, with Molly trailing behind.

seven

. . .

Zack

ZACK SURVEYED HIS DOMAIN. Surfboards stood in the sand, beach blankets casually laid out on the ground. A portable firepit was lit and crackling, sending sparks up into the fresh beach air. Wineglass holders stood ready, stuck in the sand, and a clay carafe of chilled wine sat on the travel table he had covered with a casual checkered cloth. Two canvas chairs finished the look. Yeah, he was the master of ambiance.

Giggles and laughter caught his attention. Instead of Esme strolling slowly toward him with a smile on her face and the breeze blowing through her hair, she was marching through the sand, pulling a harried Isla by the hand. Following were the blonde, the scary fitness girl, and a miserable-looking... What was her name? Molly. Uh-oh. She'd brought reinforcements.

Esme stopped suddenly and surveyed the romantic scene. "Uh..."

Zack quirked a brow in return and folded his arms, waiting for her to finish. He knew she might not have shown up; what he hadn't expected was for her to show up with an army.

Her pretty eyebrows drew down into a V, and she dropped the wrist of the woman she'd been dragging. "Hey, Zack. I hope you don't mind but I invited the other girls, who are very excited to learn about surfing."

He knew his crossed arms highlighted his biceps and, noticing his body language, she blushed. Good. He'd work to keep her flustered all night. He could turn this new situation to his advantage, put all his focus on the four new girls and completely ignore Esme. He taught that strategy to all his students. Before long, she'd be begging for his attention.

Esme continued with the introductions. "You remember Isla, Madison, Joy, and Molly?"

Of course he remembered; he had cataloged the women in his mind the first night. Isla was a fiery redhead with a slender build and musical laugh. Madison was blonde and had dangerous curves; Molly, short and spunky; and Joy was a tall, slender brunette. Joy didn't hold a candle to Esme. None of them did, but they were still four gorgeous women. Zack smiled and looked each of them in the eyes as he asked if they had fun on the boat.

"So, I didn't know we'd have company. Have any of you surfed before?"

The girls giggled and started hammering him with questions about surfboard designs, colors, and wet suit fashion trends.

Zack watched out of the corner of his eye as Esme made her way down the beach. Escape artist. It was amazing how she could just slip away unnoticed or blend into the background while everyone else blazed brightly in living color. Keeping an eye on her, he dug into the picnic set he'd hauled down to the beach, pulling out more glass holders and plastic wineglasses. He settled the four women around the fire.

"So, ladies, I promised Esme a surf lesson, and I brought wetsuits and everything. Seems a shame to not make good on my promise. Any objections if I drag her back here and use her to demonstrate for the group?"

Madison started to raise a hand but put it down when Molly elbowed her in the side. With no objections from the crowd, he set off at an easy jog down the beach. "Hey, Houdini, where are you heading?"

He caught up with her, and they stood facing the water. The corners of her mouth quirked up. "Houdini?"

"Yeah, because you're a master of escape. I need you to come back with me, or four ladies are going to be very disappointed. I promised them a surf lesson demonstration. I can't give one without a student."

"You should just use one of them as your student; it would be a good opportunity for bonding time, so you can get to know them better."

Zack stepped in front of her to catch her eye. "Come on, ten minutes. Besides, I only have one wetsuit and it's in your size, Shortcake. You don't want to let them down, do you? All they've been talking about for the past fifteen minutes is how amazing it is to hang out with a real live matchmaker. You have a fan club." Laughing, he ran a hand over his face. "I think they're convinced you have some kind of magical dating mojo."

Esme sighed and walked with him back up the beach. "Maybe I do have some kind of magical dating mojo."

"Oh, I do not doubt it, Es." Zack took her hand and pulled her along. For him, it was less about getting back to the waiting women and more about the opportunity to touch her. Her hand was small and warm in his. Maybe it was his imagination, but it felt like she briefly squeezed his back. And why was he so damn pleased at this revelation? He'd held probably hundreds of women's hands and never really longed for it. He'd tuck that thought away for now and examine it later.

Esme withdrew her hand from his and frowned. "Zack, touching is a no-no. If I have anything to say about it, your future wife is waiting for us right down the beach."

He stopped walking and stared at her, his hand cold from the absence of her warmth. His lips twitched up in a smile, and he shook his head. She was a trip. He motioned to where his equipment lay on the sand. Using his most reasonable voice, he said, "Esme, it's just a surf lesson."

Esme threw her hands up. "Fine, I'll help you demonstrate."

They stopped at the surfboards and Zack handed her a wet suit. She looked from the wet suit to him. Apparently just noticing he had his on already, the top half hanging bunched around his hips. The blush that deepened across her cheeks was extremely satisfying. Her eyes shot up to the sky, and she quickly shimmied out of her romper and wiggled into the wet suit. Holy shit. Zack distracted himself by corralling the rest of the girls around the two surfboards.

When he noticed Esme was still struggling to get dressed, Zack stepped behind her. "Here, let me help you." He tugged the zipper up her back slowly. The wetsuit was tight, required care and his knuckles brushed her spine through the fabric. She went still. He paused, his lips so close to the back of her neck, he couldn't miss the sigh that escaped her lips. Her sigh sounded almost like surrender, and something tightened in his chest. He wanted to stay right here, his hands on her shoulders, his mouth inches from her skin, wanted to see if she'd sigh like that again if he—

Esme stepped away sharply from where he hovered behind her. Disappointment hit him harder than it should have. She aimed a reassuring smile at the women, who watched them closely. "Okay, so let's get this show on the road and get a surf lesson. Woo!" Esme hopped and cheered so much, he suspected she was grateful to have everyone else there to steal some of the spotlight she seemed so intent on avoiding. The ladies hopped up and down and cheered too.

He took one of the boards and set it on the sand. They'd start simple before moving into the ocean. When he looked at Esme, he couldn't help but smile. He'd caught a glimpse of her pretty bikini as she raced to get into the wetsuit. Too bad the water was so cool tonight and required them to wear some insulation, because he'd have loved the opportunity to run his hands over her soft skin while he played the role of helpful surf instructor. Balance was important in surfing, after all.

"Okay, what I want you to do is lie down, stomach first on the board. Make sure that line on the board is aligned with the center of your body. Your toes should always be in the sweet spot, touching the back of the board. From this position, you'll be able to paddle out into the water."

Zack waited for Esme to get situated. "All right, so when a wave comes, what you're going to do is pop up. Put your hands right next to your ribcage in resting position—" He bit back a groan as his eyes followed her hands, which now rested right next to her chest. "Great. You need to follow four steps. Step one, push all the way up. Step two, go back down onto your knees." She complied. And wasn't that a picture that would burn in his mind for the rest of time?

Kneeling beside the board, he tried to catch her eye so he could figure out how engaged she was with him. But she managed to look everywhere else except at him.

"You're doing great!" he went on. "Now step three, bring one foot forward, and your back foot is already there for step four, which is to stand up."

Esme wobbled as she stood up on the board and Zack jumped up to catch her. "Great job. You want the line on the board to travel right through the arches of your feet. And bend your knees. Do not stand straight up, or I guarantee you're going to fall." Running his hands up under her arms, he gently nudged them up in the air. "And now arms out, in classic surfer dude pose." He could smell the clean scent of her shampoo. Reluctantly, he let her go.

"All right, now it's time to try to catch some waves." Zack held out a hand to Esme. He needed to get her out in the water, away from the gawking women she'd dragged down to the beach with her.

Esme hopped off the board. "Thanks, Zack! That was fun, but you know what? I'm beat. Ladies, I'm going to leave you all in Zack's very capable hands. Enjoy the rest of your night." Waving, she grabbed her clothes and ran for the stairs that led up to the house.

"Wow," Isla breathed. "Now I really want to learn how to surf." Smiling at Zack, she pointed to the board. "May I?"

After watching Esme make her way up the stairs, he returned

his attention to the remaining women. "Absolutely. Here, let me lay the second board down, and you can all take turns."

The girls giggled and took turns on the boards while Zack talked them through the steps. All four of them were beautiful and funny and clearly interested. This should have been pickup artist heaven. So, why wasn't he enjoying the chance to basically feel up willing girls on the beach? Instead, all he could think about was the way Esme had looked in that wetsuit before she'd bolted. The little sigh she made when he zipped her up. The brief squeeze of her hand that he was definitely not imagining. He was losing his edge. And worse, he wasn't sure he cared. But the cameras were aimed at him, and he didn't want to ruin his hard-won reputation, so it was time to turn on the charm.

"Don't worry, ladies. I'll catch anyone who might fall."

eight

. . .

Esme

ESME POWER WALKED to escape the beach, surfboards, and Zack. The ocean kept slapping the shore behind her like it had performance notes for her:

Do not kiss men with their own brands.

Do not trust men with biceps that apologize for nothing.

Do not read the book he wrote and assume it's all he is.

Ugh. Stupid notes.

She tried to catch her breath at the top of the stairs. She wasn't sure if the breathlessness was from the sprint up from the beach or from Zack's arms around her on the surfboard. Esme surveyed the scene down on the beach. He wrapped himself around each woman, one by one, playing with their hair and shooting them all his easy smile.

Her stomach twisted. Which was absurd. This was exactly what she wanted. Zack focusing on the actual contestants, finding his match, playing his player games with someone who wasn't her.

So why did watching him touch Isla's waist, laugh at Madison's joke, steady Molly on the board make her want to march back down there and shove them all in the ocean?

She told herself it was disappointment. Disappointment in her professionalism. Certainly not jealousy. She was the matchmaker. The one who should be helping Zack connect with his future wife and instead she ran away like a coward. That's all this uncomfortable feeling was. Disappointment in herself. A voice in her head whispered, "Liar." The voice sounded suspiciously like Alex.

Esme snugged her arms around herself. The man was despicable, mugging it up for the cameras. Well, at least he was happy with the other potential matches.

She could still feel his fingers folded over hers when he had held her hand. Her stomach did flips at every smile he beamed her way. The man was sinfully handsome. And how she'd missed the fact he was wearing a wetsuit with the top hanging down at his waist and the bottom emphasizing his rather fine backside and muscular thighs were beyond her. Her hand snaked up to touch where his warm breath had coasted across the back of her neck, and she hoped her sigh of pleasure hadn't been too loud.

Zack was a dangerous distraction, and she needed to focus on the game. She still wasn't one hundred percent sure which woman was the woman for him. Secretly, she was rooting for the effervescent Isla, who seemed the most grounded by strong family ties. Zack's story about how he grew up had tugged at Esme's heart, and she could picture him with someone from a deeply rooted family.

A PA jogged past with a tray of bottled designer waters, three different flavors of fruit and mineral-laced fanciness. Somewhere behind her, a laugh she was trying not to recognize ricocheted off the house's wood and glass. Zack would probably call it "banter." She pressed a palm to her sternum and willed her heart to stop its marathon session. Once it had steadied, she whispered to it. *You're not a lifeguard. You do not have to sprint every time that surfer looks handsome.*

"Professional," she whispered to the salty air. "We are a professional."

As she walked toward the house, dread pooled in her stomach. Tomorrow she was expected to spend the day with Zack for a lesson in the art of the pickup. In her opinion, there was less art happening in Zack's game than in the painting she'd done last week during girls' night out. For the sake of the game and Ferris's sanity, she'd humor everyone and follow along, although she had zero intentions of trying to meet anyone. Esme was swearing off men forever, starting with one Mister Zack MacKenzie.

nine

. . .

Zack

ZACK COULDN'T KEEP the grin off his face the next morning when Esme came down the stairs in pants which, from afar, looked like they were patterned with colorful paisleys but up close turned out to be whimsical fish. Her white T-shirt was crooked, half tucked in, as if she'd thrown it on fast.

He stood as she crossed the room. "Normally, I'd say whoa, those are some crazy fish pants. But you make them look cute." He reached out quickly to tug her shirt into place. Oops. He knew he shouldn't touch her but couldn't help himself.

Esme stepped back and arched an eyebrow at him. "Do you even realize when you are doing it?"

"Doing what?" He had no idea what she was talking about. While he worked to puzzle it out, she sighed a very exasperated sigh.

"Hitting on women. Tossing out witty lines trying to impress them or throw them off-balance or whatever."

He ran a hand through his hair and studied her. Was she serious? Yep. Her hip was jutting out to one side and her arms crossed. An eyebrow was still doing its best Spock impersonation. She was serious. Only, he couldn't take her seriously in fish pants. She was too adorable. He couldn't help the laugh that escaped his lips, even when the result was a tapping foot joining the hip and the eyebrow. Nor could he stop the next thing that came out of his mouth. A total neg.

"Jeez, Es. Are you always so uptight? I was simply complimenting your unique clothing choice and fixing your crooked shirt, not asking you to go to bed with me. Relax a little."

"Relax?" Esme threw her arms in the air and walked out the living room door. She spun on her heel, eyes blazing. "Relax? How am I supposed to do that when there are cameras following me, production assistants stalking me for interviews, and you're constantly saying nice things to me when I can't even tell if you mean it or not? And my name is not Es."

She glared at the tiny orbs recording the room. He'd completely forgotten about the cameras and didn't really care that they were even there, recording everything he did.

Well, this relationship certainly was not off to a great start. Was his reputation so bad that Esme didn't believe anything he said? Zack shook his head, hands held up in retreat. He backed up and tried a smile.

"Okay, we got off track here, so let's start over. Good morning, Esme. How are you?"

She dropped her arms and frowned at him. "I'm fine, thank you. Hungry. Could use some breakfast but other than that, just fine." Seeming to forgive his transgressions, she came back into the room and studied the coffee table. "It looks like a party store threw up in here."

He ignored her use of the female "I'm fine" bomb—which in his experience meant she wasn't fine—and sifted around the items scattered on the table. Sashes, glasses, and other kitsch the producers had left for him after completing yet another one of his shopping lists. He picked up a tiara and stuck it in her hair. "Props, for your pickup artist education. Could come in handy on our next cast trip out. Or one of your dates." He handed her a wand with an LED star on top.

"So, you want to dress me up like a fairy princess?" Esme studied the wand, waving it around in the air.

"Not necessarily, unless that works for you." It could work for him, he thought, imagining Esme dressed in fairy wings, the tiara, and not a lot else. He plucked the wand from her hand and set it back on the table. He studied the props while performing mathematical equations in his head to stave off the raging hard-on the imagery was encouraging. "They're conversation starters. Instead of an opener, you could—"

"What's an opener?"

Zack forgot she wasn't up to speed on all the PUA lingo—there was a lot of slang and acronyms—so he clarified. "Opening line. Instead of an opening line, absurd headwear and props can be a great icebreaker and draw people to you instead of you hunting for someone to talk to all night."

"And that really works?" Esme eyed him, her voice thick with skepticism.

"Aren't these crazy clothes you keep showing up in the same thing? Conversation starters?" He looked pointedly at the fish pants.

Her cheeks flushed red, and she squared her shoulders. He had poked the bear again. "No! I told you my friend Summer owns a boutique. I made an error in letting her pack my bag. After unpacking, I can say with confidence I will be wearing more weird animal prints before our time is through, but not by choice."

He smiled and honestly wanted to make her more comfortable, so instead of standing awkwardly by the table, he took her hand and tugged her over to the breakfast bar, where coffee and Danish had appeared from the food fairies who seemed to keep the house stocked with delicious meals and snacks. At least the contestants were not going to starve during their solitary confinement.

"Here, sit." He pulled out a stool for her.

"Thanks." Hopping up, she propped an elbow on the counter and rested a cheek in her palm, watching him with interest as he slid a buzzing phone from his pocket.

Ping.

Dad — patient portal notification: Lab results posted

Esme tipped her head. "Is the algorithm rewarding your charm?"

"Spam thinks I have a warrant for unpaid tolls in Florida," he said lightly, tucking the phone away. "Any interest in an excerpt from *How to Mingle and Stay Single* on the details of openers?"

Esme made a face that said she'd read him and his book and wasn't impressed.

"Okay, so no excerpt. Got it."

She did look like a fairy princess with the tiara sparkling atop her dark, loose curls. Zack's fingers wanted to run through and get tangled in those waves. But his hands were better served by getting some breakfast into his hangry roommate.

"How do you like your coffee?" Shit. Did she like coffee? He studied her. "You do like coffee, right? Or have I made another bad assumption that you are going to yell at me about?"

Her laughter washed over him like warm waves on a perfect surfing day. She actually smiled. "I wasn't yelling at you."

"Hmmm. Okay, lecturing me then? Or sternly putting me in my place?" He grinned to let her know he wasn't mad. "You look like a cream and sugar kind of gal. Am I right?"

"Why? Let me guess. Because I'm so sweet?"

Zack groaned. Getting past her preconceived notion of him as a pickup artist was going to be tough. "I legit just want to know how you take it, so I can fix it for you. It's not some seduction technique or intel gathering move so I can manipulate you into something."

"Cream, no sugar. Please."

He added cream to the hot coffee and slid the mug over to her. As she took a tentative sip, he laughed. "See, I am capable of being human. Here, grab a bite to eat, and I'll be right back with some more props." Maybe if he got her blood sugar up, she'd mellow out a bit and have some fun with the stuff he'd put together.

He returned and draped a sash over her head, guiding it under an arm. Next, he replaced the tiara with a veil and dropped a feather boa over her head and added a necklace with a giant pendant that read *Bride*.

"Oldest and best props in the book, the classic bachelorette party look. If a guy asks why you are alone—and trust me, one will ask—say you left your friends because you're having second thoughts about the whole till-death-do-you part thing. Immediately, the guy is going to want to go into rescue mode, and—"

Zack stopped, surprised by the tears streaming down Esme's face. "Oh shit. Uh, here, don't move." He removed the headband and the feather boa, and tossed them onto the couch. She was still crying, so he ran into the powder room off the hallway to wet a face towel in the sink.

He was such a moron. Sometimes, stupid things just came out of his mouth before they could filter through his brain. The woman had been humiliated by her ex-fiancé in an episode that was probably even worse than being left at the altar. The thought of being so insensitive and bringing her to tears made him cringe. He rushed back to Esme and handed the cool cloth to her, along with a handful of Kleenex he'd grabbed. "I'm sorry. I'm an idiot and wasn't thinking."

She sniffled and wiped at her eyes with the cloth, nodding. "Don't worry about it, Zack. It's not your fault. I'm just not having a great day. I'm going to go see what the other girls are up to and hang out for a bit before we head out to the bar event tonight." She slipped off the stool and made her way across the room.

Zack followed her out and watched her walk up the stairs, considering his actions and feeling bad that he had hurt her. He didn't want to make her cry. Instead, he wanted to make her laugh, because he could look at her smile forever. And wasn't that interesting?

Before any more introspection could weave its torrid way through his brain, a cold hand grabbed his arm and yanked. Surprised, he found himself hauled into the laundry room off the kitchen by Olivia, who looked certifiably grim in Executive Producer chic: black pants and a sleeveless black button-up vest with nothing underneath. Her five-inch heels nearly brought her to his height.

"What the hell do you think you're doing?" she hissed.

"I'm sorry, Olivia. I'm not feeling up to sparring today. What are you talking about?" Zack considered leaving but for a very skinny woman, she was surprisingly effective at blocking the only door out. When he realized this was going to take a minute, he opted for nonchalance and hopped up on the washer.

"You are not supposed to be making your costar cry! Our viewers want fun, fantasy, and romance. Not sad reminders of failed weddings and crying contestants. You need to fix this and fix it now!"

Zack could practically see the steam escaping from Olivia's blinged-out ears, she was so furious. Nobody had told him when he woke up that it was going to be everyone-yell-at-Zack-day. He needed backup, but Esme had already fled the scene.

"Okay, Olivia, I'll fix it. Tonight the cast is going out to a bar so we can see everyone's style when trying to find dates. I'm sure you want the audience to really see Zoom in action. I'll give them what they want, all right?"

Olivia dropped her arms and cocked her head to the side. "I just want my show back on track."

"I promise I'll be good for your ratings. I'm a good-looking dude and charismatic as hell. I promise I and the other guys will put on a good show."

Olivia stared at him so long he started to feel the need to squirm. Zack never squirmed. Squaring his shoulders, he stared back.

"Okay. I think you're going to fall flat on your face. Whatever scheme you are brewing up in your head to win the girl won't work. Which means you are going to be mine, Zack." Olivia stepped up to him and ran a hand down his chest. He felt her nails through his T-shirt. "To humiliate in front of an audience or ingratiate to them... Whatever my whim. I will enjoy it. So much."

She walked out of the laundry room and the house, closing the front door behind her, and Zack shivered. If he had any doubt as to how miserable it would be to spend ten years indebted to Olivia, it was now gone. Time to get his game back and stop fucking around.

Esme

ESME CLOSED her bedroom door and leaned against it, her wobbly legs barely holding her up. Stupid Clayton and their wedding had doomed her into reality television in the first place. Now she was breaking down and crying in front of the cameras. In front of Zack, which bothered her almost more than public humiliation. The look in his eyes as he handed her Kleenex had been almost apologetic. Afraid he was about to reach for her, and she'd like it way too much, she had run out of the room like a maniac.

She traced a hand along her collarbone where his hands had brushed when he tugged her T-shirt into place. Zack MacKenzie was a conundrum. One minute he was making fun of her clothes with glee, and the next he was trying to comfort her with food and coffee. Esme never had problems figuring people out. But even trying to come up with women to match with Zack was complicated and difficult. The normal tingle she'd get in the tips of her ears or nose, which meant she was letting her intuition guide her, hadn't been there at all when she'd interviewed the other female contestants. Barely even an itch. The only tingle on the beach had been the one zipping along her skin when close to Zack. Not only was she ostracized by the matchmaking community on the East Coast, but now she'd lost her gift. If she didn't win this competition, all would be lost.

No, she wasn't a quitter. Her matches would hold up, and Zack was going to fall in love with one of the women in the house if it was the last thing she made happen.

Love charms! She'd have the producers pick her up some supplies and load the women up with as much knowledge she could muster, plus a little bit of magic.

Esme might have been a great matchmaker, but she sucked at dating. There was no way she was going to pick up any man in any bar, even in an event staged by producers for ratings. Her game was lame, and that was fine by her. Diving for her bag, she dug around in it until she found what she was looking for. She clutched the charm necklace Alex had given her to her chest. Maybe a little magic of her own would get her mind off Zack and onto someone else.

ten

· · ·

Esme

TUESDAY NIGHT. Bar night. And Esme was already regretting every life choice leading up to this moment. She and Ferris stepped out of the car on the tarmac at John Wayne Airport. The rest of the cast had left the house earlier, and everyone was meeting up to take a chartered flight to Palm Springs for the evening.

"I could get used to the travel aspect of reality television." Esme smiled at Ferris. "Private cars and airplanes, they are decent perks."

After giving directions to the driver to meet them for the drive back to the house later, Ferris started for the stairs up to the plane. "Sure, that along with free room, board, and a daily stipend. All you have to do is give up your freedom and privacy."

"Gee, Ferris, you make it sound so glamorous." Esme followed him through the door and into the plane's cabin. Zack was already there, sitting next to Kent. Both men stood up. Whereas Zack's features were classic California surfer boy, Kent's were all hard planes and lines.

"Hey, Es, looking good tonight."

Zack lifted her hand and brought it up to his lips. Esme might have blushed as Zack swept his blue-green eyes over her simple black dress and might have felt a little thrill shoot through her as he held her hand … if she hadn't been immediately distracted by his appearance.

"You're not going to stop calling me Es, are you?" She

stopped in the aisle and examined the two guys. "What on earth are you two wearing?"

Zack's clothes were typical night-out garb: nicely fitting jeans and a black button-up shirt. He had a knit beanie pulled over his sun-kissed hair and over the hat he'd tugged on a pair of aviator goggles. Kent wore black jeans, a crazy red-and-gold long coat, and a cowboy hat. Esme shook her head.

Before Zack could explain, she said, "You know what, I don't even want to know. I'm just going to sit back there and read my book." She tried to extract her hand from Zack's, but he held on tight.

"Hey, wait a sec, Kent's helping out tonight as a wing. And this"—Zack waved his free hand up and down his body—"is called peacocking or dressing for attention."

Her eyes narrowed, and she looked at Ferris, who sat across the aisle. "I don't even want to know what a wing is and why they get to dress so ridiculously."

Ferris shrugged. "I guess because they asked?" The host stuck headphones over his ears and settled into his seat.

Zack cocked an eyebrow at her. "You know, nicknames are a PUA's rite of passage. What are we going to call you, sweetheart?"

"Uh..." Esme's words failed her. She should be irritated at the endearment, but all she could focus on was his smooth voice and charismatic smile. Between Zack and Kent, any women they met were doomed tonight. "Definitely not sweetheart, for starters."

Zack continued, unfazed. "How about Fox, because you are one foxy lady?"

Esme groaned. Spell broken, she pushed Zack gently on the shoulder and back over to his seat. "I'll just stick with Esme. Or, if you like, you can call me by my full name, Esmeralda." Pausing in the aisle, she gave one last look at the goggles on his head. "I really don't understand why you need those. Aren't you enough?"

He frowned at her and sank back into his seat.

Settling into a seat in the back, she thought her last comment over. Why did guys like Zack and Kent, who were not just good-looking but downright hot, dress themselves up in ridiculous costumes to try to pick up women? She knew there was a kind, gentle side to Zack buried beneath his ridiculous exterior. What had happened in his life that he went through the rest of it making a complete spectacle of himself?

Esme opened the book she'd brought along for the quick flight. Why did she care what Zack did and why? Maybe the ridiculous peacock thing worked though, because here she was focused on his stupid clothes instead of her own plan for the evening. Which was to stay in the background, take notes, and go with the flow.

She didn't have to worry about the cameras on her. Zack and Kent were going to keep the cameramen engaged just fine.

ESME FOLLOWED THE CAST, Ben, and the camera crew through the door of a bar called Joe's Pub. Ferris was happily monitoring the video and audio feeds from a rented van out on the street, able to give commands to Ben through their headsets and take notes for any host commentary. The place was a typical nightspot. Red walls, thumping music, and the heat from too many bodies standing around in one room. Drink specials were handwritten in chalk on boards behind the bar that stretched from counter to ceiling. As if a switch had been flipped in each of them, Zack and Kent transformed into Zoom and his sidekick and worked their way through the crowd. She spied Joy and Madison dancing with Joel while Molly, Trey, Wes, and Isla held court at the dartboard. Cameras followed each group, drawing a crowd.

The two men approached a group of women standing off to

one side of the bar. Esme followed behind, nobody paying her any attention.

"Hey, ladies, can I get your opinion on something?" Zack smiled at the group. "My buddy here just got new glasses, but he's embarrassed to wear them. Can you tell him what you all think?"

On cue, Kent pulled a pair of dorky looking glasses from his back pocket and put them on. The girls giggled. Kent took the glasses back off.

"So, what do think looks better, glasses on or off?" Zack asked.

"I like them on." Girl number one laughed, moving closer to Kent.

Kent put the glasses back on and gave the girls a goofy glare, then swiped them back off again, to more giggles.

"No! I like them off better." Girl number two slipped up to Kent's other side.

"I don't know." Zack tapped his chin, examining Kent, who put the glasses back on. "Our friends all think he looks a little like Clark Kent with the glasses on."

"Yeah, he really does." Girl number one hooked her arm through Kent's and beamed up at him. "You should wear them."

Kent smiled down at her. "Why do you like it when my glasses are on?"

"I think it makes you look like a sexy cowboy."

Esme had heard and seen enough, and they hadn't even been there ten minutes. Nobody even noticed when she sidled away and found a spot at the bar. Zack and Kent were too deep in the game, and Ben had his eye glued to the camera, no doubt trained on the hot chicks flocking over to give their opinions on Kent's glasses.

"What'll you have?" The bartender tossed a coaster on the counter. He tilted his head at the crowd in the corner. "What's going on over there?"

"De-evolution." Esme looked at the drink board. "What's good?"

"Well, I consider myself an alchemist when it comes to bourbon. How about a sour cherry old-fashioned?

"Sounds great. I'll take two."

Laughing, the bartender mixed the two drinks and set them in front of her before making his way down the bar to serve other customers.

Esme drank the first old-fashioned in one gulp, wincing only slightly from the burn of the liquor as it slid down her throat. She took her time with drink number two; she sipped at it and surveyed the bar. Zack and Kent, now joined by Joel, were in the middle of a group of women three deep performing, what, magic tricks? She watched as women flocked over to Zack while Kent worked a deck of cards. The two men performed as if they had been a team for a very long time. Just how long had Kent been Zack's student? Joel seemed to be working some type of crowd control as he drew women in, probably with bad jokes. Looking down, she was surprised her second drink was already gone.

"Can I buy you another one?" The man sliding into the seat next to hers set his drink down and held up his hand to get the bartender's attention. "Two more of what the lady is having. Thanks, man."

Esme considered her new companion with suspicion and looked around for cameras.

"Hi, I'm Greg. You looked like you could use some company."

"Esme. Nice to meet you."

The bartender remained attentive as a third drink appeared in front of her. "So, Greg, do you ever dress up in funny costumes to meet women?"

Greg laughed. "No, can't say I've ever done that. I'm here on business and was bored in my hotel room, so I thought I'd pop over for a nightcap. Lucky me, I came across you looking like you could use a friend." Picking up his glass, he held it up. "Cheers?"

Esme clinked her glass against his. Why not? "Cheers."

Engrossed in conversation with Greg and on her third... No, fifth... No, fourth drink, Esme didn't notice Zack at her back until he reached in between her and Greg and took the glass out of her hand. He set it on the counter. "I think it's time to go."

Looking up at him, Esme giggled and pulled the ridiculous beanie and goggles off his head. She wanted to see his pretty, sun-streaked hair, which made the blue-green of his eyes stand out. "What, is the magic show already over?"

Zack snatched the glass, which had made its way back into her hand again, and pushed it down the bar. "Excuse me." Placing himself firmly between her and Greg again, Zack turned her stool so she was facing him.

Apparently not wanting to argue with Zack, who looked like he could tear someone's head off right about then, Greg shrugged and stood up. "I've got to get going, I have an early morning meeting. It was nice meeting you, Esme."

Zack sighed and took the hat and goggles from her. "Look, the only reason I am even here tonight in this getup is because you're supposed to be observing my dating style. I thought having Kent and Joel play along would make you feel more comfortable, since you seem to hate being alone with me."

Esme looked up at him. She didn't hate being alone with Zack. In fact, the exact opposite was true. She liked being alone with him too much.

"I don't hate being alone with you." Esme groaned. She normally wasn't so forward, but the alcohol coursing through her veins didn't really care for decorum. Honest juice was what it was.

"But you always run away." Zack gave her a half smile and stepped aside so she could get past him.

And he was right, because that was her cue to go, before she could embarrass herself anymore. Her own personal brand of magic—the disappearing act.

eleven

. . .

Esme

WEDNESDAY MORNING, Esme gripped the railing for balance as she followed Ferris and Madison downstairs to the lower level of the house. An invisible hammer hit her in the head each time she took a step, reminding her of every single drink she had last night. Esme sighed.

"You okay back there, Esme?" Ferris stopped at the bottom and peered up at her.

"Oh, I'm super." Forcing a smile, she concentrated on trying to trot down the rest of the stairs to catch up with the others.

Ferris spun on his heel and waved both arms in a follow-me gesture. "C'mon, sinners, for we are on our way to film an interview via the confessional!"

"Ooooh, that sounds like fun. What's the confessional?" Madison sashayed after him, blonde curls bobbing and bouncing around her shoulders.

"Think of it as a tiny truth palace. Sometimes you may be by yourself or in groups. It's just you, the lens, and a very judgmental ring light. You may be interviewed by a producer or given prompts to respond to on your own." Ferris led them down the hall that branched off past the kitchen—past the breakfast bar and bathroom and what she'd assumed were the guys' bedrooms—to a door Esme hadn't noticed before. He stopped. "This used to be an oversized storage room, but the transformation is amazing, right?"

Track lighting had been hung from the ceiling over an overstuffed two-person couch, casting it in soft light. To the side of the sofa were two plush and soft-looking ottomans that could be pulled up for extra seating if necessary. Ferris perched himself on a simple wooden stool positioned under a mirror that hung on the wall opposite the couch.

Ferris waved at the couch. "Have a seat, you two. I'm going to ask you both a series of questions. All you have to do is sit back, get comfortable, and answer them honestly." He pointed up to the mirror. "Cameras are behind that glass. These babies are running twenty-four seven, so anytime you want to come in and vent or explain something to the audience or producers, help yourselves."

Madison plopped down on the couch, looking cool and collected and ready to spill anything Ferris wanted to know. Esme, on the other hand, lowered herself gingerly and perched on the edge of the couch, already on guard and giving the mirror the evil eye.

"Okay, let's get this show on the road!" Ferris shuffled a stack of note cards he had produced from the satchel he brought.

Esme raised a brow at the satchel. Ferris was wearing tight, brown plaid pants and a brown T-shirt, which was a total changeup from his uniform of skinny jeans and button-downs. A red cardigan sweater with white patterning at the lapels and along the forearms added enough quirk to the ensemble that she'd swear Summer must have dressed him.

She missed Alex and Summer. The two of them would have cut her off after two of those cocktails last night. And they'd give her advice on how to handle Zack. Remembering the look on his face last night made Esme wince.

"Esme, cheer up, you look like you've been sucking on lemons. Ready to do this thing?" Ferris snapped his fingers at her.

Sitting up straight, she pushed the thoughts of Zack out of her head and nodded to Ferris. "Absolutely, let's get rolling."

"Okay, so we're here to talk about Madison's date tonight with Zack. Madison, why don't you introduce yourself to the audience?"

"Hi everyone!" Madison waved at the mirror. "My name's Madison Parks, and I'm so excited to be here. Let's see... I'm an LA girl, born and raised. At night, you can find me working at the Cobalt Lounge in West Hollywood, where I'm a master mixologist. I love to hang out there with my friends. I'm looking forward to showing you all what I can do!" Madison flipped her hair back and smiled at the mirror.

At least someone was comfortable in front of the cameras. Esme fought the urge to fidget on the couch and keep her face as neutral as possible. Even being in front of invisible cameras was making her twitch.

"Great! Our audience was given a few options to choose from when deciding what you should do on your date. They thought it would be fun to have you and Zack spend some time behind the bar at the Cobalt Lounge before you head off to a romantic dinner."

Madison squealed and clapped her hands. Ferris cleared his throat.

"So, Esme. What do you think about Madison as a potential match for Zack?"

Esme looked over at Madison and plastered on a smile, even though that knowing tingle still wasn't happening. Even though she suspected her matchmaker superpowers might be broken, this question was completely in her wheelhouse. She spoke with utter confidence.

"What draws me to Madison as a potential match for Zack is... Well, first of all, she's absolutely gorgeous, isn't she?"

Madison giggled. "Aww, you're so nice."

"And she is really involved in the LA nightlife scene. A point that could work in her favor. Both of them are very social people who spend a lot of time in the same type of nightspots. Both of them have jobs requiring them to be in front of a lot of strangers. They share a lot in common."

Ferris nodded encouragingly. "Yes, that makes complete sense. What are you hoping will happen on their date tonight?"

Esme thought for a moment. "What I'm hoping will happen on their date tonight is the two of them will find a connection with one another they can explore more deeply on a second date."

"Madison, what do you hope will happen on your date tonight with Zack?"

"Oh wow. I mean, what don't I hope will happen on my date tonight with Zack? He's pretty cute, you know? I'm hoping we'll have fun when I take him to see where I work and what I do for a living. It's one of the hottest spots in town, and I'm sure he's going to love it! Maybe he'll kiss me good-night. That would be totally hot."

Esme squirmed on the couch in annoyance but then mentally reined herself in. She had no right to be annoyed by the thought of Zack kissing Madison. She didn't even care who Zack had already kissed, which was probably half of the United States of America, give or take a few women. Last night had been educational, and left Esme wondering how much she did not know about the male gender. She was supposed to be a dating expert, but she felt like everything she knew was being turned upside down, all because of one arrogant pickup artist. Maybe she really had lost her matchmaking mojo, and this entire show was going to make a mockery of her.

"What do you think about kissing on the first date, Esme?" Ferris threw the question at her from left field.

"In regard to any displays of affection during a first date, I counsel my clients that they should read body language and signs from the person they are with but not feel pressured into things like good-night kisses. If they are feeling anxious, they can take control by holding out a hand for a good-night handshake or giving their date a quick hug. But if the chemistry is there, I see nothing wrong with hugging and kissing."

And now she was thinking about kissing. And Zack. And kissing Zack. Groaning inwardly, she looked at Madison. "Do you want my advice for tonight?"

Madison nodded eagerly.

"Let the man take the lead. Be engaging, answer questions, and ask him questions too. Keep your focus on him. Don't drink too much. Don't discuss religion or marriage or kids. All those things can be talked about on subsequent meetups. You should avoid any awkward pitfalls."

Madison smiled and grabbed Esme's hand. "Thank you, Esme! I'm so excited for this opportunity."

Esme looked at her hand clasped in Madison's. Something wasn't quite right about the Madison and Zack match, but she couldn't put her finger on it yet.

Ferris popped up from the stool. "Well, fingers crossed it all goes well tonight. Esme, you'll be in the van with me so you can take notes during the date. Any questions?"

Feeling sick to her stomach from either anticipation or the cocktails from last night, Esme nodded and ran for the bathroom.

Stomach completely empty, Esme rinsed her mouth and opened the door right as Zack was about to knock on it.

"Zack, hey. What are you doing down here?"

He frowned at her. "Hey, Shortcake. I ran into Ferris and Madison outside, and he said he thought you might be sick. Are you okay?"

Esme's stomach did a flip-flop, but not from queasiness this time. After fleeing the bar last night, she'd barricaded herself in the airplane lavatory so she didn't have to face him. And now he'd come seeking her out hours and hours later.

"I'm great, thanks for checking, Hobie Wan Kenobi."

Zack chuckled. "Clever. Hobie, like the surfboard brand. You're a funny one, Es. Ferris says to be out front in an hour so you can tag along with him in the van during my Madison date."

"Okay. I'm just going to, uh, run upstairs and change and grab my stuff." Esme looked up into those eyes, which seemed more sea green than blue in the dim light of the hallway. "Are you ready for tonight?"

"Yep, ready and willing," said Zack, grinning. He stepped back to let her out of the bathroom and followed her to the stairs. "Let's do this thing."

Of course he was willing. What man wouldn't be ready and willing to go out on a date with a knockout like Madison? Her height made Esme look like a Smurf, and her curves? Well, Esme just couldn't compete.

She shook her head to clear it of those thoughts and moved past Zack, catching her breath as her shoulder brushed against his arm. "Right, let's do this."

Esme climbed the stairs, aware of Zack right behind her. She ran up the next set of stairs to her room as fast as she could. And was just a little disappointed when he didn't follow her up.

twelve

. . .

Zack

ZACK CLIMBED into the back seat behind Madison and closed the SUV's door. Any other day, he'd be dancing with glee at being trapped in the back of a private limousine with a hot, curvy chick like Madison. The tight navy-blue dress she wore, with its series of complicated straps and a plunging neckline, left very little to his imagination. And Zack had an impressive imagination. Every guy in his network would kill to be in his place. But instead of blonde curls, he wanted to run his hands through deep chocolate waves. No other woman had ever left Zack as perplexed as Esmeralda Adams. But tonight, he needed to focus on his objective, which was to throw this date without being obvious. Because if he couldn't woo Esme, he would miss out on some much-needed leverage with Olivia.

"So, Madison, what is on the schedule tonight?" Normally, Zack would throw in a cute nickname or a backward insult, but he just wasn't feeling up to it tonight. Maybe it was the company.

"I'm so glad you asked." Madison literally bounced to life. "We're heading to my part of town—West Hollywood! The audience voted for me to show you around the bar I work at, and afterward we can have dinner there if you want. I figured it would be a good way for you to learn something about me. Plus, I don't think you've ever been by our place. I'd totally remember if you had."

"What's the name of it?" Zack asked, not really caring.

"Cobalt Lounge. It is so tight. Wait until you see it. I arranged things so you can work behind the bar with me for a while. How cool is that?"

"Cobalt... No. I don't think I've been there. Looking forward to it. Hey, do you want to listen to some music on the way?" Zack fiddled with the audio controls, filling the back of the car with Top Forty Pop.

"OMG, I love this song!" Madison bopped to the beat while Zack settled back for the ride.

Twenty more OMG-I-love-this-songs later, they finally arrived outside the Cobalt Lounge. Zack hopped out and raced the driver around to open Madison's door. Ben was already there on the curb with the cameras, and Zack didn't want to seem like a schmuck who didn't open car doors for ladies on national television.

Madison glanced up at him and held out her hand. He helped her out of the car, and she latched onto him to catch her balance. "Oops, sorry, I didn't mean to grab you." Her hands lingered, and she squeezed his bicep. "Wow, you really do have a lot of muscles."

Giggling, she let go and headed toward the front doors. Why couldn't Esme fall into his arms every time she got out of a car? Zack shook his head and followed Madison into the bar. While quiet now, Zack assumed the place would be hopping in about thirty minutes.

"Hi, everyone!" Madison waved to the servers as she swung up to the counter of the bar and walked around behind it, grabbing two aprons from a hanger under the bar and tossing one to Zack. "Are you all ready to be on television? Let's make magic tonight, people, and show the world how we do things here at Cobalt!"

Zack tied the apron around his waist and stood, perplexed. He'd spent countless hours in bars and nightclubs but honestly couldn't remember ever being behind a bar. He knew the basics from watching hundreds of bartenders do their things but realized he had no idea what to do. This had to be the weirdest date he'd ever been on.

"So, this is where you work?"

"Yeah! Cool, isn't it? I'm the master mixologist, and this here" —Madison knelt under the counter and punched in a code on a digital safe, from which she pulled out a leather-bound book— "is my drink bible. Everything I've ever concocted is documented in here, and people come from all over the state to try things out. I was supposed to get my own reality show a year or so ago, but that kinda fell through. So Olivia called and suggested I audition for this one."

Zack paused from inspecting artistically stacked glasses, and a cold, invisible finger ran its way up his spine at the mention of Olivia's name. "You know Olivia?"

"Sure. Who in LA doesn't know Olivia? She creates some of the hottest reality television. Plus, she's friends with my older sister; they went to film school together."

"What would you say if I suggested we do something else— go somewhere quiet where we could talk and get to know each other better?" Zack looked around, suddenly not super enthusiastic about helping Madison launch her reality television career. Plus, his track record in bars while Esme watched wasn't going very well.

Madison laughed. "Oh Zack, you are so funny. Wouldn't that be boring? Just wait until this place gets kicking! You won't believe how many people come through here in a night. I'm really surprised you've never been to Cobalt." She wandered off to look over a row of strategically lit bottles.

Buzz.

Sis: *He joked with the nurses today. Ask him about the BMW later.*

He opened Venmo and entered $23.17 to send to Dad with the memo: *BMW mirror 1998 + inflation.* Just that morning he'd stared at the journal page about the car until his eyes watered.

The lights in the bar dimmed, the music pumped, and all of a sudden Madison was on. She leaned over the bar, whispering in patrons' ears, both male and female. She tossed those curls and laughed jovially. Zack closed the book and retreated to the other end of the bar to escape the theatrics. He was getting into a groove of pouring beers and talking with guests when hooting and yelling drew his attention back to Madison's end of the bar. She was balancing a shot glass between those glorious breasts, offering it to the highest paying customer.

Now this was a change. Usually Zack was the center of attention, for better or worse. But here he was, wiping off the bar and trying to ignore Madison's antics.

He wondered what Esme was making of this shit show. He could picture her pretty lips pursed, and her elegant eyebrows raised in humor at his situation. Madison was definitely not acting like a lady or anything he expected Esme would approve of in a client. If he were a betting man, he'd wager Esme was pretty pissed right about now. He would have so much fun, sitting out in the van listening to Esme tick off everything that was wrong with this situation.

What the hell was he thinking? He was here, in an amazing bar, with access to free liquor. And the hottest chick in the place was his date. And then there were the scores of other women in the place. Esme had made it clear after last night she was embarrassed by his behavior, so until he regained some ground with her, a relationship with her wasn't an option. He couldn't let Madison have all the attention, could he?

Just like that, Zoom was in the house. Ripping off his shirt, he smiled at the women at his end of the bar. "Anyone interested in body shots?"

Esme

Esme watched one of the small screens in the back of the van, horrified, her mouth hanging open in an O. What were these two imbeciles doing? Madison had ignored everything she had told her. She'd taken the lead, talked all about herself, gotten drunk, and thrown herself at every man and woman waving money at her from across the bar. Now she was standing on top of it, wearing a pair of angel wings she'd procured from a guest and pouring liquor from up high.

Her hands flew to her lips, and she shook her head. "Oh no, no, no. This is getting totally out of control."

Ferris squawked. "Are you kidding? This is amazing!" He leaned closer to his monitor, chewing on the end of a pen.

Leaning closer to the monitor, Esme gasped. Zack was shirt-less—of course he was shirtless—pouring drinks for women ten deep at his end of the bar. God, he looked good without a shirt. She should have known something like this was going to happen.

Ferris vibrated with excitement as Ben and the camera guys managed to capture the entire chaotic scene. Nodding, Ferris swiveled in his chair to look at her. "The crew will stuff Zack back in his shirt soon and wrestle Madison off the bar. This stuff happens all the time."

Esme sat back and observed Ben try to haul Madison and Zack through the crowded bar to the front door. Never in her career had something like this ever happened. The clients she worked with were sane and kept their clothes on in public. They didn't wear costumes or props and behaved like grown adults. Maybe it was the difference between East Coast and West Coast. Or maybe it was just this cast.

She ran a hand down her face, then peered through her fingers at the monitor to see a production assistant push Madison none too gently into the car and drag Zack around to the other side.

"So, that went well?" Ferris asked.

"Ferris! She completely ignored everything I said in the confessional. I knew something was off earlier. Remember during the interview, she made a comment about looking forward to showing the audience what she could do? Then when she and Zack got here tonight, she mentioned being excited at the chance to do another reality show. I don't think she's really invested in this process."

"Nooooo." Ferris feigned shock. "Really?"

"What? You already knew? And you let me go on in our interview about how she could be a good match for Zack?" Esme picked up a pen from the counter in the van and threw it at him. "Why would you let me do that?"

"Honey, what did you think reality television is all about? This is what gets ratings. And you provided the editors seriously fantastic footage to work with."

"Gee, thanks, Ferris. I'm just going to be the laughingstock of the world after this show is over."

Ferris stood, reached up to the ceiling panel, and flipped the power switch to the monitors. "Not the entire world. We don't broadcast in every country."

Esme sighed and fastened the seat belt buckle across her lap. Tonight had been a disaster. Sure, Zack and Madison's antics probably created incredible footage that would make a reality show editor sing with glee. But for a matchmaker whose career was already ruined, this was not a shining moment. Madison and Zack had made a complete joke out of their date.

She was sure neither of them realized the impact of their actions on her stake in the show. Why would they care? She'd gotten herself into this mess, and nobody in the cast or crew owed her anything. The best thing about the night was when the cameras were focused on Zack and Madison, and not on her. Nope, scratch that, she thought as she looked at the camera mounted in the corner of the van.

Ben opened the back door of the van and peeked in. "Hey, Ferris? Do you mind driving? I'm going to ride with Madison."

Why was Ben going to ride with Madison? Before she could even ask the question out loud, Zack climbed into the back of the van and Ferris climbed over equipment to get in the driver's seat.

Settling into the seat Ferris abandoned, Zack swiveled it back and forth a few times, then stopped. "So, that was interesting."

"Interesting? Zack, a documentary about ancient mummies in Egypt is interesting. That was just embarrassing."

Zack chuckled and swiveled in the chair again. "Oh, come on, it wasn't so bad. I have to admit, she's a wild one, Madison. I don't think I can compete."

"You aren't supposed to compete with her. You're supposed to connect with her." Esme raised her head from where she'd been hiding her face in her hands. "Is connection even possible for you?"

Zack stared back at her. Unbothered, he reclined back in the chair. "I don't know the answer to your question. Maybe you can help me. You know, connect?"

Esme's breath caught and the flip-flops started in her stomach again. She could think of several ways she could pleasantly connect with Zack, if he weren't such a jerk. The trick was figuring out how to get him to connect with someone else. God help her.

"How about we start with you keeping your shirt on in public and staying out of bars?"

Zack laughed. "Okay, but do I have to keep my shirt on in the house?"

No, please don't, Esme thought to herself. She poked Zack in the chest. "Yes, in the house too."

thirteen

. . .

Esme

THE NEXT MORNING, Esme went in search of Zack. All night, she had turned the events of the evening over in her head. Madison's motives and behavior had been a total surprise, but what was Zack's excuse for essentially abandoning ship and joining in with her chaos?

After checking the whole house, including his room, she found him on the beach, facing the water. Shirtless. Water glistened over the smooth planes of his back. His legs were crossed, arms resting on his knees. When her shadow moved over him, he looked up in surprise.

"Hey, what are you doing out here?" Zack grabbed a towel lying on the surfboard next to him and spread it out in the sand on his other side. "Want to have a seat?"

Esme lowered herself onto the towel and looked out across the perfect waves. On such a clear day, it was hard to discern where the ocean ended and the sky began. Kicking off her sandals, she buried her feet in the warm sand. She spared a quick peek from under her lashes at Zack, who was back to staring out across the waves.

"I was hoping we could talk more about what happened last night."

Zack shook his wet hair. Droplets traveled from his hair to shoulder and navigated their way down peaks and valleys of lean muscle. Resisting the urge to lick his arm, she hugged her knees and clasped her fingers together for good measure. Sitting so close, she could smell his sunscreen and the scent of ocean salt on his skin. Why it drove her crazy and made her long to smoosh her nose up against his neck to inhale was something best left tucked away and unacknowledged. She'd never wanted to do that with Clayton—or any other man, come to think of it. Maybe all the pickup artist behaviors were getting to her, and she was losing all sense of decorum. Which brought her thoughts back to the events of last night.

Zack dropped his hand, resting it casually over a knee again. "Did you really think Madison could be a match for me?"

Esme leaned back, surprised he'd thrown that question back at her. "Well, she scored high in the areas of socialization; she's definitely an extrovert. You seem to spend a lot of time in similar circles, so I thought maybe you'd have a lot in common. Obviously, I entirely missed her desire for fifteen minutes of fame, but—"

Zack burst out laughing. "You think?"

"You didn't let me finish. I was going to say I'm not sure it's a problem, seeing as you seem to want your own fifteen minutes of fame." Esme poked a finger at him. "You are always on, even more than Madison. And maybe I'm having such a hard time picking out a match because I'm not sure who you are."

"An interesting observation coming from you, the person who manages to disappear at every opportunity." Zack smiled but it didn't quite reach his eyes, which were the bluest of blue under the clear sky. "But right, we're talking about me. Who am I?" Zack stood up and held a hand down to her. "Walk with me?"

Esme reached for him but thought better of it and stood on her own. If she started holding his hand, she might want to do more, like run her hands all over him. She wished she had included indoors and outdoors in the whole wear-a-shirt-rule.

Zack pointed at posts stuck in the ground along the beach. "Cameras, just so you know. Not sure when the crew put them up here, but I guess they're weatherproof and everything. Obviously we're not wearing microphones, so I doubt there is audio.

Must not be too big of a deal, or the crew would be down here hounding us."

"I didn't think you cared much about the cameras or what is caught on audio." Esme walked alongside him, kicking her feet in the surf gently rolling up the sand.

"I don't. I was pointing those things out for your benefit." Zack laughed and turned, walking backward to watch her. "Because that's who I am, Esme. The guy who doesn't care what anyone thinks of him. I'd rather be that guy than be invisible."

Esme studied his face before he moved to be side by side with her again. "You keep insinuating that I prefer to be invisible, which isn't true. I just prefer to maintain control of my image."

"Your image or your feelings? Don't you ever want to take risks and put yourself out there? Do something wild and crazy, and be free?" Zack stopped.

Esme bristled. Clayton and Lucas acting crazy, wild, and free was what got her into this whole mess. Crazy, wild, and free didn't make careers or lasting relationships. Her father had been a crazy, wild, and free man, and she'd learned early on you could not depend on anyone whose life philosophy was so unrestrained. "No, I don't subscribe to that kind of behavior. Acting without thinking gets you nowhere."

"Yeah?"

"Yeah."

Before she could move, Zack hoisted Esme up over a shoulder and ran with her into the surf. She pounded on his back with her fists. "Let me down! Zack, what are you doing? Take me back and put me down! Don't you dare throw me into the water!"

Shuffling back through the waves to shore, he let her down slowly. She had no choice but to grab onto his shoulders to keep from falling face-first into his chest. Zack's hands rested on her hips, and for a minute she forgot how to breathe. Smiling down at her, he chuckled. "That was fun."

"Oh my God, you are so infuriating. I was attempting to have a grown-up conversation, and you are acting like a teenage boy, trying to throw me into the water."

Zack's hands tightened on her hips so she couldn't shove him away. "Maybe I was acting like a teenage boy so I could get closer to you."

Esme froze and her breath hitched. How easy it would be to stand there, embracing Zack on the beach, inches from being able to kiss his amazing, full lips. Coming to her senses, she shook her head and pushed out of his hold. "I have to go find one of the producers; I need them to run an errand for me before tonight."

Zack stepped back and let his hands drop, to show Esme he wasn't going to try to stop her. "You all set for your first date?"

Esme nodded. "I will be. Gotta run, catch you later." She jogged back up the beach to the stairs that led up to the house.

Invisible, she mused to herself. He was wrong. She simply thought before she acted, and he wasn't the only person who could be in the spotlight. She was going to take a page out of Zack MacKenzie's playbook and show everyone just how invisible she was not.

fourteen

• • •

Esme

THURSDAY EVENING, Esme mused at the clothing options laid out on the bed. After learning her date was taking place at a country western bar, she had asked one of the production assistants to take a request to Summer for some wardrobe help. And as usual, her BFF did not disappoint in the selections she pulled and sent back with the staff. Tonight, Esme was being turned loose in a bar for an evening of dancing with Trey, and she wanted to take a page out of Zack's book and dress the part.

Why anyone would want to engage in half the things she had observed Zack and his ex-students doing was beyond Esme. In her experience, good old-fashioned conversation went a long way. Parading around in costumes and performing magic tricks and fake psychic routines looked exhausting.

Esme had given Zack's debut book, *Players: How to Mingle and Stay Single*, a cursory glance before the shooting started. Okay, that wasn't true. She had read the whole thing from cover to cover in a day. She'd been shocked at the degree of success he and his followers had at picking up women with ridiculous escapades. The whole experience was making her rethink her target audience for matchmaking, because those women could use her help.

Of course, Zack was an extraordinarily attractive man and charismatic as hell. She knew firsthand how hard it might be to resist his charms. At least she had found a magic ward against his tactics—Zack had made good on his promise and had kept his shirt on in the house.

Carefully, she pulled the red tank top on, holding the fabric away from her hair and makeup. She tugged it down and shimmied into the artistically shabby denim cutoffs. Summer was right; the Daisy Duke shorts accentuated her legs and made them look longer. A rhinestone-blinged belt and buckle added a nice touch. Esme didn't recognize herself in the full-length mirror. Paired with her own well-broken-in cowboy boots, the effect of the outfit was startling. She looked sexy. Before she could change her mind about appearing on camera in so little clothing, Esme grabbed her ID, stuffed it in her pocket, and ran down the stairs.

"Holy shit." Zack looked up from his seat at the breakfast bar. "I mean... Wow. You look great. But are you sure that's what you want to wear out tonight?"

Esme matched his stare, refusing to look away from those eyes, blue in the current light. She flipped her hair over her shoulder. "Why not? I think this fits the whole peacock approach to the evening, don't you?"

Zack shrugged. "Yeah, but are you confident you know how to wield such powers?"

"Watch me." Esme marched out to the waiting car.

Zack

ZACK DRUMMED his fingers on the counter in the van and peered closer at the monitor. They were parked outside the country western bar the producers had set up for tonight's filming. Trey had sauntered in the front door with Esme on his arm, and every cowboy in the place had come to attention. Even with him by her side after they settled at the bar, the other guys were drawn to Esme like moths to a flame. They drifted over and engaged her in conversation.

"Our girl's not doing too badly in there tonight, eh, Zacky?" Ferris tossed a stress ball up in the air and caught it.

Snatching the stress ball out of the air on Ferris's next toss, Zack snapped back to the monitor with a grunt. "Not too bad."

Zack glared at the monitor. Trey had excused himself to the restroom for barely a minute, and now Esme was being led to the dance floor by a tall guy dressed in blue jeans, a red button-up shirt, and a black cowboy hat.

Zack's eyes followed them around the dance floor. Sweat dripped from his brow. Why was it so hot in the back of the van? Looking over at Ferris, he noticed the host now had headphones clenched to his ears.

"Hey, Ferris." Zack lifted one of the cans. "Can you hear what's going on in there?"

"Uh, yeah." Ferris rolled his eyes behind his dorky glasses. "Duh. What kind of two-bit production do you take this for? Olivia expects us to monitor you guys and make sure everything is staying on track, and I need to take notes for my hosting duties."

"Right. I need those headphones."

Ferris shook his head. "I don't think so. Only crew gets to wear the magic headphones."

Zack stood up in the cramped van and plucked the headphones off Ferris' head. "Good thing you're the host and not crew. I'll help you with your notes later."

"Hey! What are you doing, Zack? Give those back to me, right now."

"No." Zack sat down and pulled the headphones over his ears, leaning forward to stare at the monitor again. Esme had been passed off to yet another tall, lanky cowboy wannabe, and they were two-stepping their way around the dance floor.

The conversation was your average two-relative-strangers-on-a-dance-floor discussion. What's a matchmaker do, anyway? What's your favorite thing to do?

Esme handled it all like a champ. "I'm a dating coach. Research."

Zack couldn't take his eyes off her shorts and legs every time she was danced backward toward the cameras. He'd always been a sucker for cowboy boots on a woman. And the swish-swish of those long, black waves of hair across the back of her tank top every time she laughed at something her dance partner said—oof. He clenched the stress ball in his right hand and squeezed.

He took the headphones off and handed them back to Ferris. "How much longer are we going to stay here? All they're doing is going in circles around the dance floor."

"Oh, I don't know. I'd say things are picking up. I can only imagine what he's whispering in her ear right now. Their mics aren't picking it up over the music." Ferris chuckled and wrote down the film marker on a notepad. "I want to be sure to point this dance out to the post edit team and ask about it in an interview."

Zack stopped breathing when he looked back at the monitor. Trey stood by the dance floor now, and the stranger had drawn Esme in closer. He was a good-looking guy, about Zack's height, with his hair pulled back in a neat tail. At some point he'd lost the cowboy hat. Esme was laughing as he whispered in her ear, and Zack growled as the guy's hand trailed down her back and over her perfect, denim-clad ass. Why wasn't Trey doing something? He certainly wasn't going to sit here and watch from the back of a van while she got manhandled.

Time to act. Zack jumped up and shoved his way out the van doors. Ferris halfheartedly tried reaching for his arm and missed.

Ignoring him, Zack hopped out of the van and headed for the bar, storming through the front doors. He plowed a straight line to Esme on the dance floor and tapped the man on the shoulder, edging between them. "I'm cutting in."

The other man must have seen the fire in Zack's eyes because he didn't argue.

Taking Esme's hand, he ran his other hand down her back to the power pack for the wireless microphone she was wearing and flipped the switch to off. With a growl, he clutched her hip and hauled her against him.

"Zack, what the hell are you doing?" She didn't try to get away; she just looked up at him with those beautiful, dark eyes, where sparks of anger flew.

"Dancing with you. Don't think. Just let me do this, Es."

"You're supposed to be in the van with Ferris. Oh, I see he's in here too now."

Zack nodded at the host, who stood grinning on the side of the dance floor next to a fuming Trey. Zack didn't care. Esme was his for the taking. He had a plan, and it wasn't going to be sidelined by some smooth guy in cowboy boots and a ponytail. Olivia would forgive his transgressions. He was making her great television.

Burying his face in Esme's hair, near her ear, he whispered, "Sorry. I couldn't stand the thought of you in here all alone getting grabbed by that guy. We should work on your date technique."

"I thought I was doing just fine," Esme murmured back, letting him lead her around the floor.

As they passed the band, Zack let go of her hip long enough to spin Esme with one hand and use the other to dig a bill out of his pocket and shove it in the band leader's hand. He leaned closer to the guy and asked for a nice slow song—or three—to get played next. None of the guys in this place had Zack's game. He was the master, had done this a million times.

Esme

As the music slowed, Esme followed Zack's lead as he changed pace. He draped her hand around his neck and tugged her even closer. The scent of the ocean on his skin teased her nose, but now it was mixed with cedar and sandalwood. Esme concentrated on breathing shallowly, so she wouldn't be completely undone by how fantastic he smelled.

Alpha Zack was mesmerizing. She'd seen him as soon as he'd barged through the doors, looking as though he owned the place. In less than three seconds, he had spotted her and was on the floor, cutting in and seamlessly picking up the two-step in time with the music.

Heat burned her skin everywhere they touched. His black T-shirt stretched tightly across his chest and shoulders and did little to hide the ridges of muscle pressed against her. Zack's hand trailed down from her shoulder blade to her waist, leaving a trail of electricity in its path. She shivered.

Zack leaned back to look at her. "Are you cold? Because I can think of some ways to warm you up." A slow, lazy smile tugged at the corners of his mouth.

"What are we doing, Zack? This is practically mutiny; you've hijacked the filming schedule."

Zack closed the distance between them again and smirked against her ear. "Judging by the looks on their faces, I figure we have one more song left before the crew drags us off the dance floor and back to prison. I mean the beach house. The whole no fraternizing allowed outside of your arranged date rule. Just go with it, Esme. What have you got to lose?"

She sank into him, resigned. What did she have to lose? Just everything. Her future, the career she was trying to rebuild, and her reputation in the matchmaking world. She'd be the matchmaker who fell for the scheming pickup artist. Nobody would want to work with her. Her brain was telling her one thing, and her body was completely ignoring her incredibly smart brain.

She stepped back and dropped her hands to Zack's arms. "We should be going. It's getting late, and you know it will be forever before we get to sleep due to the interviews we have to have to film with Ferris."

Ben noticed the break in movement and was bulldozing his way across the dance floor.

Zack reached for her again. "Who said anything about sleep?"

Surprise registered in his eyes as for the second time in two nights, he got hauled out of a bar. Laughing, he let Ben lead him outside, where Esme imagined Ben stuffing him into the back of the production van.

Trey appeared at her elbow, looking equal parts amused and irritated. "Well, that was something. Guess I'll catch a ride back with the camera crew." He kissed her cheek. "Good luck with that one, Esme." With a wave, he headed for the production van parked behind the bar.

Ferris raised a well-groomed eyebrow at her. "Have a nice evening? If you all manage to get me fired, I'm going to die. And then my ghost is going to haunt you forever. But something tells me Olivia is going to looooooove the mess you all are making on camera."

Hooking her arm through his, she started for the door, towing the host along with her. "It has been an interesting evening."

"Interesting? That's the best you've got, sister? I'd say it was hotter than Channing Tatum in here tonight."

"Oh, Ferris, I was just doing what Zack taught me. It's not my fault he's what I managed to reel in tonight. At least I have a lot to think about before we pick matches for the match ceremony."

"I see. So, all of this was just research, that's what you're telling yourself?" Ferris shook his head. "Can't wait to see that next date. Should be entertaining."

"Don't worry, Ferris. I know what I'm doing. I'm a professional, remember?" Esme ducked into the back seat of the waiting car. "Are you riding with me?"

"Uh, yeah, I'm riding with you. No way do I want to drown in the testosterone that'll be oozing from Trey and Mr. Dancy-pants the whole ride back to the beach house." Ferris motioned for her to scoot over and jumped in the back seat. "I just hope you know what you're doing, that's all."

Me too, Esme thought. *Me too.*

fifteen

. . .

Zack

HANDS LACED BEHIND HIS HEAD, Zack lay in bed smiling at the moonlight patterns dancing across the bedroom ceiling. Had tonight gone as anyone planned? No. But how it'd turned out suited Zack just fine. Esme hadn't pushed him away; in fact, she had melted—fucking melted—right into him as they danced. It was the first time he'd had her in his arms, and she didn't even try to bolt right away. Progress.

Zack could still smell her fruity shampoo as he'd buried his face in her glorious hair to whisper in her ear. Undeniably, there had been something burning between them on the dance floor, and he couldn't get the image of her in that red tank top and those shorts out of his mind. With a moan, he jerked the pillow out from under his head and pulled it over his face. Fighting a boner that wouldn't quit, he should just take care of business and move on. A little self-maintenance might help in the short-term, but the only thing more satisfying would be setting eyes on her again. He needed to see her. Talk to her. Maybe he could convince her to go for a moonlit walk on the beach. Chicks loved walking on the beach at night.

Zack rolled out of bed, tugged on a pair of board shorts, and started for the door. Remembering the shirt rule, he doubled back to the dresser and got a T-shirt from the top drawer. He yanked it over his head and as he opened the door, he was surprised to catch an armful of warm woman. Madison's boobs smashed against his chest, and her lips crashed into his, her momentum driving him back into the room. Her hands tangled in his hair, and he couldn't do anything but try to grab for her hips, which only gained him a handful of her ass.

Managing to dislodge his mouth from hers, he wrenched his head to the side. He tried to ignore the burn of pulled hair and got a hand on one of her shoulders. "Madison, whoa. Stop." Zack worked harder to untangle himself from the squirming woman and won a couple feet of distance.

"What's the matter, Zack?" Madison pouted up at him. "I thought you would be bored and up for a little company."

Madison advanced like a cat stalking a delicious mouse. Still free of her grasp, Zack stepped to the side, conscious of the bed behind him. "It's late. And you aren't supposed to be in my room. You're going to get us both busted."

Madison giggled. "I see. You're playing hard to get. Like Olivia's going to care about PDA happening on her cameras."

Zack circled wide and slow around the crazed sex kitten from Hell and worked his way to the door. "Come on, Madison, let me walk you out. I mean, you are gorgeous, but this isn't fair to your fellow contestants who haven't even had their first dates yet." Forcing a smile on his face, he added, "Besides, I'd like to save a little mystery for our next date." Like he was going on another one with this bunny-boiling nut. First thing in the morning he'd make sure to be very clear with Ferris, Esme, and the crew he and Madison were not happening. Nothing. Nada. No way Jose.

But, damn, a hot girl wanted to kiss him. Why would he want to fight it?

No, he had to stay strong. He had one objective, to win his bet with Olivia. Kissing another woman wasn't going to help.

"Next date? Mmm, I like the way you think." Madison sashayed, her signature move, out the door just as the lights in the hallway flipped on and Esme stepped off the stairs.

Zack looked from Madison's barely-there tank top and pajama shorts to Esme's face. *Aw, shitballs.* Most days, Zack didn't give a crap what people thought of him. Tonight wasn't the first time he'd ended up in an awkward situation between two ladies. But for some reason, this time it mattered.

"It's not what you think, Es. Madison stopped by for a little chat and I was just showing her out, seeing as it's the middle of the night and all." He squirmed under the laser beam glare Esme aimed his way.

"I was out for a walk with the other girls and came to see if Zack wanted to join us," Madison said.

Esme ran a cool eye over Madison's attire. "Don't mind me—couldn't sleep, so I was just getting a cup of hot tea. You two go on with whatever it is you were doing." She smirked, rolled her eyes, and headed into the kitchen.

Running into Esme was the worst thing that could have happened. Zack watched the progress he'd made unraveling with each step she took away from him. Her back was straight, shoulders squared. The temperature in the hallway had dipped by a solid thirty degrees. Esme was going to ice him out and he was back to square one. And the worst part? He hadn't even done anything but try to be a gentleman—for a change.

"I don't think she likes me very much," Madison said.

She pursed her lips and was about to follow after Esme, but Zack placed a hand on her back and gave the girl a none too gentle nudge toward the back door.

"C'mon, Madison, let's go find the other women."

Zack and Madison had barely made it off the back porch onto the path when squealing erupted.

"Oh my God, Madison! We were so worried about you." Joy and Isla appeared on the path like apparitions in the night.

"Oh. Hey Zack," said Isla as she gave him a shy wave.

Joy shot invisible eye darts at Madison's head. "Fancy meeting both of you out here." She huffed and crossed her arms. "What exactly were you two up to, anyway? And why are you out here in your pj's, Madison?"

Madison smiled back at the two women, although it didn't

reach her eyes. "Oh, I had a question for Zack so thought I'd just pop over and ask."

"Right." Arms still crossed, Joy glowered at Madison and Zack. "Because it's normal to sneak around and ask questions at two o'clock in the morning in your freaking pajamas. You're such a bitch, Madison."

Isla gasped. "Joy! That wasn't very nice!"

"Don't you get it, Isla? She's playing us." Joy poked a finger at Madison.

Zack realized this was going nowhere fast and coughed to get their attention. Three sets of eyes landed on him. "How do you ladies feel about a walk on the beach, since nobody seems able to sleep?"

Three dreamy sighs answered him. Because chicks loved moonlit walks on the beach.

Esme

ESME TOSSED the tea bag into a mug and tapped her fingers on the counter while the electric kettle warmed up. She'd been unable to sleep because she couldn't get thoughts of Zack out of her head. Now she felt like an idiot after running into a nearly naked Madison and a rumpled-looking Zack coming out of his bedroom.

What the hell did she know about anything, let alone matchmaking? First, she'd blown it big time not seeing any red flags with Clay. And then she'd sighed and rubbed herself—in public —against Zack, who she knew was bad news from the start.

The kettle's red light clicked to green, and Esme poured steaming water into her mug. Walking out on the back porch to sip her tea and listen to the waves, she couldn't help but hear giggling down on the beach. What now?

She pulled her wrap tighter and gripped her mug, descending the steps to the beach. Her thoughts wandered as she sipped tea. Seriously? Zack was out frolicking on the beach with not only Madison but Isla and Joy too? Frowning, she watched the foursome. Joy and Madison were the more aggressive women; she'd known that from the start. Isla was sweet and reserved, more wholesome than the other two. Molly, shyer than all of them, wasn't around. Almost a week in the house and Esme had no idea of which woman would, let alone should, win Zack's heart. At least she didn't have to wonder about who could win his bed. Okay, that was bitchy and not really fair. Zack was a big boy; he could do what he wanted on camera and off.

Shrugging off the thought of Zack and Madison doing the deed, she dropped her empty mug off in the kitchen sink and made her way back up the stairs to her bedroom. If Madison didn't want to take her dating advice, so be it. First thing in the morning, she and Zack were slotted to do interviews together as the intro for the first Love Shack results announcement. She crawled back into bed. Esme needed sleep before she could even think of facing him on camera.

sixteen

. . .

Esme

RELIEF WASHED over Esme when she beat Zack to the patio set they were using for the Love Shack announcements and weekly matching ceremony. Waving to the rest of the cast, who were already seated on the risers placed on the beach next to the porch area, she planted herself square in the center of the small wicker sofa reserved for the interviews.

Zack and Ferris arrived together. Zack, being an intuitive man, took one look at her and opted to pull up one of the ottomans on the porch as a seat. Ferris's eyes widened from behind his glasses.

"Wow," said Ferris, "this whole time I thought I was living and working in California, but turns out I'm in Antarctica." Pretending to shiver, he perched on his wooden stool. "What gives with you two? Something happen between Keith Urban and now that I don't know about?"

Huffing, Esme shrugged. "Nope, I'm good. Zack?"

Zack gave a noncommittal grunt from his seat three feet away.

"Ooookay. Well, look, you two—Olivia wants a sunshine and rainbows interview today for the first Love Shack opening sequence. So suck it up, buttercups. I need you to be shiny happy people and I need it now. Esme, scooch over and let Zack sit on the sofa."

Esme huffed and slid over.

Ferris nodded. "That's better." After flipping through his note cards, he pointed at them both. "You ready to play nice?"

Esme watched Zack shrug, and gave Ferris a curt nod. If Zack could play aloof, so could she.

Ferris cleared his throat, moving the stool aside to stand at the heart-shaped podium the crew had placed between the cast and the interview couch. "Welcome, everyone, to the first Love Shack vote results announcement. But first, we have a little treat today—a get-to-know-you interview with our two resident love experts, Esme Adams and Zack MacKenzie! First question is for Esme. Esme, what drove you to become a matchmaker and dating coach?"

Esme sat up straighter. The question was easy enough and something she'd answered in a thousand interviews. "I was born into it. My grandmother was a matchmaker, and so was her mother, and her mother, and so on. We can trace it back several generations. Except for my mother. She doesn't seem to have inherited the gift."

"So, this is something that runs in your family?"

"Yes, it's a talent. You see, my family's descended from the Romani. My ancestors were really into arranged marriages. I believe my grandmother and I were the first two to monetize the talent. She runs a small dating business in Los Angeles. When I was living in New York, I saw a real need for helping very busy people find love."

"You said the talent skipped your mother. Can you expand on that some?" Ferris looked up from his cards, going off script if Esme didn't know any better.

"Mmm. Yes, my grandparents had a nice young man picked out for her, but she had other ideas and eloped with my father. My grandmother tried to bring her into the business, but she kept running off clients. She's … a lot to take in sometimes."

Please don't let him ask any more questions about my parents. She didn't want to get into her father leaving.

Still not referring to the cards, Ferris studied her until she felt like squirming. "So, are your parents still together?"

Esme groaned and felt lightheaded. She stayed quiet, thinking about how to answer the question.

"No, they've been separated for a long time now. It's one of the reasons I know the talent skipped her." Aware of Zack next to her on the couch, Esme smiled widely for the cameras. "Which is why my motto has always been: 'Matchmaking—saving the world one happy ending at a time.'"

Esme prayed Ferris was finished asking her questions.

She caught Zack taking in her clenched fists, and he shot her a concerned look and jumped to her rescue. "That's a good one, saving the world one happy ending at a time. I can think of some happy endings that rocked my world."

Crude, but she'd take the save. Esme breathed a sigh of relief as Ferris's attention shifted to Zack.

"All right, your turn, Zack. What led you down the path of becoming a, uh, professional pickup artist?" Ferris emphasized the word professional.

"What led me to become the most renowned pickup artist ever? I was giving advice to guys I met in bars, and it was resonating with a bunch of dudes who needed my help. Before I knew it, I had a following and guys were paying me money to teach them how to meet ladies. I was bored one day and wrote a book about it so I could reach more guys."

"Your parents are very successful entrepreneurs, running several thriving corporations. Yet you have been a professional surfer, and now you own a male strip club and run your pickup artist business. Most people would probably wonder why you didn't follow in their footsteps."

Zack froze at the question for just a moment, and then he was back on for the cameras.

"I didn't follow my parents into the family businesses because... Well, that would be boring, wouldn't it? I mean, you can't spend the day at the beach surfing and nights partying, for one thing. And I am a business owner in my own right. I own a cool bar with my buds. Why not invest in male strippers? The place is a chick magnet, and all the women you could ever want flood the place every night. Now and then, I might even get onstage and give a little show, you know?"

Zack grinned for the cameras. Ferris dropped his cards and stared at Zack. So did Esme. While Ferris was probably hung up on the image of Zack dancing on a stage, she was thinking about his current body language and how he'd stiffened when asked about his parents' business. She made a mental note to ask him about it later.

"Holy shit, you're living the dream, man. Right on." Kent said, interrupting the silence. Some of the other guys chuckled in agreement.

Molly rolled her eyes. "Shut up, Kent. You are such a douche." Her cheeks flushed. "Excuse my language. I've been hanging around Joy too much."

"Right." Ferris scrambled to pick up his cards. "Esme, Zack, why don't you join the rest of the cast on the risers, and we can get on to the announcement."

Zack

ZACK HAD to get out of the hot seat before the shit-eating grin he'd plastered on for the camera broke his face. He took a seat next to the other guys, and Kent gave him a fist bump.

"What a week we've been having here at Heart House!" Ferris beamed a smile at the cast. "Madison and Zack painted the town on Thursday night and then on Friday, Esme, Trey, and Zack showed us how the two-step is not done! The audience had the opportunity to vote on whether to send one of the couples to the Love Shack this week to confirm a match." Ferris looked over at Madison. "How do you think they voted, Madison?"

Wiggling in her seat and sitting up straighter, Madison

bounced to life. "I'd like to think they voted me and Zack into the Love Shack, because we have serious chemistry."

Zack raised a hand to his mouth to muffle the choked cough burbling up from surprise. The girl really was delusional.

"What about you, Esme? How do you think the vote will go tonight?"

Zack's breath quickened as she caught his gaze. He watched her eyes narrow and slide over to Madison. "Honestly, Ferris? I think the vote will be to not send anyone to the Love Shack tonight. I don't think enough connections were built to entice the audience."

"Well, let's find out!" Ferris opened the envelope lying on his podium. "Esme, you are right! Nobody is going to the Love Shack tonight. Better luck next week, everyone, and I'll see you all tomorrow night for the matching ceremony. Zack, Esme—you both have a lot of work ahead of you to try and light up as many matches as possible."

"Ferris, we need to talk." Olivia's voice rang out from the house.

Zack's attempt to bolt from the patio was foiled when Olivia intercepted him, and he was forcefully deposited into an armchair in the living room seating area. She stomped back outside to capture Esme and Ferris. Esme was delivered to the other armchair. Ferris was unceremoniously dumped on an ottoman.

Olivia crossed her arms, walked a circle around the seating area, and glared at everyone. The woman must have a never-ending supply of black pants, heels, and sleeveless blouses and vests. Her dark eye makeup and deep red lips were intimidating, and she was one silver hair streak away from an amazing Cruella de Vil imper-sonation. Zack sank farther down in his chair, getting the impres-sion this could take a while since she hadn't said a word yet.

"I'm on break from the set of my other show, *Forever After*, and am here to observe the setup for the Love Shack vote and matching ceremony." Olivia pointed her finger at Ferris. "And it's finale week over there, Ferris. After you screwed up last year's reveal, I can't spare being away, so you better keep making this good."

Zack cringed inside at the look on Ferris's face. He was pale, tears threatening to spill any second. He knew the little dude was working hard and just wanted to impress Olivia Marcum. Her attitude was not cool.

Zack stood up, hands raised as if approaching a wild beast. "Olivia, calm down. What the hell is wrong with you? You shouldn't just stomp in and start yelling at everyone when we haven't seen you for days. Ferris and the crew have been working real hard, keeping everything going."

"What the hell is wrong with me? You have no idea what last year's mistake on the *Forever After* finale cost me, Zack. To get a second chance on a mega-hit show that I created was a gift. And to get the green light for a second romance-angle show after that disaster, well, it's just a miracle."

Ferris stood, hip jutted out. Color had spilled back onto his face. "Olivia, I've got this."

Olivia stalked toward the slighter man. To Ferris's credit, he didn't shove his dorky glasses back up on his nose. Shoulders squared, he stood defiantly. Zack was impressed; he didn't think the kid had it in him.

"One more thing, Ferris," said Olivia. "As much as I looooove the drama behind the scenes on the dates, the crew is complaining about keeping track of too many contestants. I don't want to hire more camera operators. From here on out, Esme and Zack do not go anywhere near each other's dates. They can watch on the livestream with the rest of the house-guests and observe without being tempted to interrupt or interfere."

Zack froze and resisted the urge to growl at the producer. He and Olivia had a deal, so why would she come in guns blazing and squash his game? "Olivia, how about you and I take this outside..."

Ignoring him, she continued with a pointed look at Zack and Esme. "And you two, I need more chemistry and drama on these dates. We want the audience to vote on Love Shack because they are dying to know if their match guesses are right. I want show-mances galore all over this house. Ferris, maybe we should send two other wild card couples out on dates too. I think it will be more fun for viewers."

"Aye-aye, Olivia." Ferris offered her a quirky salute. "Esme, come with me and let's go tell the rest of the cast you are free to get ready for the '80s prom party the producers are throwing for you tonight."

Esme shot Zack a wry smile and made a beeline after Ferris for the patio.

Zack studied Olivia, wary of her mood. She stalked toward him, and her mouth smoothed up into a cruel smile. "You didn't think I was going to make it this easy, did you, Zacky? If none of these girls work out, I'm going to need a bachelor on next year's *Forever After*." Olivia trailed a sharp finger down his chest, and he resisted the urge to shrug her off. "I think you'd do just fine."

Smiling, she grabbed her bag. "I'll see myself out. Enjoy your day."

Zack ran a hand through his hair and watched her saunter out the door. What was it Ferris had said? A party in the house tonight? Game on. As he headed straight to his room to get ready, he thought about his next move. If there was one thing Zack had learned from Esme's date, he enjoyed dancing with her. And if he played it right, could he make that happen again tonight?

Esme

DETERMINED to hide out and decompress after the drama of the morning, Esme made a beeline for her room.

She made it halfway up the stairs when she heard a "Pssst" from behind. Turning, she found Zack at the bottom of the stairs, his T-shirt rumpled and obviously hastily pulled over his head. She laughed. "Following the shirt rule. I'm so proud of you."

Zack started up the stairs, stopping a step below her. Even then, she still had to look up into his smiling face.

"What's up? Shouldn't you be in the shower by now?" she asked. An image of him popped into her mind: water dripping down his face on its way lower. She could keep this professional despite the fact his lips were within the most kissable distance they'd ever been.

"Hey, Shortcake. Just wanted to say I like your dinosaur skirt."

"Thanks. I'm pretty sure it glows in the dark." Esme held up a hand before Zack could utter a word. "No, there is no need for us to find out."

He put a hand on the railing. "About this morning, with Madison. I just wanted you to know nothing happened. She slid into my room uninvited, and I was just trying to get her out of the house."

Showmances. Olivia's words echoed through Esme's head. Everything in her being wanted to take Zack's hand, pull him up into her room, and nix the shirt-on-indoors rule. But that was not why she was here. Career first, always. Nothing was more important than getting back on track, and a relationship with Zack would end in disaster when he went back to his real life, and she went back to hers.

She waved him off. "Don't be silly, Zack. Even if you did want her in your room, there's nothing wrong with that desire. It's the whole point of being here, right? To build a romantic connection with one of the women on the show?"

"I may not be the matchmaker here, but I'm going to go out on a limb and say I'm pretty sure Madison is not my perfect match."

"And how do you know?"

Zack pinched the bridge of his nose and laughed. "Don't make fun of me. It's just a feeling I have; she's definitely not The One."

"I have those feelings too sometimes. I think you're onto something."

"Yeah?" Zack leaned closer and her heart may have skipped a beat or two. "So, you wanna help me at the party tonight? We should set up a mini speed dating session. What do you think? Get to know the rest of the cast better and compare notes?"

Drowning in the gaze of those eyes staring so intently into hers, Esme agreed. "Uh, sure. Sounds great. I'll be rooting for you tonight. I'm just going to"—she pointed up the stairs—"catch some downtime before we start tonight." She trotted up the rest of the stairs and disappeared into her room.

Romantic connection. Zack started back down to his room to get changed. Rooting for him? What did she mean by that, anyway?

seventeen

. . .

Zack

ZACK HAD to hand it to the crew; they knew how to throw a party. Not necessarily a cool party, but beggars—as well as prisoners of a reality television show—couldn't be choosers. The downstairs of the house had been transformed with hot-pink and teal lighting that screamed '80s and in the background, Cyndi Lauper reminded everyone all girls really want is to have fun. Esme looked like she was doing just that, dancing with the other girls on the makeshift dance floor, furniture pushed aside to make room.

He had to give props to the '80s for making revealing women's clothing popular. Esme's short, zebra print skirt showed off her amazing legs, and the teal off-the-shoulder top was really sexy. Her silly animal print clothes made him smile, and the thought of taking them off her made him burn. His breath caught when her gaze found his, and she headed over his way.

"Hey! Jake Ryan called, and he wants his clothes back!" Grinning, she poked at his sweater vest.

"Who's Jake Ryan?"

Everyone in the cast had been provided with a gigantic wardrobe and screen captures of '80s pop culture icons to help them choose theme-appropriate outfits. Zack thought the guy leaning on the red sports car looked cool in his classic sweater vest over a button-down with sleeves rolled up, well broken in blue jeans, and black combat boots.

"Just the hottest guy from one of the most popular '80s movies. Haven't you ever seen *Sixteen Candles*?"

"Handsome guy, red sports car? He may have been my inspiration for the evening. So, you think I look hot?" Unable to help himself, he leaned closer. "Because I think you are smokin' tonight."

He watched her cheeks explode with color. "Thanks. So, do you still want to get everyone together and see if they're willing to do a speed dating round tonight? I agree it would be a good way for us to get to know the other contestants."

He bit back a growl of frustration. If changing the subject was a sport, she'd be World Champion. Why was this woman immune to his well-honed charms? Refusing to be ignored in a boring round of speed dating, Zack grabbed her hand.

"I have a better idea. Come with me." Draining the bottle of beer he'd been drinking, he tugged her across the makeshift dance floor to the sound system, which was being run by Joel, who not only was a graphic novel artist but also had some skill at spinning sounds around Orange County as a decent DJ. After Zack's wild gesturing and shouting, Joel cut the music volume and handed Zack the microphone.

The other guys, who were parked by the snack table, looked up.

"Who's down for a classic party game of Spin the Bottle?" When Esme gasped, he grinned. "Or better yet, Seven Minutes in Heaven?"

Esme narrowed her eyes at him and grabbed the microphone. "Kissing optional." Covering the microphone, she said to him, "I read the chapter in your book on kissing and games. Did you plan this with the other guys in the house?"

Faking a pained sigh, Zack acquiesced and took the microphone back. "Fine, kissing optional." Although he hadn't planned anything with the guys in the house, he was going to make sure he got his seven minutes with Esme.

Zack slung an arm around Joel's neck. While he handed the microphone back, he whispered, "When it's your turn to spin, do your best to land on me, man."

Joel gave him a grin and a nod. Esme looked between the two of them with a frown. "You two are up to something."

Zack chuckled as Madison swooped in for the save.

"Oh my God, I love this game!" Madison plopped down on the floor, pulling Isla down with her. "I make how to kiss tutorial videos on YouTube, and my most favorite one I filmed is how to kiss in a game of Seven Minutes in Heaven!"

"Seriously? That's a thing? Kissing tutorials?" Wesley's surprise climbed up his face.

"Duh! It's super important to know how to kiss well, and kissing games are the best practice." Madison grinned as Wesley's face turned bright red.

Isla cleared her throat. "Um, how many kissing tutorials could you possibly have to film?"

Madison counted off on her fingers. "Well, there's How to Make Out in the Back Seat of a Car, How to Kiss in a Movie Theater, Where to Put Your Hands When Kiss—"

Wesley cut her off. "Wait, why not how to make out in the front seat?"

Madison rolled her eyes. "Um, the gear shift gets in the way."

"All right. Thank you, Madison, for that enlightening information." Lowering himself to the floor in the center of the room, Zack said a little prayer that he wouldn't end up in the closet with Madison. "I'm putting my own spin on the rules, no pun intended. Because he's been spinning some righteous eighties tunes tonight, I nominate Joel as first into the closet. I'll spin the bottle, and whoever it lands on will join him in there for seven minutes. When time is up, Joel will come out and he'll spin, and that person will join whoever's in the closet. And so on and so on. What you do in there is up to you."

Kent raised his beer. "I'm just warning you ladies now, seven minutes might not be enough time with the Kentimator."

Molly glared at him and raised a hand. "Can we leave sooner than seven minutes?"

No matter how hard he tried, Zack just couldn't convince

Kent to give up the lame nickname he'd chosen for himself. Some guys were really beyond his help. "Sorry, ladies, minimum of seven minutes, no exceptions."

Joy shared a knowing look with Molly. "Don't worry, Mol, seven minutes is enough time for the Joyinator to kick the Kentimator's ass, I'm just saying."

"Okay, I'm modifying the rules," said Zack. "What you do in there is up to you, except for ass-kicking. No ass-kicking." Zack took off his watch and held it in the air. "Bottle spinner is in charge of the timer. The person who exits the closet becomes the new bottle spinner. Everyone ready? Wait, Joel needs a blindfold. Isla, give him your scarf."

"Hell yeah!" Joel grabbed the scarf and entered the closet.

Esme pulled at one of her ears. "Hey, Joel, are there cameras in the closet?"

"Negative," he called back. "I don't see any in here. Blindfold's on. Closing the door now."

Zack spun the bottle. Round and round it went, and when it stopped it pointed directly at Esme, whose expression alternated between suspicious and pleading.

Madison huffed. "Darn, I really wanted to go first!"

Zack interrupted Esme before she could offer. "Nope, nuh-uh. Rules say whoever the bottle points at has to go." He made shooing motions with his hands. "Off with you. Timer isn't starting until the closet door closes."

Narrowing her eyes at him, Esme got to her feet to join Joel in the closet. "At least there aren't cameras," she muttered under her breath.

Esme

SEVEN MINUTES IN CLOSET PURGATORY, then she'd be free. Esme slipped in to join Joel in the cramped and dark space. At least she could use the time to get to know him better and actually strategize around the real game, which was making matches and not figuring out the best way to make out with other people in the house. She considered it an extra bonus that there were no cameras in the closet. Sadly, the producers would probably remedy the situation as soon as they watched the party footage.

The only light in the small space filtered in from under the door. Her eyes adjusted to the dark and Esme jumped as Joel's hands grabbed her face.

"Hey, who won the first spin?" he asked.

She clasped his hands in hers before they could roam anywhere else. "It's Esme. I think you can take the blindfold off now."

Joel gave her a sheepish look as he pulled off the scarf. "So, what do you want to do for the next six and a half minutes?"

She leaned against the wall behind her, thinking. "Want to tell me about your art?"

Joel's face lit up. "Yeah, sure! I'd love to, although it may not be as entertaining as the stories I could tell you from driving for Uber."

"I bet, but something tells me art is more personal to you, and, well, I wanted to spend tonight getting to know more about everyone. You're a graphic novel artist, right?"

"I am. Frank Miller is my idol; I love his work. I'm working on my own series right now, but I've been stuck and looking for a muse to inspire me." Joel wiggled his eyebrows. "How would you like to be immortalized on my pages?"

"Do you use that line on all the girls? You said something similar during your introduction on the first night."

The corners of Joel's mouth quirked down. "What? That

doesn't work for you? Zoom—I mean Zack—said it was a sure thing."

Esme shook her head. "Mmm, no, doesn't really work for me." But she bet it would work for Madison. She made a mental note for a possible match for the matching ceremony.

"Dang, you are stone-cold, Esme. No kissing, don't want to be drawn..." He swallowed a laugh as he counted off her negative qualities. Before he could get any further though, there was a knock on the door. "Time's up. Your turn to put this on." He tied the blindfold gently around her head. He left the closet and she was alone.

Esme straightened the scarf so it wasn't tugging on her hair and waited. She heard the door open and quietly close again, and her breath caught in the wave of electricity that filled the air. The scent of ocean, sunscreen, and sandalwood teased her nose. Hands gently untied the blindfold. She didn't need to open her eyes to know who was with her.

"You fixed the game, didn't you?" Accusing him was a better plan than kissing him.

"I didn't fix anything! The bottle wants what the bottle wants." Zack's laugh was low and warm against her ear, and her heart literally tried to beat its way out of her chest.

"I'm not kissing you in here, Zack MacKenzie."

"Okay."

"Fine."

Zack brightened. "Fine. Shall we talk?"

"Let's. Why did you freeze up last night when Ferris asked you about working for your parents?"

Zack's face faltered. "Shall we talk about something else?"

"I think we should talk about this. Knowing this kind of information about each other will help us make matches." And keeping him talking would keep her from thinking about kissing his freaking perfectly kissable lips. Lips just inches from hers, so close she could feel his breath tickle her ear. He shifted and his arm brushed hers, sending a zing of heat through her body. She shivered at the thought of his arm circling her waist, pulling her in closer.

"I covered it in the interview. Surfing, parties, and a cool bar to hang out in every night—what else is there to life?"

"So you never considered working with your parents?"

Zack slid down the wall to sit on the floor and rested an arm on his knee. She followed him and sat cross-legged opposite of him and waited for him to continue.

"My parents never invited me to help run the family business. I don't think it even occurred to them to ask." Zack shrugged.

"Why not? You've got to be the most charismatic person I've ever met. You'd be great at public relations, marketing, sales..."

His mouth turned up in a wry smile. "When I was thirteen, one night at dinner after parent-teacher conferences they had a whole conversation right in front of me, as though I wasn't even there. They kept wondering how two successful, intelligent people could have a son who was failing elementary art, of all things? Obviously the only thing I'd ever be good at was physical activities, since gym was the only class I wasn't failing."

Zack tilted his head back and examined the bar that ran across the top of the closet. "In middle school, I held Laguna Beach's record for juvenile busted for hosting the most house parties. My parents' generous financial support of the city kept me out of serious trouble. I barely graduated high school. Gym really was my best subject, and the only things we all agreed I was very good at were breaking rules and surfing. At sixteen, my parents stuck me in my own house, so I'd stop trashing theirs, and it was out of sight out of mind, like always. So, you see, I'm not really CEO material."

Esme resisted the urge to reach out and comfort him, sad for the little boy who had been so desperate for attention and praise. "Well, despite all of that, I'd say you've accomplished a lot. Pro surfing career, best-selling book—in some peoples' opinions."

Grinning at him, she nudged his foot with her toes. "And you are part owner of a wildly popular bar."

"True. How about you?"

"What about me?"

"You didn't want to answer Ferris's questions about your parents either." Zack gave her a pointed look. "Why not?"

"Because they represent everything I work to help other people avoid."

"Divorce?"

"I remember my sixth birthday so vividly. It smelled like flowers and rain outside. That year I'd gotten the best present ever—a new bike. I begged my dad to teach me how to ride it. You know, like a big girl, with no training wheels?"

Zack's lips curved up in a smile and his eyes crinkled at the corners. He had nice eyes.

Esme sighed. Try as she might, she couldn't forget the day one spring when her dad had left.

"Daddy! Is it time yet?" She'd jumped on his lap and he'd laughed, snuggling her into a hug. But something was weird, and he held her just a little longer than normal.

"Okay, pumpkin, I think you've waited long enough. Go put your shoes on while I talk to your mom." Hugging her one more time, he ran a hand through his hair and stared off to the kitchen. Head down, he went one direction, and she scampered off in another.

She ignored their raised voices while tying her shoes and finding a jacket. Running down the stairs to the garage, she'd pushed the button to open the garage door and wheeled her new bike outside.

Suitcases sat on the driveway next to her father's car. Her mother stood there, arms crossed. With a sigh, her father's shoulders sagged. "You sure you want this, Nat? Once I pull out of the driveway, I'm not ever coming back."

"We've been over this too many times, Todd. Until you decide to grow up and spend more time focusing on real issues at home instead of your ridiculous business venture with Jimmy, we have nothing more to talk about."

Esme dropped her bike in the green grass next to the driveway and ran as fast as she could, tackling his legs, holding on for dear life. "You can't leave, Daddy. You can't leave and not come back. What about me? You love me, and I love you." Tears streamed down her face and she couldn't breathe.

"Esme, come here, my love. Daddy has to go." Mommy held out her hand.

He bent down and untangled her arms from his legs. He hefted his bags into the car.

She kicked and screamed and fell to the ground, watching his car back out of the driveway.

After experiencing the pain of seeing him leave, she tried not to have to go through it again with him or anyone else. She busied herself with dance classes, schoolwork, fake illnesses—anything to avoid visits after which he'd just leave again. Eventually, he gave up and left her alone.

Esme jumped as Zack tucked a strand of hair behind her ear. "So, what, he left you and your mom on your birthday?"

Esme swallowed hard. She didn't even have to tell him, yet somehow Zack seemed to always know what she was thinking.

"Wow. That's really terrible. Guess your mom should have let your grandparents do the whole arranged marriage thing. Is that your deal then? You want to save the world from heartbreak through your own version of arranged marriage?"

A knock on the door signaled time was up. Esme ran hands over her hair and face, ensuring everything was in place. "Something like that, anyway."

Zack stood and held out a hand to pull her up. "Well, if anyone can do it, I think you're a sure bet." He winked at her and opened the door so she could exit. "Hey, Esme? Next time, instead of sharing stories of our sad childhoods, how about we just kiss instead?"

eighteen

. . .

Esme

SUNDAY EVENING. Week one, and already Esme felt like she'd been living in the house for months. She stared nervously at the heart-shaped podium. She took in the newly added row of lights pointed at the house's wall, projectors for the hearts, as well as what looked like a control console from a spaceship placed between the cast seats and the host stand.

While Ferris gave last-minute directions to Ben and the camera crew, she mentally reviewed her matches. She mused over the process. Normally, clients spent time with her in her office and filled out a variety of questionnaires. That information, along with computer-generated probabilities and a hunch, would allow Esme to know whether a couple belonged together or not. But now, minus her trusty computer program, Esme was forced to rely on good old intuition, and she just hadn't gotten to spend enough time getting to know everyone yet. The twist also loomed over her; she was matching herself too. One of these five couples had to include her name.

While the dates were fun, and the guys in the house were seriously nice to look at, the process was stressing her out. Anxiety was a constant knot in her throat and the feeling of eyes on her all the time, knowing an audience was watching, also threw her off-balance. And her future livelihood was at stake.

Ferris grabbed her by the elbow and tugged her off the bench. "Come with me, we're about to start."

Taking a deep breath, she followed him to the front of the set. Ben's booming voice called for the cast to stand on the side of the patio while they waited to be seated in matched pairs.

After a nod from Ben, Ferris lit up. "Welcome, everyone, to our first match ceremony. Quick reminder for those just tuning in: Esme and Zack will each propose five couples from our ten contestants. Esme locks in first, then Zack can swap up to two. Hearts light up for each correct match, but they won't know which ones. Zero hearts is a blackout and costs fifty grand. What a week! How about that party last night? I heard there was a lot of fun and games, if you know what I mean. Want to tell us about the time you spent in the closet last night, Esme, during that crazy game of Seven Minutes in Heaven?"

Heat flushed her cheeks and her chest tightened. Of course he'd ask her first. "Well, Ferris, a lady doesn't kiss and tell, now does she?"

Ferris shot her a questioning look. "So there was kissing involved?"

Giving him what she hoped were laser beam eyes, she smiled sweetly and tried not to bare her teeth at him. "Since there were no cameras in there, I guess that is for us to know and you to not find out?"

"Fair enough." Ferris chuckled. "But if any of you decide you do want to kiss and tell, all you have to do is pop into the confessional and have your say. The audience—and not gonna lie—I would love to know."

Madison's hand shot up and Ferris ignored her. "Let's move on to the real reason we're gathered out here tonight. Matches. Esme and Zack have both come up with their proposed pairs. Both of our experts are playing for a shared pool of a million dollars." On cue, everyone gasped and Ferris nodded. "The stakes are high. After Esme locks in her matches, we'll give Zack the opportunity to change any of them he disagrees with. After all the matches are locked in, we'll see how many hearts light up on the board. It will take at least one heart to keep them both on track to split a million-dollar prize. However, a blackout will result in the pool being reduced by fifty grand. That's the price of love, right, folks?

"And to keep it interesting, our contestants are playing for another million dollars. Same rules apply, so it is in everyone's best interest to work together."

Sweat broke out on Esme's palms and trickled down the back of her neck. Not only did she have to miraculously pull matches out of thin air this week; she had to put some trust in Zack not to cause a blackout and drop the prize pool. She sneaked a glance his way, and her breath caught. Dressed in slacks and a button-down with the tail untucked and sleeves rolled up his forearms, he belonged on the cover of a fashion magazine. When he winked at her, she jerked her attention back to Ferris.

"So, Esme, you're going to announce your matches as you enter them into the control panel. Are you ready?"

Nodding, she made her way to the silly control panel and faced the cast. She went with her gut on a match she felt very strongly about and pushed two buttons. Two headshots appeared on the big monitor above the podium. "My first match tonight is Joel and Madison."

Esme had to suppress a giggle at the look on Madison's face. No way was Esme going to match her with Zack; it was painfully obvious that would never work out, as amusing as it would be to make him squirm on another date with the wild woman.

"My second match tonight is Molly and Wesley." Then she announced Zack and Joy, Kent and Isla, and herself and Trey. While she was positive Trey was not her match, she couldn't really decide who he belonged with, so he was a wild card for sure.

Taking her seat next to him in the cast seating area, she held her breath while Ferris motioned to Zack.

"All right, Zack, this is your chance," Ferris said. "Do you want to lock in any changes to the couples this week?"

Esme clenched her fists as she waited for him to answer. The heat of his presence in the seat behind her emanated against her back. *Please don't let him say yes and cause a blackout.*

"Yes, I think I'm going to change a couple of things up." Zack stood, making his way to the console, and Esme held her breath again. "Not touching Joel and Madison, I think that is a good guess. However, I want to match Isla with Trey, Joy and Kent, Esme and Wesley, and lastly, myself and Molly."

Esme laughed and clapped a hand over her mouth so she didn't distract from the ceremony. But seriously, Zack and Molly? The cast shifted seats to sit with their new matches, and Ferris faced the lights again.

"All right, we have our matches locked in. Let's see how you did. There are ten light projectors set up facing the house. You can think of them like bat signals for love. Let's see if we have any matches tonight." Ferris turned once more and waited for the lights.

Esme bit her lip. What if they got zero matches? Her leg jiggled with nerves and anticipation. She felt a tap on her shoulder. "Don't worry, we've got this." Zack's breath tickled her ear. Ignoring him, she grabbed Trey's hand, who looked over at her with surprise. A grunt from Zack told her he'd sat back down. A breath she'd been holding escaped when a hot-pink heart appeared on the side of the house.

Kent jumped up and pumped a fist. "Yeah!" He was jerked down quickly by Molly.

"We have one light. Will there be any more?" Ferris stood at the podium, continuing to stare at the lights as if they were the answer to everything in the universe. It reminded Esme of how strange she found reality television.

One light remained steady. No blackout, thank goodness. Just when she thought it was over, another light projected onto the house, which made Kent let out another whoop. Now she just had to figure out which couples represented the two lights.

"Nicely done. Two lights. No blackout. Everyone's prize money remains intact for another week! Congratulations! Just a reminder, we've randomly selected Zack and Esme's next date partners, and as a bonus, we're sending two more couples along.

Zack and Joy will be joined by Molly and Trey. Esme and Wesley will be joined by Madison and Kent. The audience will vote on the location and activity of the dates on Tuesday, and we'll all be back here for another matching ceremony next Sunday night!"

Joy bounded up the steps to where Esme and Zack were still seated. "I'm so pumped for our date, Zack! I'm into all things fitness and love learning new sports. I hope we get physical." Joy flexed her arms. "You don't get these guns slinging drinks in a nightclub."

Esme's eyes slid over the Incredible She-Hulk. Joy was amazing. No doubt now the audience would pick a date night involving something athletic. A pang of disappointment pooled in her stomach. She wasn't sure if it was from the thought she would miss seeing Zack get his ass kicked in a physical challenge by a girl firsthand, or if she would just miss seeing Zack.

"Come on, Esme, let's get some drinks and hang out in the hot tub. Girls only!" said Joy.

Esme managed not to squeak when Joy nearly yanked her off her feet. Steadying herself, she smiled at the slightly scary woman.

"Good idea, girls only." Stealing a backward glance at Zack, Esme continued, "Let's discuss the possibility of romantic connections on the next round of dates. We need more lights."

Joy locked arms with her and beamed with delight. "Yes! Let's discuss."

nineteen

· · ·

Zack

WEEK TWO, Wednesday night. Romantic connection. Zack sighed and looked over the packing list a production assistant had handed him—the gear he needed for his date with Joy tonight. What the hell were they doing, anyway? Going spelunking? Opening a duffel bag, he threw in his wetsuit along with a long-sleeve, dry-tech shirt, pants, and the headlamp someone had dropped off to his room. He pulled on a T-shirt and athletic shorts, retrieved the bag, and headed for the car.

Zack, Joy, Trey, Molly, and the camera crew piled into the private plane the show had rented, along with a seriously stressed-out host who immediately slipped on headphones and informed them not to interrupt his meditation track. After a one-hour flight and another short car ride, Zack found himself in the desert outside Henderson, Nevada, at dusk.

A truck towing a small equipment trailer pulled up and Ferris gathered the contestants together in front of it.. Beaming at the camera, the host gestured to everyone standing awkwardly around him. "Welcome to date night, everyone! And what a night the audience has planned! You all get the pleasure of running one of the most elite obstacle courses in the country. One loop around is just five miles, and the audience wants to see how many times you can complete the course overnight. We've brought tents, in case anyone wants to take a rest"—Ferris wiggled his eyebrows—"or some privacy. I'm just going to leave you kids to it. Have a great night!"

Zack watched with a pang of jealousy as Ferris made his way

back to the heated car."Here, help me put this up." Joy handed him a tent from the trailer.

Zack wrestled with the nylon and plastic as Ben and the boom mic of doom watched every move. When it was clear she wasn't going to help, he gave his date an exasperated look, then stopped to watch as Joy launched into a routine of calisthenics and stretches.

"So, what's the plan for tonight?" he asked. Surely, she wasn't keen on camping out here in the middle of nowhere.

Joy was suspended in a wide-legged forward fold and peered at him through her legs. "Don't you know where we are? Just one of the coolest mud obstacle courses in the whole country!" Jumping up, she took the tent he was still wrestling with and shook it out, plopping it on the ground. "Five miles of obstacles galore! You brought your wetsuit, right? We don't want you getting hypothermia. I'm going to go run a few warmup miles. Want to join me?"

"Uh, no. I'm good. Hypothermia?" Zack tended to stay away from situations that started with hypo- and ended with -thermia. Born and raised in California, he preferred sunshine and clear, warm nights. Besides, the cold irritated the knee injury that had ruined his surfing career.

"Yeah, it's a risk we have to mitigate here in the desert at night. Not so bad during the day."

He thought about Esme as he watched Joy jog off for a warmup run. By now, the cast had their live feed on at the house, and she was probably curled up with a glass of wine to enjoy this while Zack ran around the freezing-cold desert at night. Tugging on his wetsuit, he wished he was sitting in Kent or Wesley's place in the house instead of in front of the camera tonight.

Twenty minutes later, Joy rejoined him at the campsite, along with a shivering Molly and determined-looking Trey. The former paratrooper probably ran these things in his sleep when he'd been in the military.

Zack's crazy date started doing jumping jacks. "You guys, this is awesome! I have a Tough Mudders team and we've been training for the world championships. Tonight is going to be an awesome practice run. I hope you are ready to have some fun! Wait until we get to jump over the flaming hay bales!"

Zack followed them all to the starting line. Why couldn't the audience have set him up on a normal date? What was so wrong with dinner and a movie? A chick flick would be better than freezing his balls off scrambling through muddy water, crawling under barbed wire, and hauling himself over walls. Not to mention it would all irritate his bum knee.

The starting horn sounded, and Joy was off before he could say *flaming hay bale*, let alone jump one.

Zack trotted at a slow jog to the first obstacle. Joy was nowhere to be seen. Trey and Molly wrestled with metal poles, in what looked like a real-life version of the game Operation. They were trying to retrieve a metal ring without being zapped by an electric charge while standing in a puddle. Shaking his head, he jogged on, surveying each crazy obstacle. He came across a wooden structure with rope ladders at wild angles to make climbing harder. He stopped to examine a 45-degree angle wall of slotted boards, its highest point twenty feet above his head. It would be at least a two-person job to get up and over. Variations of swinging obstacles dotted the course. He could tackle some of them without messing up his knee.

Everything was high. He completed the monkey bars easily enough. One obstacle consisted of several rotating wheels that spun him around when he tried to get from one to the other. Fortunately, he didn't have to try out the net that lay suspended a few inches over a freezing pool of muddy water. Panting with exertion, he spotted Joy, swinging from ring to ring high in the air like she was Tarzan's sister.

"Zack! There you are. Come on, let's go!" Hopping down from the ladder, Jenergizer Bunny grabbed his hand and pulled him along. She hadn't been kidding about jumping over flaming hay bales.

Finally, after a couple of hours, back at camp, Zack collapsed in the tent, too tired and sore to move. Joy stood over him, hands on her hips. "What? Are you done? That was just the first lap!"

Zack closed his eyes and waved her on. "You go for it; I didn't get much sleep last night." Cracking one eye open, he gave her a thumbs-up. "You'll rock it."

"You bet your ass I'll rock it!" And she was off.

Zack groaned and looked into the camera Ben was holding into the tent over his face. "I don't know about you all, but I have trouble forming a romantic connection while being thrown around like a rag doll by a woman who could kick my ass." Zack laughed. "Seriously, I bet everyone back at the house is finding this hilarious. Wish you guys were here with me."

Pushing Ben aside, Molly poked her head in the door and crawled halfway into the tent, shivering. "Ugh. I'm freezing my ass off out here. It's not fair that everyone else gets to stay back at the beach house. Can I come in here with you? Trey is being a really good guy, and he's off helping Joy scale more walls." Her expression turned thoughtful. "You know, maybe if you didn't glower at the women, your dates would turn out better."

Undeterred, Ben poked the camera back into the tent.

Zack reached up and tugged her down next to him, draping one of the survival blankets stashed in his bag around her shoulders. "Pop a squat, munchkin. We're gonna be here a while."

Molly huffed. "My name is not munchkin."

Zack tugged on one of her braids. "I don't glower. I smolder."

"Yeah, when you look at Esme." Molly gasped, covering her mouth with both hands, pretending to be surprised by her own nerve.

Zack grinned. "That's not a smolder. It's a full-on blaze."

Esme

ESME CHOKED on her wine at Zack's wink into the camera. Setting her glass on the coffee table, she picked up a pillow and pulled it over her face. Zack was the most incorrigible man she had ever met. No amount of coaching or matchmaking was going to save him from himself. And she liked him. Which meant she had officially lost her mind.

"Good God, woman. Separating the two of you only seems to turn the heat factor up." Joel looked up from his sketchbook and sighed.

Esme laughed and threw her pillow at Joel. Since getting to know him better in the closet, she realized the artist was fun to hang out with in the house. "Come on; you at least have to admit the footage is pretty funny. I think audiences will be entertained. Maybe not for the reason the producers hoped, but ratings are ratings, right?" She frowned. "Although I'm not sure that's going to get anyone voted into the Love Shack this week either."

Joel chuckled and put the pillow down, reached for the wine bottle, and took a swig. "Hey, as long as the prize pool doesn't get depleted and we keep on hitting the producers' goals, I'm cool with whatever you two do."

"Ah, yes. Show goals." Esme giggled. "Lest we forget about the show goals." Pointing at the television, she reached for her wineglass. "Can we rewind and watch the part again with the flaming hay bales?"

Joel stretched and stood up. "No, we can't watch that part again. This isn't on-demand. It's a delayed feed from the production crew. There is no rewind from this room." Pointing the wine bottle at Esme, he accused, "You're drunk. And you were supposed to be taking notes on the dates for the next matching ceremony. Anyway, I think I'm going to go join the others out in the hot tub. You coming?"

Esme tapped her head with her index finger. "Don't you worry, Joel, I have my notes all up here. And I'm not drunk. Also not feeling the hot tub right now." Rolling off the couch, she stood and executed a precise hand-to-nose touch. "See, perfect hand-eye coordination. Besides, I didn't really glean any new information from that date. Obviously, my matchmaking radar is broken."

"Well, fix it!"

"I'm trying!" Esme threw herself back down on the couch, arms crossed. "I don't know why I messed up the matches."

Joel raised a brow and stood over her and scoffed. "Really? You don't think it has a teensy bit to do with being distracted by —what did you call him earlier—Mr. Tall-Handsome-and-Shirt-less?" He plopped next to her on the couch, handing her the wine bottle.

Had she really called Zack that in front of Joel? Taking a slug from the bottle, she sat back, a hand over her forehead. "What am I going to do?"

"Flee the country and find work as cruise ship wedding planner?"

Esme snorted. "Out of five matches, I only got two right at the match ceremony, and I have no idea what the right matches were. Imagine me as a wedding planner."

"Good point."

"Hey." Esme slapped Joel with the pillow.

"Just kidding." Joel sat up. "You have to nail your date with Wesley and get yourselves or Kent and Madison voted into the Love Shack. We just need to focus on confirming some matches and win. Easy peasy."

Esme groaned. If the game was so easy, why did everything seem so hard? "Are you sure we can't rewind?"

The front door opened, and Ferris walked in, followed by an exhausted-looking group. They were back early. A muddy and grumpy Zack uncharacteristically slumped into his room and shut the door without even saying hello.

After a quick change of clothes, Molly, Trey, and Joy followed Joel out to the hot tub.

"So, no all-nighter in the desert after all?" Esme pointed a look at Ferris.

"No, thank God. I was getting bored sitting in the car, and it was too cold to stay outside. I'm heading home. You'll need to be downstairs ready to go at three p.m. tomorrow. We'll be spending the afternoon and evening at the Newport Beach Boardwalk. And dress in athletic wear."

At the sound of the front door closing, Esme settled back on the couch again. Late Wednesday night—technically early Thursday morning. Why had they all come home instead of spending the night in the desert? Chalk it up to television magic to make it look like that really happened. Glancing at the hallway to Zack's bedroom, she sighed. Why did she have this overwhelming urge to check on him? She got up and dropped the wine bottle and glass off in the kitchen on the way to his door.

She knocked softly and waited for an answer. Nothing. "Hey, Zack? You still up?" She pressed her forehead against the door and knocked again, softer this time.. The door flew open, and she almost fell right into Zack, who was wearing nothing but a towel slung low on his hips. Esme pulled her gaze up from the towel, spent 3.5 seconds staring at his abs, and forced her eyes up to his face. "Um, hi."

Zack's eyes were stormy blue. His mouth quirked up in a half smile, lacking some of his usual energy. "Hey, Es. What're you doing still awake?"

"I was staying up talking strategy with Joel in the living room when you guys walked into the house. I was surprised to see you all back tonight, and when you didn't come join us, I thought I'd check on you." She gestured vaguely back toward the main living area, visible from his doorway down the hall.

Zack looked at her, pinching the bridge of his nose. He dragged his hand down to cover his mouth as he peered at her. "The audience chose elite obstacle course racing for our date. I think they have it in for me."

"Or they have complete faith in your physical prowess."

Zack sucked in his bottom lip. "And what do you think of my physical prowess?"

I could think of some obstacles to tackle, starting with your towel, she thought. Her cheeks heated, and her fingers twitched with an urge to reach for the corner of the towel tucked in at Zack's waist. Forcing her hands to still, she grinned. "I thought you held your own, considering Joy is apparently an American Gladiator in disguise. How did the knee hold up, though?"

"She's more like a member of the Avengers. Jesus. My knee is sore. I don't think I'm going to be able to move tomorrow. Wanna join me in the hot tub?"

Did she want to join him in the hot tub? Her body screamed *yes, yes, YES.* Her body needed a reality check. "No thanks. But everyone else is out there if you want company. I need to get some sleep. Catch you tomorrow?"

"Your loss." Zack shrugged and turned to grab a pair of swim trunks from a dresser drawer, the towel sliding dangerously lower.

She fled.

twenty

. . .

Esme

ESME RAN a hand down the teal leopard-print athletic leggings she had paired with a black T-shirt. Not even workout gear was immune to Summer's eclectic touch. She turned on the cell phone she'd hid in one of her bags and dialed her friend's number. If Zack could break rules for group outings and everything else, then she could at least sneak a phone call.

"Esme! Why are you calling me?" Summer's squeal over the phone had her smiling.

"I just missed you and wanted to hear your voice." She leaned her head on the car window and watched the scenery fly by. "How's life on the outside?"

Summer laughed. "Not as exciting as it looks like yours is on the inside. I mean, could they have found any more good-looking guys to stick in that place with you?"

"Summer, I have a question and I need a straight, non-fluffy answer, okay?"

"Sure, sweetie. Of course. What's going on?" Concern colored her friend's voice.

"Am I making a fool of myself on national television? Because it feels that way."

"Oh my God, no! Of course, you aren't. You look gorgeous and of course come across as professional and knowledgeable, as always." Summer paused. "Are you having any fun at all?"

Esme thought about the question. "I've had my moments."

"Well, I think you're amazing and can't wait to see what happens next. Don't tell me. I don't want it spoiled!"

"Thanks, Summer. I love you."

"Love you too! Miss ya and can't wait to catch up when you're home."

Esme turned the phone off and stuck it in the pocket of the back seat to retrieve later. The car rolled to a stop at the boardwalk.

Stepping out, she headed to where Ferris was standing with Ben and the camera crew. After getting fitted with a microphone and transmitter pack, she joined Wesley, Kent, and Madison.

Ferris stepped up between them. "You all ready? Here we go. Count it down, Ben." Taking his cue from Ben, who silently counted them down from five, Ferris transformed from loveable dork to polished host.

"Welcome back to *Perfectly Matched*, where you—the audience —get to meddle in the love lives of two professional meddlers." Ferris slung an arm around her shoulders and repeated the gesture with Wesley. "I'm here with Esme and Wesley. Also joining us are Kent and Madison. Esme and Wes, how are you two doing today?"

Wesley looked terrified to be interviewed for the first time on camera. Swallowing hard, he took a deep breath. Esme could practically feel his nervousness radiating through Ferris over to her. "Uh, I'm great, thanks," said Wesley. "Excited to take Esme out on a date."

Ferris grinned at the camera. Tightening his arm around Esme's shoulders, he gave her a friendly shake. "We have got a great evening in store for you. The audience was given three of Wesley's hobbies to choose from and elevate it as a date activity. Any guesses as to what they chose?"

Refraining from rolling her eyes, Esme took in her surroundings. Newport Beach Boardwalk. Anything but surfing, she silently pled. Smiling at Ferris, she shrugged. "I have no idea what it could be, but I'm looking forward to finding out." Liar.

Ferris dropped his arms and stepped to the side, pulling two pairs of Rollerblades out of a bag. "You're going Rollerblading on the boardwalk!"

Esme shot a dubious but considering look at the Rollerblades. She was not looking forward to a broken arm but willing to give it a try, and she laughed nervously. "Gee, Wes, can't be into just riding a bicycle, eh?"

Wesley smiled sheepishly. "Sorry. Ever since I was a kid, I spend all my time at the skate park. At least they didn't vote for skateboarding!"

Every silver lining has a cloud. Thank God they were Rollerblading and not skateboarding. Maybe surfing wouldn't have been so bad after all. She reevaluated the shy engineer and his hidden athleticism. Maybe she was on the wrong track matching him with Molly.

Ferris handed a pair of skates to each of them and rubbed his hands together, looking into the camera. "Well, I can't wait to see what happens. You kids have fun!"

Laughing, Ferris leaned into Esme. "Don't break anything, okay?"

Ben waved one of the crew over to power up Esme and Wesley's microphones. Madison and Kent trotted off to some tables and benches. She was on her own. Looking at a frozen Wesley, she touched his arm. "So, what's our plan?"

"Oh, um, have you Rollerbladed before?" Wesley tucked a lock of brown hair falling over one eye back into his knit beanie. He had pretty hazel eyes, hair that was slightly too long in the front, and an average build. Dressed in a trash-fashion tattoo art T-shirt that screamed Ed Hardy, his outfit had Zack written all over it. "Come sit over here on this bench, and I'll help you with your skates. We can put your shoes in my backpack in case you want a break."

Esme sat patiently while Wesley slipped the skates onto her feet and tied them up, buckling the straps at the top. Her feet felt like they weighed fifty pounds each. He quickly laced his own up and tucked their shoes in his backpack. Once he stood, he held out a hand to her. In addition to hidden hobbies, he had manners. Esme took his hand, and he helped her up with surprising strength.

"Okay." He spun around on his skates. "Wait, I don't think you answered my question. Do you already know how to skate?"

Wobbling and waving her arms for balance, Esme laughed. "Wesley, I'm more of a feet-on-the-ground girl, and I've never been rollerblading before. Tonight is going to be a long night. But fun!" A long night she hoped ended with wine or a gallon of margaritas.

Wesley smiled. "Okay, well, stand there a minute and get used to the feel. You can try rolling your feet back and forth a bit like this." He demonstrated by sliding his feet forward and backward a few times. "Rollerblades are different from roller skates. They have brakes on the back instead of the stopper things on the toes. So, when you want to slow down, tip your toe up and let the brake drag on the ground. Here, I'll lead you forward slowly, and you can practice."

Esme squealed as Wesley pulled her toward him. She grabbed him around the waist for support to avoid falling on her ass. Remembering the cameras, she let go and stood on her own, tightening her ponytail. "Seriously, Wesley, why couldn't you have been into Dungeons & Dragons or video games?"

He looked around and pointed to a light post. "I'm going to go over to that light post, and I want you to try to make your way over to me. Just take your time. Push out with one foot and just kind of glide forward on the other one."

Esme half glided, half stumbled her way to the post, sort of getting the hang of skating.

"Not bad! Here, I'll go to where we started, and you make your way there. Try not to lift your feet so much and the stumble will go away." Wesley zipped off to the bench, turning in a smooth half circle to face her.

Groaning, Esme squared her shoulders and eyed the distance. She could do this. It was just roller-skating. She took a deep breath and managed to glide her way to where Wesley waited.

"I have to admit, this is a lot of fun, Wesley. And a pretty great workout for my quads!"

"I'm glad you like it, since we've got a few miles to go on the boardwalk before we stop for dinner." Wesley picked up another smaller backpack. "Picnic. Do you want to carry this one or the bag with our shoes?"

"I'll take the picnic bag." Esme shrugged into the straps. A few miles. No big deal.

Wesley held out his hand. "I can help you keep your balance, and I promise not to let you fall."

Esme took his hand. No sparks. No zip of electricity. But there were warmth and surety, and true to his word, Wesley didn't let her fall. Why couldn't she feel a zing with a guy like Wesley instead of the worst possible guy she could fall for, her archnemesis in the dating industry? Esme found herself smiling as she remembered the look on Zack's face when he saw the obstacle course last night. Did her face look like that when she saw the Rollerblades? Probably. Zack was probably getting a good laugh at her expense.

After a filling picnic dinner on the beach, Wesley helped her remove her skates, and they walked to the end of the pier to watch the sunset. He was actually charming and funny, and the experience hadn't been completely horrible. Leaning on the railing of the pier, she listened to him regale her with stories of crazy bus trips when he was in his college's drum corps and practical jokes the engineers in his office played on each other.

She tugged the beanie off his head and smoothed his hair down. "You know you're a really great guy, right? Why are you on a reality dating show?"

Wesley stuck the beanie in his back pocket and ran a hand through his hair. "Honestly? I have serious problems approaching women. That's how I met Zack: I read his book, sought him out, and was amazed at his formulas for openers and closers."

"I think you're doing just fine without those things." Esme looked at the sky, streaked with dark orange, deep purple, and light pink, the colors reflecting off the soft waves.

"Why are you on a reality dating show?" Wesley slid his gaze over to her.

"I ask myself that same question every day." She laughed and turned toward Wesley, surprised to find herself lip to lip with him. And it wasn't horrible. Actually, it was pretty great as far as kisses went, but did they have time for this? If the date went any later, they'd hit traffic on the way home, and she'd been hoping to get through a load of laundry before bed. She also had to come up with next week's matches...

Yeah, there were just no sparks between her and Wesley.

Wesley jumped back, brushing his hands down his shorts. "Sorry, I shouldn't have done that, but you just looked so pretty in this light, and—"

She put a hand on his arm and squeezed. Not wanting to hurt his feelings, and also not wanting to encourage him, she shrugged. "Hey, it's okay. It was nice. Thank you for a fun date."

Wesley smiled shyly back at her. "Yeah, it was fun. We should probably get back, huh? Car's probably here to pick us up."

Esme vowed to find Wesley the best match in the whole world.

Zack

ZACK PACED BACK and forth in front of the television. What the hell was up with that terrible deal-closing kiss? A great kiss was the number-one goal after a successful meet. That's what he taught in his classes. Wes's technique was embarrassing and needed some serious work. Zack wavered between feeling proud of his protégé for at least trying and wanting to kick his ass for touching her. Watching the live feed had been … annoying. Why weren't they back yet?

The front door opened, and Zack threw himself down on the couch, kicking his feet up on the coffee table, trying to create a picture of cool relaxation, not maniac anxiousness. Of course he hadn't been pacing a hole in the floor waiting for her arrival, like he had a right to do so. Esme stopped when she saw him on the couch. Fuck calm and collected. He should have been the one to kiss her on camera. It was where he belonged. In the spotlight.

He jumped up and grabbed her hand. "Let's go for a walk." Without giving her a chance to respond, he led her over to the back door, down the stairs, and out to the moonlit beach. "Fun date?"

Esme shook her head. "You saw the footage. What do you think?"

Zack kept walking. Eyes on the sand ahead. "I'm thinking a lot of things I probably shouldn't think. Like how hot you looked in those pants and the adorable way your ponytail bounced when you roller-stomped down the boardwalk."

Esme stopped, bringing him to a halt. She shivered and rubbed her arms. "You noticed the stomping, huh? I was hoping it would come across more smooth on camera." Esme held a hand to her face. "How embarrassing. I envy Joy's athleticism. And the whole country gets to watch me be lame. Or whatever." Peeking through her fingers at him, she raised a brow. "Did you watch the whole thing?"

Zack answered with a grunt and started walking again.

Esme sighed. "I'll take your lack of support as a yes. No way will the producers edit that out either. Zack? Where are we going? Can you slow down? I'm not joking about the athleticism thing. My legs hurt." She vowed to get more cardio in. Starting tomorrow.

He stopped and looked back the way they'd come, gauging

the distance. Far enough from cameras and microphones. Esme started to retreat.

"Wait." He reached for her again. "You're cold, put this on." He shrugged out of the light jacket he'd been wearing over his T-shirt and draped it over her shoulders.

She didn't step away as she snaked her arms into the sleeves and pulled her hair out from under the jacket. Thanks to the moonlight, her brown hair fell in midnight-blue waves around her shoulders. Her eyes were black pools. Zack walked her backward up against a retaining wall. "I saw it all, but he did it wrong."

"Did what wrong?" Her voice came out breathless, and this close to her, pressed against her, he could feel her heart beating hard.

Zack wrapped a hand behind her head and ran his thumb over her perfect lips, leaning down to whisper in her ear. "You deserve better." He inhaled the fruity scent of her shampoo as every part of his body tightened. He tilted her head up, and when her eyes closed and her lips parted... Damn, she was the sexiest thing he'd ever seen. The first brush of his lips against hers was gentle. Teasing. But when she made a small sound in the back of her throat and her fingers found the hem of his shirt, something in him snapped. He deepened the kiss. She tasted of coconut lip balm and bubble gum and something that was pure Esme. She snaked an arm around his neck and was kissing him back with an intensity that made his knees weak.

His body was on fire, and her hands were tangled in his hair. The heat made his heart thud in his chest, and he didn't want to stop kissing her. Whoa. This had never happened to him before. He always kept control. Always stayed detached. But Esme made him forget every rule he'd ever taught, every formula he'd ever followed. She made him forget everything except the way she felt in his arms and the small sounds she made when he kissed the corner of her mouth, her jaw, the soft skin beneath her ear. Resisting women, being in control—that was his specialty. He had to stop before he looked like he was too into this girl.

Zack ran his hand down her neck, trailing it down her back. He forced himself to slow down, to pull back, to remember this was a game. Smiling against her mouth, and even though it felt like a lie he drew back. "See? That's how you kiss a woman. Shall we go back? It's getting late."

Esme gaped at him, one hand rising to her mouth. With a little growl, she shoved past him and stomped down the beach.

Satisfied he had at least erased the memory of Wesley's kiss, Zack adjusted his pants and began a very uncomfortable walk back down the beach.

twenty-one

. . .

Esme

Sun streamed through her bedroom windows. Esme pulled on yoga pants and a tank top and added a lightweight wraparound sweater. Hours after Zack had led her onto the beach, her lips still tingled and she could still feel his lips on hers. How dare he kiss her? Esme groaned and threw herself face-first on the bed. How dare he stop kissing her? She didn't care. Did she? Flipping over, she looked askance at the ceiling.

"What am I doing here? This is insane."

When the funky chandelier didn't answer, she sat up. Kissing. Zack's book talked about it as being part of his stupid game. The kiss close. She'd fallen for it twice yesterday. Wesley wasn't her fault; he'd completely surprised her. But Zack? She should have seen it coming from miles away.

Ugh. She did care and that was a problem. Zack's kiss had felt different. Not like Clayton's kisses, which had been pleasant and comfortable and utterly forgettable. Not like Wesley's surprise kiss on the pier, which had been nice but no sparks. Zack's kiss? Zack's kiss had set her on fire. Had made her forget where she was. Forget who she was. Forget why she couldn't let herself want him. And the worst part? When he'd pulled away with that smug player smile and his condescending line about how to kiss a woman properly, she'd wanted to grab him by the shirt and kiss him again just to wipe that smile off his face.

She was in so much trouble.

Blowing out a breath, she yanked open her door and headed downstairs for the Love Shack vote. Fingers crossed that the audience voted to send a lucky couple in so the cast could avoid another charming visit from Olivia.

Esme wasn't surprised to find Ferris, Zack, Wesley, and Kent in the kitchen munching on breakfast left for them by the catering service. One bonus of this reality show: they didn't have to cook for themselves. She grabbed a bowl of apple slices and headed into the living room, which was the day's designated filming spot. All the other girls were squished onto what Esme had grown to think of as the girl couch. The camera crew stood around eating too.

As she crunched a few apple slices, she watched the girls with interest, not even able to guess how the audience might have voted after last night's episode.

Keeping out of the spotlight was impossible with cameras everywhere, and telling herself it was just a TV show and not a big deal wasn't working anymore. Everything was becoming complicated. Interestingly enough, Zack had made sure they were off camera before he kissed her. She chewed another piece of apple and thought that through. Why did he act like it was all a game but was considerate enough to make sure they weren't filmed? Zack walked in and she scowled into her bowl. It was embarrassing how attuned her body was to him, how it shimmered to life in response to his presence. Ugh.

As Ferris walked into the room, production assistants swarmed on the cast members, gathering dishes and glasses and clearing the area of everything except contestants. Arranging himself artfully in the "host chair," Ferris waved the guys onto the boy couch. Esme joined Zack in their assigned armchairs on each side of the host chair.

"Welcome back, everyone, to *Perfectly Matched*—a battle of hearts. How are we doing today?" Ferris beamed at the room like it was the most fun place to be in the whole world. Host Ferris was really creepy. "Joy? How are you feeling after the other night?"

"Awesome! I couldn't be more pumped right now." Joy beamed back.

Everyone was just so beamy. Esme wanted to throw up.

"Sure looked like a lot of fun out there on that obstacle course." Ferris tapped the envelope he was holding against his other hand. "How about you, Wesley? Have a good date?"

Wesley blushed and the rogue lock of hair fell into his eyes again. "I had a great time with Esme. She's a lot of fun to spend time around."

"And she's not too bad on wheels, either!" Ferris beamed around at everyone again. "Well, we're going to get right down to the Love Shack vote … right after a brief commercial break. We'll be right back!"

Ferris glared around the room, not so beamy. "Can we get a little bit more enthusiasm and energy, contestants?"

Esme fidgeted in her chair. She needed a confirmed match because they needed more lights in the next ceremony.

"Let's get this done, so all of you can go back to sleep, which is where you apparently belong right now." Ferris nodded to Ben to start rolling again.

"Welcome back! America had the chance to watch the dates unfold and vote. They were given a choice to vote one lucky couple into the Love Shack tonight to see if there is a confirmed match among any of our lucky contestants. Madison?" Ferris turned his beam to the girls' couch. "How do you think America voted?"

Madison giggled and smiled wide at the camera. "Oh gosh, Ferris. I really couldn't even guess! I just hope it's me! Please, America? You are all amazeballs!"

Esme wanted to roll her eyes into the back of her head so hard, but she fought the urge.

"How about you, Esme? Any guesses?" Ferris turned the spotlight on her.

She considered the question. Although she was positive

Madison and Joel were a match, voting her and Kent into the Love Shack would confirm a few of the other matches for her. "Actually, I'm with Madison on this one. I hope America voted for her and Kent."

"Zack?"

"Oh, I couldn't even begin to guess." Zack flashed a grin for the cameras. "But I'm sure America knows what they're doing."

"Well, let's find out!" Ferris made a show of opening the envelope. "Okay, America, you voted and here are the results." He whistled and put down the card. "Esme and Wesley, you have been voted into the Love Shack!"

"Seriously?" Esme sat gripping the couch. Frenemy Madison grabbed her in a hug.

Wesley stood awkwardly, shoulders hunched. Esme felt bad for him. She knew they were not a match and made a silent vow to call him after the show was over to offer pro bono matchmaking services. Some lucky girl—or boy—was just waiting for Wesley out there somewhere, Esme was sure. She'd seen the slight lean into Ferris when he'd slung his arm around their shoulders yesterday on the boardwalk. Someone with a bright and funny personality would be perfect for the shy and reserved engineer. She eyed Ferris thoughtfully. He was bright and shiny...

"Esme and Wesley, step on into the Love Shack!"

Following Wesley out the back door and down the path of flagstones, she stood outside the small guest house that had been transformed into the Love Shack. Cameras followed, of course. Permanent shadows, recording her every move.

Trying to smile instead of scowl, she grabbed Wesley's hand. "Ready?"

He nodded, and they walked through the door into the small room that was outfitted with two giant monitors on a wall and nothing else. The left monitor displayed Wesley's headshot, and hers was on the right. She jumped when the overhead lights dimmed, and a spotlight caught them both in a circle. Music was piped in through speakers, and they stood while funky-colored lights hung from the ceiling swung around, adding drama to the room. Suddenly the music and lights stopped, and a red bar flashed up on the screens with the words *No Match*.

twenty-two

. . .

Zack

Zack clapped Wesley on the shoulder in solidarity while the rest of the guys consoled him on the No Match result. Filming took all day. He grabbed the bottle of wine Esme had left open in the kitchen and went in search of the MIA matchmaker.

After the Love Shack ceremony, everything had happened so fast. One minute she'd been in a conversation with Ferris after the cameras had cut, and the next she was on her way out the back door with a glass of wine. He paused by the hot tub to ask if anyone had seen her pass by and followed their waves to the stairs that led down to the beach, where he found her huddled on the sand, wineglass clasped in front of her knees.

"I thought you might want more of this, so I brought an emergency supply with me." Zack held out the wine bottle, and a wave of confusion washed over him when she lifted her tear-stained face. Crying women were his kryptonite.

Fighting the urge to run from an emotional catastrophe, he immediately fell back on humor. "Wowza, maybe Wesley wasn't such a bad kisser after all. I didn't realize you would be so devastated at not being a match."

More tears welled up in her eyes, and he felt like a real jerk for making her cry more. Jokes weren't going to save him this time, and he couldn't leave her sitting on the beach alone in this state. He crouched down and reached out a tentative hand to swipe a tear away with his thumb. "Hey now, it's too beautiful of a night on the beach for tears. But you had the right idea with the wine, great night for wine. Want some more?"

She sniffled and nodded, holding out the glass. Zack topped

it off. "Okay if I sit down?" Not waiting for an affirmative, he plopped down next to her and dug his feet into the sand. Nothing he loved more than cooling sand after the sun had set and sitting with a beautiful woman on a beach. He studied the moon hanging in the sky. Tipping the wine bottle up to his lips, he took a draw and slid a glance sideways at Esme. Thank God the tears had stopped, and she was tentatively sipping the wine. An overwhelming urge to wrap an arm around her and tug her in close to his side bubbled up from who knew where.

"Want to tell me what's wrong?"

"Nothing's wrong. I'm fine." Esme's gaze was focused straight ahead on the waves.

Zack couldn't help laughing and held up a hand in acquiescence when she turned to glare at him. "Sorry. You may not think I'm the most intuitive or couth guy, but I am smart enough to know the words 'I'm fine' generally mean the wrath of a woman is about to be rained down upon the Earth." He met her gaze. "I'm just not sure who or what has you upset. I'm just hoping it's not me."

With a shake of her head, her lips quirked up into a rueful smile. "Not you, you're safe. For now."

Zack let out a breath and put a hand to his chest in mock relief. "Whew. I feel better." She picked at the edge of her long-sleeved T-shirt. "But seriously, what's going on?"

"After we finished filming, I was talking to Ferris about how fast time seemed to be flying by, since we're already wrapping up week two. And he mentioned today was the fifteenth. October fifteenth." She threw a hand up in the air as if that explained it all. His face must have registered completely blank because she sighed. "My wedding day. Today was supposed to be my wedding day."

"Ahhhh…"

"I don't know why I'm crying about it. Clayton getting caught was probably the best thing that could have happened to me. What if I had married him and then ten years and two kids later, he confessed he was into guys? Or worse, carried on with Lucas behind my back the entire time. It would have been my worst nightmare. How can I call myself a matchmaker or dating coach? I'm good at reading people, but I completely missed something was not right. God, when we were together, was he thinking about Lucas? The worst part is I've started to believe love is just a sham. And I don't want to believe that."

She met his eyes, her own beginning to well up again, and Zack tried not to panic. "But the thing is, I knew how my life was going to play out. Today was supposed to be, and then was not supposed to be, my wedding day. Now I'm on this crazy reality show and completely out of my comfort zone."

Zack watched in silence as she slugged back the rest of her glass of wine. He untangled her words in his head. She expected to be married today. And tomorrow. And the next. But now she was single, not married, and crying on the beach.

"And I don't know what's going to happen after this show or what I'm going to do. If I won the money, I was going to over-haul my grandmother's matchmaking business, bring it into the twenty-first century. But what if I don't win? Then what?"

He was so in over his head yet enthralled at the same time.

"Want to hear something crazy?" he asked. She nodded and sniffled. "I'm completely impressed with your ability to read people and know if they're right for each other or not. My whole career has been dumb luck. Coming on this show was the first intentional thing I've ever done in my life. Winning would be an accomplishment I could be proud of."

Planning for the future was not his strength. And right now, he just wanted to hear her laugh and for her to not be so down. "Look, I don't know anything about planning. I tend to jump first and ask questions later. Live in the moment." He stood up. "We should go swimming."

Esme looked at him as though he had two heads. "What? It's too cold to go swimming at night. Plus, we don't even have on swimsuits."

"So? You're going to let that stop you from having fun?" He waved the hand he was holding out to her. "Just come on. Be a little wild and crazy for once."

After a brief hesitation, she took his hand, and he helped her up to her feet. Tucking her hand close to his side, he started off down the beach past the camera line.

"Zack, where are we going? We're going to get into so much trouble." She took her hand out from where it was tucked into his arm and stopped, arms crossed.

He shrugged. "So? The rest of the cast is busy consoling Wesley and partying tonight. Ferris and the camera guys left. It's not like this is a high-class production. Olivia is spending the bare minimum on this production, so I doubt anyone is even monitoring the feed."

Stopping at a set of steps leading up from the beach, he waited for her to catch up, then started up the stairs.

"Zack," Esme hissed. "What are you doing? We're going to get arrested for trespassing."

When he got to a gate at the top of the steps, he punched in a code to unlock it and held it open. But she refused to walk through it, so he went anyway. He crossed the large patio and ducked behind the outdoor bar to flip a switch, which lit up the infinity pool and highlighted the thin layer of steam hovering above the heated water. Next, he grabbed an arm full of fluffy towels and tossed them on a lounge chair, grinning at Esme, who had tentatively joined him.

"See, Olivia asked me if I knew of any property owners who'd be willing to rent out their place for her production. My long-time neighbor, Martin, spends most of his time on business in China, and his place is always empty."

"This is your house? You've got to be kidding. This whole time you've been, what, a ten-minute walk from home?" Narrowing her eyes at him, she poked at his chest. "So that's why you weren't worried about trespassing when we were making out against the retaining wall down below. It's your wall!"

A thrill shot through him at her choice of words. "So, we were making out, were we?"

Her face flushed red, and he couldn't help but think about how cute she was when embarrassed.

"No! Yes! I mean—" Her words cut off when he yanked his T-shirt over his head. Her eyes followed his hand to the button he was unfastening on his shorts. "Zack MacKenzie, I am not going skinny-dipping with you."

"Suit yourself, but nobody said anything about skinny-dipping. What's the difference between swimming in a bathing suit and swimming in your underwear?" To emphasize his point, he slipped off his shorts and tossed them on a chair. "See? Perfectly harmless boxer briefs."

He sensed her inner debate and decided to ignore her hesitation. "I'm going to get in the pool now, and you can decide what you want to do. Just stick your feet into the water. For once, do something unexpected and see how it feels. After all, a year ago you were planning to get married today, but instead you're partially skinny-dipping with a hot TV star. Not too shabby, right?"

Esme

THOSE BOXER BRIEFS were anything but harmless. She was positive the label probably read *Danger—Handle with Extreme Caution*. Esme felt jitters in her legs as she watched Zack dive into the pool and resurface. Who was she kidding, though? The man was pure muscular grace. A perfectly proportioned, drool-worthy specimen. How had she gotten here? One minute she was feeling sorry for herself on the beach, and the next she was standing awkwardly next to his pool at his house. He had led them on a perfectly executed, yet ridiculously easy jailbreak. No cameras. No expectations to meet. Except Zack's. And she wasn't exactly sure what his were. Stripping down to her underwear in front of him felt wrong but exciting at the same time.

Turning her back to him, she pulled off her shirt and laid it neatly on the back of the chair where he'd tossed his shorts. She shimmied out of her shorts and laid them on top of her shirt. She took a deep breath and froze. She felt the heat behind her and heard the dripping water. His breath tickled her ear, and she shivered, goose bumps breaking out on her arms.

"Too slow," he said.

She squealed as a wet arm snaked around her middle, and she was lifted and tossed into the pool. Zack followed behind. Surfacing, she splashed him with water. "What are you, twelve?"

"On the inside." Grinning, Zack held up an arm to shield himself from the onslaught of her splashes. "Don't you feel better though?"

She slowly paddled to the edge of the pool to look out at the silver ocean. Sweeping her wet hair back from her face, she realized she did feel better. Maybe there was something to taking a walk on the wild side sometimes. And right now, she wanted to do that with Zack. Her lips on his lips ASAP was what she wanted. He stood there, three feet away, steam swirling up his abdomen in the shallow water. Water dripped from his hair and ran down his chest, and she wanted to lick it up. His cobalt eyes fixed on her, looking uncertain.

"You okay, Esme?"

Sensible Esme would say, "I'm fine," and wave him off. She didn't want to be sensible Esme tonight. She wanted to be bad-girl Esme, the one who ran away from the reality show she was supposed to be filming with her super sexy castmate. But Sensible Esme began to win, and she started to move toward the steps ... then stopped. Screw sensible Esme. Alex was right. She did need revenge sex. No, she deserved revenge sex. And her avenger had hand-delivered himself to her. She wanted to do something unexpected.

"Kiss me, Zack."

The words barely left her lips before he was there, hands threading into her hair as his lips brushed against hers. She wrapped an arm around his neck and her legs around his waist, and he backed her up against the pool wall. Desire lit every muscle in her body on fire, and she moaned against the softness of the kiss. Zack lifted his head and trailed a hand down her cheek. His voice was barely a whisper.

"You are so beautiful. And kind. And caring. I don't know how Clayton could have given you up, but I don't want to be your distraction or the tool for your vengeance. I didn't bring you here tonight to have sex or do anything shady, I swear. And if the time comes that we decide to go there, I want it to be because you want to be with me. Not because you don't have him."

Who'd have imagined Zack MacKenzie would be the voice of reason between the two of them tonight? Esme untangled her arm from around his neck. "You're right. Sorry, I got carried away."

Zack clasped his hands behind her head and used his thumbs to lift her chin. "Hey, I kind of like it when you get carried away."

Zack

WALKING down the beach toward Heart House, Zack caught Esme's hand and pulled her to a halt. It had taken everything he had to stop what she had started in the pool. But for the first time in his life, he didn't want to take advantage of someone else's weakness. And he didn't want the moment to be about him. Shocked by this revelation, Zack's mind couldn't stop spinning out ideas. He wanted to help her.

"Hey, what if we form an alliance?"

Esme pursed her lips and stared at him. "An alliance? How would that work, exactly?"

"Easy. You and I put up the same matches every week. We get the rest of the cast involved, to help work out the matches. We split the five hundred grand in our prize pool, and they win their five hundred grand when we declare all the correct matches."

Her laughter rang out along with the sound of the waves lapping against the shore. "Oh, Olivia is going to hate that, Zack."

Zack nodded. Olivia was going to hate it, but he'd win either way. Although now he wasn't as interested in winning as he was in getting the girl. "Well, that's why she can't find out. Don't get me wrong, we have to make a big show of being at odds and competing. Not our fault that poof—we come up with the same matches. Let's go see if the others are still awake and get them on board."

He was stopped by resistance when she didn't follow him. "What's wrong?"

"How are we going to get everyone on board without the production crew hearing the plan? You can't keep sneaking people down the beach off camera. Someone is going to notice."

She had a point, Zack mused. Then he snapped his fingers. "Easy. The closet. You go find Wesley and drag him into the closet with you. When Ferris asks what you are up to, just tell him you were consoling Wesley on the No Match thing. Or you can tell him you were making out. Up to you."

"I'm not telling Ferris I was making out with Wesley in the closet!"

Zack laughed. "Just get him in the closet and tell him the plan and ask him to pass it on to someone else. I'll take a couple of the girls in there and get them on board."

Esme quirked one of her perfect brows at him. "A couple of the girls?"

He smirked. "Come on, Es, I'm a player, remember? Everyone expects me to be doing shit like that all the time."

Her face softened and they resumed walking back to the house.

"You shouldn't let others' expectations define you. I think you're better," she said.

Smiling like a fool at the stars in the sky, he felt like his heart was swelling in his chest. "Yeah? I'll give it some thought."

twenty-three

. . .

Esme

ESME PULLED her hair up in a ponytail and studied her reflection in the bathroom mirror. She dug through her makeup bag to finish getting ready for the matching ceremony. Zack's plan to form an alliance and get the cast on board was well underway, and she couldn't help but be impressed at how it came together as he worked his magic, finding ways for everyone to pass messages back and forth.

He had brains and muscles. Lots of muscles. The way he'd felt when she'd wrapped herself around him in the pool... Just ... wow. Her heart raced just thinking about that moment.

She took care to dab extra lip gloss on, not that she was trying to impress anyone, especially not Zack. Blowing out a puff of air, she laughed. Okay, maybe she was trying to impress him. Zack MacKenzie was showing he had deep, deep layers, and she wanted to uncover them all. What if he was her match?

"No, that's crazy talk. Two kisses and you have lost your mind." She waved off her reflection and headed downstairs.

Everyone was already outside on the patio, Ferris and the crew included. Ben waved the cast to their seats on the benches.

Ferris smiled wide from behind the heart-shaped podium. "Hi, everyone! Welcome to your second matching ceremony. Love Shack, baby, am I right? Wow, I was on the edge of my seat waiting for the results. And then, No Match! I mean, that had to be tough, right, Wesley?"

Wesley straightened, startled. His face flushed slightly under Ferris's stare. "Um, I mean, I guess? Esme's great. I'm at least glad to have gotten her friendship out of this experience."

"Friendship." Ferris's lips quirked up in a sly smile. "So, there was nothing going on when you two sneaked into the closet last night?"

Esme perked up at that comment. So much for Zack's theory on cheap production limiting or delaying the crew's review of footage. Feeling bad as Wesley stammered, she cleared her throat. "Now, Ferris, we already talked about the whole kissing and telling thing."

Ferris laughed. "And so we did, Esme. So we did. All right then, let's get to it, shall we?"

She fidgeted in her seat, nerves starting to get the best of her. Everyone had agreed since Zack had two matches last week, they should both use the same list this week. From there, everyone would start working with each other to help determine more matches, while continuing to take what the audience and the producers threw at them all.

"Just to recap, Esme and Zack are playing for a shared pool of a million dollars. Once their matches are locked in, we'll see how many heart lights appear." Getting serious, Ferris looked straight at the camera. "A blackout will result in the pool being reduced by fifty thousand big ones. Last week, Esme had one match and Zack had two. How will the hearts fall this week, folks? Let's find out. Esme, please go to the control panel and lock in your matches."

She stood and walked to the console, where she tapped the cast headshots to make her matches. As she walked back to her seat, Zack gave her a reassuring smile as he stood to take his turn.

"Just to remind everyone, the rest of our couples have a lot of skin in the game too. They're all playing for another million dollars." Ferris surveyed the cast. "Let's see how your two love experts did this week. Esme's matches will light up in pink, and Zack's will light up in blue. Fingers crossed we see lights!"

Suspenseful music piped in over the hidden speakers. Esme clenched her teeth. Reality television was so weird.

A pink heart lit up on the wall. More music. A second pink heart lit up on the wall, followed by two blue ones. The cast cheered dutifully.

Ferris stared at the lights, and the large screen hanging above the lights came on to show everyone the week's matches.

"Well, isn't that interesting?" Esme couldn't miss the hint of sarcasm in Ferris's voice. "You both not only picked the same matches, but they're the same ones Zack chose last week. I don't understand why you wouldn't make any changes?"

Esme suppressed a giggle at Zack's sheepish grin and shoulder shrug.

"If it's not broke, why fix it?" Zack leaned back in his chair, the picture of casual confidence. "I need more time to get a vibe, so I went with what I knew."

Ferris nodded. "Interesting strategy, Zack, I've got to hand it to you. But don't forget, if you don't have all the matches figured out by the end of the six weeks, you don't get any prize money. It's all or nothing here on *Perfectly Matched*."

"Don't you worry, Ferris, baby! We got this!" Kent said, pumping a fist in the air.

Madison giggled at his antics.

Ferris pegged Esme and Zack with one last glance and nodded to Kent. "I'm sure you do. All right, so let's get down to the business of this week's random dates. Zack and Molly, you'll be joined by Madison and Trey. Esme and Kent will be joined by Joy and Joel. Audience, voting for the location and activity of the Tuesday dates is now open by text or phone. Go forth and find love, friends! See you here for the Love Shack ceremony later this week!"

Everyone jumped out of their seats, but a loud whistle from Ben had them all sitting back down. Esme looked expectantly at Ferris, who was still at the podium.

"Listen up, cast! The production crew is throwing you a luau on the beach tomorrow night. Swimwear encouraged—Olivia wants everyone looking sexy. Aloha!" Waving, he made his way back into the house.

"That went well, I think?" Zack's breath tickled her ear from behind and a little zing of electricity flew through her entire body, lighting everything—everything—on fire.

"I'm not sure," she murmured. "I think Ferris is suspicious."

"Nah, he looks like that all the time. Let's go get some people together and play some pool."

Her face flushed at the word pool. She wanted to play some pool with him all right, the kind they played last night. She was in so much trouble, because she couldn't stop thinking seriously bad thoughts about Zack.

twenty-four

. . .

Zack

"WHAT DO you have to say for yourself?" Olivia stomped a high-heel clad foot, and Zack resisted an urge to laugh. She'd come storming into his bedroom just as he was finishing getting ready to head down to the beach for the luau of the damned. Remembering to honor the shirt-on-in-the-house rule, he yanked a T-shirt over his head.

"Look, Olivia, I didn't realize there was a rule against using my same matches from the week before. I was stumped and knew I had two lights last week, so I went with what I knew."

Her shrewd eyes narrowed under those blunt cut bangs, her mouth pinched, and the foot began tapping. Olivia wore her usual outfit; the sleeveless blouse was dark blue today.

He tried a sheepish grin. "Did I mention that color of blue compliments your complexion?"

"Oh, cut the crap, Zack. Why did you and Esme-Little-Miss-Perfect-Adams decide to throw up the same matches? I know something is going on, I can feel it. I have producer radar, and it is going off."

Zack tensed at the tone of her voice when she brought up Esme, and the need to defend her roused something new inside him. Commitment? A need to protect someone? Shaking his head, he focused back on Olivia. The time for introspection was not when facing down a she-devil. He didn't mind attention on him for being lazy or repeating his matches. No, that didn't bother him; he'd been singled out for much worse. But Esme, she was off-limits as far as he was concerned.

"I'm sure it was an honest choice. Esme's awesome, and

she'd never do anything to put your show or the process in jeopardy. She's the most committed person I've ever met to pairing people up with their true love. It is her freaking mission in life—saving the world one divorce at a time, or something. So be pissed at me, but you leave her alone." Crossing his arms, he returned her glare.

Olivia's eyes lit up, and a bark of laughter loosened her pinched lips. "Oh, Zack. Look, I know you're seducing her for the show because of our little wager. You don't have to keep up the act when it's you and me." She stabbed a finger to his chest. "When it's you and me, you need to drop the pretty-boy shit and get your brain working on how to increase the ratings for this show. I need a decent budget for the next show you'll be starring on."

Zack cringed inwardly. Olivia was intuitive and smart. She had a knack for reading people and knowing what audiences wanted, which was what made her successful in the reality television show business. Even her cheap productions were strongly received by viewers. She thrived on manipulation, and he'd just fed the beast.

Scoffing, he grabbed his beach towel. "Whatever, Olivia. Maybe you should get some rest. The match ceremony is all on me. I can be convincing, and I spent a lot of time this week rambling on about my theories on the couples. Esme probably just picked up an idea or two, which influenced her matches. Nothing more than my original plan is going on. Picking the same matches makes it look like we're in sync, which will get your viewers all thirsty for a showmance." He tossed her a cold smile. "And all is going according to plan. I have no doubts about my abilities, and you'll just have to find yourself another bachelor next season."

Olivia tapped a perfectly manicured finger—bloodred, of course—against her lips and eyed him with what he suspected was thoughtful contrivance. Great.

Clearing his throat, he put on his best bored expression. "Are we done here? I've got an army of hot women waiting for me on the beach. Can't let the other guys get ahead of me in the method, now can I?"

"Oh, yes. Your method. Right, that's what you and your army of seduction minions call what you do. Maybe instead of casting you as the bachelor in the next season of *Forever After*, I'll pitch a new reality show that follows a bunch of hopeless men being coached by the nation's best pickup artist."

Zack shrugged. "Do what you need to do, Ollie. I gotta go and make you more reality television. Don't want to let the fans down, do we?"

Olivia's smile widened, and Zack swore he felt the room temperature drop. "No, we wouldn't want that, would we? Have fun at the luau."

The click-clack of her heels faded as she headed for the front door and Zack sighed, throwing a hand up against the door-frame while the rest of his body sagged in relief. Olivia was a force to be reckoned with, and dealing with her took everything he had in every encounter.

But it wasn't like she could do anything. He and Esme were both under contract, and there was nothing in the contract or the rules that indicated who they could and couldn't put up as matches. It wasn't his fault Olivia's production and creative staff had overlooked a loophole in the absurd game they had created. All he needed to do was get Esme through to the end and the payday.

Zack surveyed the beach and took a drink of his beer. It looked like a party store had exploded. Tiki torches were everywhere. Alternating palm-tree and flip-flop lights were strung between poles stuck in the sand. In a portable firepit, flames flickered lazily. A volleyball net was up, and the house was having a rousing match of boys versus girls. His eyes settled on Esme, watching as she dived to save a half-hearted spike from the other side of the net by Wesley. Were those...? He squinted. Yes, tiny green frogs dotted her yellow board shorts. Zack laughed. As if she heard him, her eyes found his, and she smiled and gave him a half wave.

He was already feeling better after his run-in with Olivia, but the clouds rolling in from the ocean were concerning. Looking around, there didn't seem to be any production crew around, which figured. They had probably run for the hills when Evilia stepped on the premises.

A luau with a side of tropical storm, perfect. Whose idea was it to schedule an outdoor activity with no backup plan?

Kent strolled over from the volleyball game and grabbed a can of beer from the cooler. "Want another?" he asked, holding one out to Zack.

Realizing he held a crushed can in his hand, he lifted a nonchalant shoulder. "Nah, I'm good. Thanks, man."

Kent popped the top of his beer and took a sip. Whistling low, he tipped his chin at the girls, who were now pummeling Joel, Wesley, and Trey in the game. "Lots of sexy on this beach tonight. And I don't mean you and me, bro."

He kept his eyes on the game. "Yeah, lots of sexy. So, who do you think is your match?"

Kent snorted. "Who the hell cares, man? I'd fuck any of them six ways from Sunday, and then all over again. Can't wait for my date with Esme. She's hot, don't you think? Can't believe Wes managed to stick his tongue down her throat."

An urge to growl and pound Kent into the ground surged through Zack, but he kept his eyes on Esme and tried to count frogs instead of grabbing the other man by the throat. "Don't you ever get tired of the Rico Suave act, Kent?"

"Who's Rico Suave?" Kent's brows puckered, and he stared into his beer can as if to find the answer there.

"Never mind. What I mean is, don't you ever get tired of the game? Being a lady-killer and all? Do you ever just want some-thing that lasts past tangling up the sheets?

"Who are you, man? You feeling okay, Zack?"

Not taking his eyes off Esme, he nodded. "Yep, I'm great. Gonna get in on this game before the storm hits."

Esme

ESME LUNGED for the ball that Joel had lobbed over the net in her direction. Even though he stood several feet away with Kent, she felt Zack's eyes on her, and she had to admit it gave her a little thrill. And the incentive to put a little extra effort into her game. She had excelled at volleyball in high school and even played some in college, and it felt good to play again.

"Need some height on your team, shortcake?" Zack had moved closer to the game, standing on the sidelines.

She laughed and tossed the ball to Madison, who was decent at serving. It turned out Esme wasn't the only high school volleyball champion in the house. "I think we've got it handled, big guy."

A broad smile lit Zack's face, and her face flushed with heat as he stepped closer. "I mean, like big shot, not—"

"Uh-huh. Sure."

She socked him in the arm. "Stop teasing me!"

As he took his place in front of her near the net, he leaned over and whispered, "Can't. I love it when you blush."

And her face was on fire. Not two minutes, and he'd already undone her. A drop of rain hit the top of her head and broke the spell, and she noticed the wind had picked up. So much for the rockin-luau-beach-party the producers had dreamed up.

"Looks like the game's over, everyone!" Joel grabbed the ball and trotted around the net. "We better get inside. This storm looks ugly." He stopped to help Wesley douse the fire with water buckets provided by the crew.

"What should we do about all the stuff?" Isla waved a hand, gesturing to the decorations, coolers, and the volleyball net flapping in the increasing wind. She swiped a lock of red hair out of her face and tucked it behind a petite ear.

"Leave it for now. The producers can pick it up later. What's left of it, anyway." Zack looked up at the sky. "Nothing like a tropical autumn storm to liven things up. Everyone should probably buckle down in your digs until this passes. That way, we know everyone is safe and accounted for and can get to you quickly if it worsens. Although this street is above the normal flood lines, it still gets dicey sometimes."

"How do you know that?" Joy raised a brow at him.

Zack shrugged. "I grew up around here."

"Okay, in that case, I'll take your word for it and head for high ground." Joy tossed Isla her swimsuit coverup, and they jogged after Madison and Molly, who were already a good distance away, near the houses. Esme felt Zack's hand wrap around hers, and he tugged at her. "Let's go. It's going to start pouring any minute."

She ran with him back to the house. Zack was right—no sooner were they through the door and he'd slid it shut than the sky opened and water pounded against the windows. There hadn't even been a sunset; one minute the sun was dimming in the early evening, and the next clouds had rolled in, and the beach was drenched by the storm.

Esme shivered and was touched when Zack wrapped a light blanket around her shoulders.

"Want a glass of wine?" he asked.

"Sure, that'd be great."

Zack had found candles somewhere and lit a few on the coffee table in the living room and a few more on the kitchen counter. The large house shook with the rumble of thunder. Everyone else was tucked into their rooms. She pulled the throw tighter around her shoulders and eased down onto the couch, tucking one leg under her.

After accepting the glass of wine he offered her, she settled back. Zack sank down onto the floor and propped an elbow on the edge of the couch next to her. Looking up, he studied her face, and she resisted the urge to squirm from the intense attention.

"So, played some volleyball before, have you?"

"Mm-hmm." She took a sip of her wine and sighed when he raised a brow and waved a hand for her to continue. "In high school, my team was state champ every year. I played volleyball, softball, basketball, and gave swim team a go at one point."

"Wow, that's a lot of sports."

"Yeah, plus I was on the yearbook staff and belonged to a ton of clubs. I took dance lessons, but that was more Alex's thing than mine." At his questioning look, she continued. "Alex is one of my two best friends. We grew up together. I got into college in New York, while she landed an opportunity as a principal dancer with the New York Ballet Company."

"That's a lot of activities; I bet your parents loved driving you back and forth between all that stuff."

Esme felt a lump in her throat and took another deep gulp of wine. "Uh, yeah. See, that's the thing. All those activities kept me from having to spend a lot of time with my mom and guaranteed I didn't have to spend any time with my dad."

She had tried out for every team, every school play, and joined every club she could as an excuse to be invisible to her parents.

Zack dropped his arm, and his fingers brushed against her bare leg, making her shiver. Those eyes, stormy blue and intense tonight, focused on hers.

"Probably made it easier than having to say goodbye to him over and over, huh?" he asked.

"How did you know?" She searched his eyes with wonder. The more she got to know him, the more she realized just how deep his hidden layers went. And she wanted to dive into those layers.

"Esme, there's—" His voice cracked, as if on a word he couldn't say. "There's something with my dad…" The armor he pulled out every time he was about to be vulnerable seemed to slide back over his skin.

"What about him, Zack?"

Zack picked up his wineglass and took a long draw, breaking the silence. "In school, I had the exact opposite problem, you know? My parents didn't split up, but they spent every waking minute together, away on business or vacation."

His brow crinkled, and his eyes bored into the liquid inside his glass. She shifted, and he set the glass down and ran a hand through his hair. "I did everything I could think of to get their attention. The parties. Bad grades. They hired drivers to take me to school until I was old enough to drive. Then my dad bought me a sports car. I sold it and bought a bike, thinking it would get a rise out of him. Instead, they bought me two more cars and paid my insurance for the whole year. After I threw too many parties and trashed their house, they bought me the beach house. Though once I realized no amount of partying was going to make them care they had a son, I kept the beach house and paid them back in installments with my winnings from surfing. Didn't want to be indebted to them anymore."

Esme examined the liquid courage in her own glass as she thought about his words. Yes, the pickup artist bad habits were annoying, but Zack MacKenzie had so many good qualities she hadn't expected to find. He kept coming to her rescue, and she'd never had anyone take care of her like that before. Clayton had always been all about himself. She had been so caught up in creating her own love story, she hadn't realized how wrong theirs truly was. Maybe Zack wasn't such a bad guy, and it was her paradigm that needed to be shifted.

She reached out a tentative hand and threaded her fingers through his hair. It was soft, and her fingers flowed through easily. A bright flash of lightning and a clap of thunder made her jump, and the power went out, plunging them into darkness, save for the soft glow of candlelight. Her heart started to race.

"Zack?"

"Yeah?"

"Remember what you said about the next time we found ourselves sharing stories of our sad childhoods?"

He nodded, chuckling softly. "Yeah."

"The cameras are off."

She joined him on the floor.

Stormy eyes met hers and a muscle ticked in his jaw. Leaning forward, she brushed it with her lips. A low growl started in Zack's throat, and his words came out strangled.

"Esme—"

Trailing her lips along his jawline to his ear, she whispered, "How about we just kiss instead?"

twenty-five

. . .

Zack

AS HER INCREDIBLY SKILLED tongue teased his mouth, Zack resisted the urge to stop and cheer because kissing Esme was a flipping dream come true. He groaned when she stopped, her brown eyes large and lips swollen. Zack drew her closer and teased one of her perfect ears with his mouth, moving down to her perfect neck. She gripped his shoulders, and he smiled against her warm skin. His hand tangled in all that gorgeous hair. Her skin was so soft. When she rose from the couch and reached for the string on his board shorts, he all but came undone.

He grabbed her hand. "Not here."

He tossed her easily over his shoulder and carried her to his bedroom. In a perfect world, they'd be at his house with no cameras—power or no power—and no risk of what was surely going to be the best sex of his life being recorded in the annals of reality television history. But, he thought, with the strength of the wind whipping around outside, the electricity wasn't going to be coming back anytime soon. Shoving the door shut with a foot, he let her down and found her mouth again with his. He walked her backward until the back of her knees hit the bed and followed her down, amused by her little moan of surprise.

Zack laughed when Esme pulled at his T-shirt. Finding his first words since she had demanded a kiss, he spoke against her neck. "Sure you want to break the shirt-on-in-the-house rule?"

"Zack!" She wiggled beneath him, and if that wasn't Heaven, he didn't know what was. "Stop teasing," she demanded with another tug. "Off!"

He rose, backing off the bed and pulling his T-shirt over his head. Zack allowed his eyes to roam over the vision before him. Esme's dark hair was fanned out against the white of the comforter, and one arm was tossed above her head. Her skin glowed a light olive color. Delicate facial features and a generous mouth hinted at her Roma roots.

"Damn, you are the most beautiful woman I've ever seen," he murmured with sincere appreciation, and was rewarded with a smile.

He crawled back over her on the bed, sliding his hands up under her T-shirt as he kissed her again. Pleased when he was rewarded with another little moan from the back of her throat, his hands found her breasts, and he skimmed his thumb over the satin fabric of her bra. Patience was not something Zack had ever been known for, and he reached for the bottom of her T-shirt. Esme's hands flew to the hem, helping pull the shirt over her head. He tossed it away, not caring where it landed. Finding the front clasp on her bra, he snapped it open and ran his hands over what was absolute perfection.

His mouth trailed down her ribs, and he nuzzled against her belly as she squirmed beneath him. "As cute as I think these shorts are, I need to take them off you. Now." He unbuttoned the frog shorts, which were even more adorable this close up, and slid them down her hips only to reveal owl-printed panties. He raised a brow and looked up to find her watching him.

"I believe I've developed a new interest in animal print underwear," he said, sliding a finger beneath the elastic to see what else he could uncover. Humor left her expression as she threw her head back and Zack became a man on a mission.

Owl panties discarded, he held her thighs open and got to work. He lowered his mouth to her, experimenting as he discovered what made her gasp, jerk against him, and what made her hips buck wildly off the bed. Even after her orgasm had her writhing, he continued until he had wrung every ounce of pleasure from her and her only movement was the rapid rise and fall of her chest.

Hands unclenching the comforter, she reached for his shoulders, tugging him up and fumbling for the tie on his board shorts. "I need you inside me, Zack."

Sweeter words had never been spoken. He raised his hips so she could push his shorts down, and his left hand fumbled with his wallet on the nightstand. Once he found the condom he was looking for, he growled as he slid inside, filling her completely. The warmth of her tightness around him felt good—too good. He had to hold still, or he was going to come way too soon, and he wanted this to last.

All coherent thought failed him at the sexy noises coming from the back of Esme's throat.

"Zack, please, don't stop."

Raising himself on his elbows, he grasped for her hands, still thrown over her head, and threaded his fingers with hers. "Baby, if I move right now, this is going to be game over."

Her mouth parted. "Oh. I won't tell anyone…"

The concern in her eyes was touching, but Zack couldn't help his laughter, and he kissed the tip of her nose when she frowned. "No, I'm not worried about my reputation. I just don't want this moment ever to end."

Shooting him a sly smile, she wrapped her legs around his waist, capturing him tight. He moaned. Her mouth found his, and she engaged him in a kiss that would have been to die for if she wasn't already killing him, the sensation of pressure and pleasure rushing through his entire body. Sliding out slowly, he took as much time as he was physically able and relished the small ahhs and murmurs Esme made. And when he thrust back in harder, and she cried out his name, his release rocketed through him, and he nearly passed out from oxygen deprivation. He collapsed on the bed, tucking her in close to his side and kissing the top of her head.

"I'll be right back, don't move." Zack hopped out of bed and strode into the bathroom to rid himself of the condom.

Esme

ESME WATCHED in appreciation as Zack stood. His shoulders were just the perfect width and sleek, sculpted muscles teased the eye down to slender hips and the most amazing butt she'd ever seen.

Returning as quickly as he'd left, he slid into bed next to her, snuggling back in close. He wrapped his arms around her and kissed the top of her head, murmuring, "You okay?"

She snuggled in against him, feeling drowsy and satisfied. Zack was a surprisingly attentive lover, he smelled good, and it was nice to be held in strong arms. "Mmm," she said. "More than okay." *If this is what revenge sex felt like, sign me up for more,* she thought and smiled.

"What's so funny?"

"Mmm, nothing." She propped herself up on an elbow and placed a kiss on the side of his frown. "Just something Alex said once." She glanced at the alarm clock glowing on the nightstand next to the bed and sighed. "Power's been out for a while; I should probably get dressed and out of here before the electricity comes back on." She laughed. "Or I could stay, and we could shock and awe Olivia's audience with the showmance of the century."

Zack rolled over to face her, eyes intense. "Would that be so bad?"

Tempting as it was, it would not serve the show, her contract, or her reputation. She could see the entertainment magazine headlines now: *Matchmaker Screws Pickup Artist on Last Night's Episode of Perfectly Matched.* She and Zack both needed to see things through properly, not only for the prize money but also because she couldn't let the rest of the cast down either.

"I don't think it's a good idea," she said. "We should keep pushing forward with our plan to figure out all the matches and finish out the show, so everyone wins."

She felt him take a big breath against her.

"You're right," he said. "Hey, tomorrow night is my date with Molly, along with Madison and Wesley. And you and Kent go out with Isla and Trey. Any ideas of what I could do to try and figure out if Molly might be more of a match for Kent or Trey?" His fingers trailed down her arm, and she shivered against him.

Sitting up, she pulled the covers around her. "Hmm. You and Molly are not a match. And Madison and Wesley... Just no. But Molly and Trey..."

Zack grinned. "You've figured something out, I can tell."

"Really? How?"

"You rub your nose. It's your 'I'm onto a match' tell."

Surprised he was so intuitive, she stared at him for a moment. There was a lot more to Zack MacKenzie than pretty looks and smooth moves. "Well, it's just I think whoever the secret consultant is who came up with the matches intended Isla and Wesley to be a match. I'm positive they're one of the two lights we've gotten right both weeks."

"But?" Zack said.

"But I'm almost positive Wesley is gay."

Zack sat back against the headboard. "Huh. Really? That would throw a wrench into things, wouldn't it?"

She shrugged. "Maybe. Maybe not. I don't think he's ready to admit it to himself, let alone anyone else. It's a hunch. But in all fairness to the anonymous matchmaker, I could see him and Isla together. They do complement one another."

She jumped when Zack leaned forward and nuzzled her neck, his words whispering against her skin as he said, "Like we complement one another?"

Laughing, she pushed him away and stood up, taking the

sheet with her to look for her clothes. "Is that what you call what we did? Complementing one another?"

Zack followed her off the bed and yanked her back to him one more time. Staring into her eyes, he shook his head. "I call it making a connection. Meet me on the beach after I'm back from date night?"

twenty-six

. . .

Zack

ZACK STARED WORDLESSLY AT FERRIS, who bounced on his toes and brandished his microphone as they stood outside the Los Angeles Convention Center.

"Welcome to date night, Heart House fans! And what a date you've voted for today! We're standing here outside the LA Comic Convention. Are you super stoked, Molly, that the audience chose this as your date?"

Wearing a long, red wig and mermaid costume, Molly beamed and nodded enthusiastically. "Oh, I'm so glad because I thought I was going to have to miss it this year!"

Ferris's smile grew wider. "Can you tell us a bit about your costumes? I'm curious why you and Trey look like a matching pair when you're on this date with Zack."

Zack wasn't curious. He'd taken one look at the Speedo-inspired Aquaman costume and grabbed the Captain America outfit, sticking Trey with other one. Why this incarnation of Captain America wore a shirt that was slit from under one arm at an angle to the other, leaving his abs completely exposed, was beyond him. Still, better than Speedoman.

Molly twirled a lock of her wig around a finger in thought. "Well, my costume is Mera, the Queen of Atlantis from the Justice League franchise. I thought it would be a fun competition for us to go with an Avengers versus Justice League theme." Molly's gaze trailed over to Madison. "But that got a bit offtrack. First, Zack decided he wanted to be Captain America instead of Aquaman, and I mean, there isn't exactly a female angel on the team—"

Madison had insisted on wearing the angel wings she'd acquired on her and Zack's date and was prancing around in little else, completely in her element. She edged her way in between Molly and Ferris, bumping the smaller girl out of the way.

"I'm an avenging angel of ecstasy," she cooed, staring into the camera.

Zack noticed Trey shiver next to him, and he was pretty sure it was from terror and not excitement. Trey was a strong dude, but he wasn't comfortable in the spotlight. Madison loved being center stage, and she was amazing at it, but it put poor Trey right out of his comfort zone.

Zack leaned over and spoke in a low voice. "Stick with me and Molly, man. Madison is going to be so in her element. Once cameras start clicking and people want a photo with her, she won't even notice us."

"Molly looks good in a mermaid costume, don't you think? Who knew all of those curves were hiding underneath T-shirts and jeans." Trey tipped a chin toward the slight woman who, Zack agreed, minus the braids was a serious vision in mer-wear.

"You know what? Why don't you spend some time getting to know her more while you've got the chance?" he told Trey. "There are plenty of interesting panels to attend. I mean, what guy doesn't like comic books and awesome sci-fi television? I can hang out with Madison; she's going to love all the long picture lines to stand in."

Trey gave him a fist bump. "Thanks, Zack. I owe you one."

"Sure." Zack whistled and waved his shield. "Hey, Maddie, let's go mingle and get some photos taken together with some of the guest stars."

"Great idea. I know just where we're going first!" Madison grabbed his hand and hauled him through the convention center doors. She stopped at a buzzing crowd of women.

After twenty minutes of standing in line, Zack watched Madison pose with the actors from a popular network television show about brothers who hunted down demons and other supernatural baddies. He approved of their T-shirts, leather jackets, and jeans. Why couldn't Molly have been a fan of their show instead of superheroes? Something fuzzy brushed against his arm and a hand grabbed his ass. Turning, he found himself face to face with a... What the hell was it, a fox? A cat?

It held a paw up to its face and giggled. "You're cute. I love a man in uniform."

Another fuzzy something brushed against his other arm, and he was effectively sandwiched between the fox-cat and a ... uh ... rabbit-raccoon?

"What have you caught here, Jaxy? He's cute." The rabbit-raccoon swished her tail around and also giggled.

"You know how much I love Captain America. And especially this Captain America."

Thank God Madison chose that moment to bounce up to them, before any more furry creatures could join the party.

"OMG, I love your fursuits!" Madison nodded in appreciation at the two fuzzy ladies.

"Thanks! I am totally in love with your wings. They are so Victoria's Secret." The rabbit-raccoon jiggled from head to toe next to Madison.

"Aw, thanks, that's totally what I was going for." Madison twirled and preened.

"Right. Well, ladies, it has been nice chatting with you. Madison and I better go find our friends."

"Well, Captain America, if you ever want to explore a fursona, you just call me up at Jaxy's Furry Friends. I make the best suits in the city." The fox-cat curtsied, draped her arm through the rabbit-raccoon's, and they both skipped off.

FIVE HOURS and two hundred party pics later, Zack stood on the beach outside his house in the shadows, having ditched the Captain America costume for a pair of shorts and a cotton hoodie. He heard footsteps behind him, and his breath caught when he turned. Moonlight turned her silver. Fuck. She was hotter than any mermaid or angel of vengeance he'd ever seen in any comic book or movie.

"Hey, Captain America, where's your shield?"

Smiling at her, he nodded. "Guess you all watched the footage. I don't get why so many of the costumes are missing half or all their shirts. I mean, you'd think a superhero would want maximum coverage. And what's up with all the Lycra? I'd want Kevlar if I were a superhero."

"Hmmm, I think I know the answer to that question."

Esme stepped up to him and ran her hands up under his shirt and over his stomach. He crushed her to him and captured her mouth. Stepping back, he grabbed her hand. "I'm sure I can borrow the costume if it works for you." He laughed at the flush in her cheeks. "Come on, let's go to my place for a while. Nobody is going to miss us."

She worried her lower lip with her teeth and hesitated. "I don't know, Zack…"

"Come on, Es. It's not a big deal; we can watch a movie and spend some time together like normal people, and then we'll sneak back into the main house later. I told Trey when we got back that I was going to check the outside of the house and see what's up. And I walked the other way down the beach and around the long way to get here, so we wouldn't be caught on camera."

Relief filled him when her lips spread into a slow smile. "Wow, you thought this all through. You're smart and pretty."

He shrugged. "You think I'm pretty?"

"Pretty crazy, but you're growing on me."

Which was good, he thought, because she was growing on him too.

twenty-seven

. . .

Esme

ESME PLACED a hand on her stomach and willed the battalion of butterflies kung-fu fighting inside her to calm down. Sneaking out, meeting guys in secret, and breaking the rules—she was definitely out of her comfort zone. Walking on the wild side was both exhilarating and terrifying. What would her friends say? Summer would shrug and tell her to go with the flow. Alex was going through something with her spot in the ballet company and had a serious rebellious streak; she'd probably say screw it, why bother sneaking around?

She ran her fingers lightly over a surfing trophy shaped like a shark fin nestled on a shelf with other various medals and plaques awarded to Zack throughout his years as a surfer. It was all a glimpse into his past. Before he became an infamous pickup artist and messiah of desperate single guys. Why had she agreed to meet him at his house? Yeah, he was pretty amazing looking and expertly attentive in bed, but he was also sweet, and she told herself this was an opportunity to get to know him better so they could figure out the final matches before time was up.

Research. Hands-on research.

"Hey." Zack was solid and warm against her back as he wrapped an arm around her, and his lips grazed her temple. The butterflies kicked up again, determined to boogie the night away in her belly.

With a sigh, she leaned back into him and waved a hand at the shelf of accolades. "Do you miss it? Surfing?"

"I used to, but not so much anymore. I thought my life was over when I was injured and I couldn't imagine doing anything else, ever. Then Jake came along with an offer to help him open the club. Helping him and Cody out with that business can be fun at times. I like the marketing aspect—we get to put our heads together and come up with fun ad campaigns. And the guys who dance there are cool. Writing books and attending conferences also keeps me busy." He chuckled softly. "Jesus. I guess maybe I did inherit some business geekiness from my folks. But living on the beach leaves me time to catch waves, so I still get to surf."

"I miss my clients." Her throat tightened.

As if he sensed the shift in her mood, Zack hugged her tighter and murmured against her hair. "Want to tell me about it? Come on, let's sit on the couch and relax. Carrying a shield and avenging evil was hard work."

A giggle bubbled up through the tears she was choking back, and she let Zack lead her to the soft gray sectional he used to divide up the large open concept room. Dark wood floors, white walls, and clean lines created a very contemporary feel, accented by the wall of windows facing the ocean. She fell onto the couch with him.

"Wait." Zack jumped back up. "Thirsty? I feel like we should have something to drink. How about some hot tea? Stay there and don't move." He trotted off to the kitchen, and she heard him rummaging around. "You okay with lavender chamomile? My stock is a bit low."

Zack drank hot tea? The surprises never ended. "Sounds great," she called back, picking at the sleeve of the cardigan she'd thrown on over a tank top.

Returning with two steaming mugs of tea, Zack set them on the glass and metal table. "I have been known to be a really good listener."

She knuckled him in the ribs. "Yes, I seem to recall that from our first night in the house: your aptitude for listening to women's conversations and taking notes."

He tugged her in close to his side. "Hey now, you asked me

why I chose to invest in a male strip club, and I was honest about the benefits!"

Esme realized that without cameras or an audience, Zack was down-to-earth and relaxed. Like a switch got flipped, and the Zoom persona shut down. "Hey, Zack, if you were to plan a date, what would it be?"

"Why? Are you going to agree to go on a date with me when this mess is over?" She heard the grin in his voice.

"Depends on the date, but one hundred percent yes if you take me to a comic convention and wear the Captain America outfit again."

"I was thinking more along the lines of a moonlight paddle-boarding adventure. The way the stars reflect off the water is breathtaking; you almost can't tell where the sky ends and the water begins. In the fall, the beach is quiet. We could have a picnic. I'd bring blankets, just in case we fell asleep on the beach listening to the ocean."

"Sounds simple and romantic."

Esme lifted her head from his shoulder as Zack drew back. Earnest turquoise eyes met hers. "I'm a simple guy, Esme. My reputation says otherwise, but deep down, yeah. Simple."

With a will of their own, her fingers traced up the side of his face. How many women had he wooed with those same words? Did she care? What she was doing with Zack was revenge sex, nothing more. When this show was over, she and Zack would go their separate ways. For now, he was all hers, at least until she figured out who his match was. Then she'd have to hand him over to the lucky lady. Until then, though…

Her hand gripped his neck, and she swung her leg over him to straddle his lap. Trailing her lips down his face, she enticed and nibbled until they were lip to lip. A soft growl from Zack's throat had her legs clenching his hips. He grabbed her ass, grasping her tighter, and she couldn't help but notice the hard length of him through his shorts.

Her cardigan slipped down her arms as Zack's clever hands

caressed up her back and eased over her shoulders, tracing the straps of her tank top. Her breath came fast with anticipation. He slid a finger under a strap and slipped it off her shoulder, replacing it with his lips, and explored down to the tops of her breasts. His breath was a whisper against her skin, leaving a path of fire as he kissed his way to the other strap.

Growling again, he lifted her off his lap and set her on the couch. "Stay. Hold that thought. Condom. Be right back."

She shrugged out of the cardigan, even though she missed the warmth of his arms around her. Not wanting to sit still, she stood, wanting to find him and tackle him. But she stopped in the foyer at the bottom of his stairs when she heard the front door open and the sound of laughter. Frozen, her cardigan in hand, she stood with a hand to her mouth. She should hide, but her feet were rooted in place, expecting the producers to walk in and say, "You're busted!"

Instead, a man came through the door walking backward, guiding a pretty blonde into a scathing kiss against the wall, front door left open and forgotten.

The woman turned her head and, seeing Esme, gave the guy a good shove. "Jake, stop. We've got an audience."

The man took in Esme with a look from head to toe, and a wide grin broke out, lighting his entire face.

"Wow. What a surprise." He held out his hand for her to shake, seeming nonplussed with her half-dressed, yeah-I-almost-just-had-sex look and vibe. "Esmeralda Adams! Nice to meet you. Jake. Jake Preston."

Footsteps on the stairs behind her announced Zack's arrival to the impromptu party.

Jake ducked his chin and gave Zack a sheepish grin. "Hey, man. I didn't know you were going to be home. I thought they had you on lockdown over on the set. My place is still being renovated, and my girls are having princess night with Uncle Cody, so Ashley and I drove out here for some peace. But, uh, we can leave, since you two seem to be busy…"

Esme clasped his hand and finally found her voice. "Jake, nice to meet you too. I've heard a lot about you." Waving hi to Ashley, she turned to look at Zack, who had lost his shirt somewhere between the couch and coming back downstairs. His swim shorts were unlaced and hanging precariously. "Uh, Zack and I were just taking some time away from the set to talk strategy for the upcoming match ceremony."

The quirk of Jake's eyebrows and the amused smile on his face said he knew exactly what kind of business she and Zack were up to, but he wasn't going to call them out. "I've been watching the show."

Esme's face heated from the scrutiny of Jake's steady gaze. With whiskey-colored eyes and soft brown hair that fell in long curls, he could have easily been a leading man on his own reality show. Maybe one where he busted people in lies and stared at them until they willingly confessed to all their sins.

"Yeah? What do you think so far?" Zack leaned casually against the wall, calm and confident in all his shirtless, half-dressed glory.

"The editing is well done. It's been pretty damn entertaining, to tell you the truth. Can't believe some of the stuff the producers have you all doing. The desert? Now that was some funny shit, Zack."

Glancing her way, Zack gave a reassuring wink and pushed off the wall. "Well, hey, we probably should get back to the house before the producers send out a search party. I think we've finished discussing enough for tonight. You guys are welcome to stay here tonight. Jake—got time for a word outside real quick about the bar?"

"Uh, sure?" Jake followed Zack out the front door where Esme was sure he was restricting Jake's visiting hours for the foreseeable future.

"You look so good on TV." Ashley smiled tentatively at her. "Your hair is just gorgeous, and you glow. I love your clothes too. Though—" Ashley tilted her head sideways like a curious puppy. "You are so different from Zack's usual type."

Holding up a hand to stop the madness, Esme interrupted before Ashley could continue. "Oh, no, I think you're mistaken. Zack and I are just coworkers on this show, with a mutual interest in winning the prize money." She shrugged into the cardigan that had been forgotten in her hands.

"Oh." Ashley gave her a polite head tilt. "Of course. I just thought there seemed to be a real spark between you two. Maybe it's the editing."

The butterflies were back with a vengeance, trading in kung fu for sumo wrestling. Exactly what were the editors doing to the broadcast footage?

The front door opened and Zack stepped in, catching her eye. With a frown, he brushed past Ashley and stood in front of her. "You okay?"

Willing the fluttering in her chest to stop, she nodded. "Yep. Just need some fresh air. It was nice to meet you, Ashley. Jake." With a wave, she headed to the back door with Zack hot on her heels.

Stepping out into the cool night air, she started to head back to the set. Zack gently caught her elbow and turned her around. "Hey, sorry about that. I forgot Jake's rental was being painted, and I told him he could stay here while I was tied up with the show. I didn't think he'd take me up on it; most nights he's busy with his daughters. The single dad thing keeps him pretty tied up when he's not at the club."

He reached for her, and she steadied her shaking hands against his chest. His very naked, hard and toned chest. Damn the man and his penchant for losing his shirts. "It's been a long day; we should get back anyway. I have a big date tomorrow."

Zack stiffened. "About that date."

"What's wrong?" Was he jealous of Kent?

"Nothing. Just watch out for Kent. He can be a real asshole sometimes."

She laughed and relaxed into his embrace. "Don't worry. I'm pretty sure I can handle the Kentimator."

Zack tipped her chin up with a finger. "I know you can, but that doesn't mean it is okay for him to be a disrespectful jerk to you or anyone else. I hate leaving you to walk back by yourself." He squeezed her one more time. "Night, shortcake. I'll see you tomorrow." He brushed his lips against hers and then he was gone. Esme started the moonlit walk back to the house, missing the warmth and solidness of him beside her.

As she quietly sneaked up the steps from the beach, she ran into Joel and Madison on the back patio. Madison still wore her angel wings and costume, posing coyly while Joel madly sketched, drawings littering the ground at his feet. Humming to herself and tickled by their obliviousness to her presence, she continued inside and up to her room.

twenty-eight

. . .

Esme

ESME LOOKED UP, perplexed, at the sign flashing above her head. *Candi Land Gentlemen's Club* blinked in pink, then red, then pink, then red. Her eyes followed the arrow to where Ferris stood with Kent and Joel on the sidewalk outside of the pink-and-white striped building. Ben and the rest of the crew stood there too, cameras pointed at Ferris. Next to her, Joy puffed up in agitation and before Esme could grab her arm, she marched over.

"You." Joy pointed her finger at Kent, whose eyebrows rose in surprise.

Ferris slung an arm around her waist and tucked her in next to him while giving Ben the signal to start filming. Another crew member appeared at Esme's elbow and guided her to stand between Kent and Joel.

"Happy date day, guys and gals! Kent and Esme, Joel and Joy… I hope you're ready for a super surprise, because the audience has voted and you are about to spend the day—"

"We are not spending our day at a strip club!" Joy's voice rose in pitch with each word as she wrenched herself out from under Ferris's arm and circled back to stand in front of Kent.

Ferris shot the camera a grin that was maybe meant to be sheepish, but Esme knew better. She'd spent enough time around the host and the rest of the crew to smell a dramatic setup.

"Whoa, wait a minute." Kent's hands flew up in defense, and he looked up at the sign, then spun back to Joy just as quick, eyes wide with realization that they thought he was taking them to a strip club. "Hey, I don't know what's going on. I haven't been to this part of town since the show started, and last time I was here, this was an innocent burger joint called Freddie's!"

Joy narrowed her eyes at him.

Kent turned to Esme. "Honest. I was so excited to be here and for Ferris to introduce the date that I didn't even notice the business had changed."

Joy stepped in between Esme and Kent again, poking him in the chest. "Are you being serious?"

"Dead so." Kent made a crisscross motion over his heart, which looked silly when done by a grown man. "Cross my heart."

Joy's icy gaze fell on Ferris, which had the host taking a step back. Smart man. Joy was a force of nature when she put her mind to something, and if her hands on her hips were any indication, she was digging in for a fight.

"Ferris. Did you set this up?" Joy faced off with the host.

Joel leaned over to whisper in Esme's ear. "Uh, you think we could just sneak off? I don't think they'll miss us right now, and this is awkward." He smiled wryly at her. "So far, my date is facing off with everyone but me."

Clearing his throat, Ferris smoothly placed Joy in between himself and Kent, not missing a beat and knowing he should fear for his life. "Ladies and Joel, it is your lucky day! In addition to being a sales exec by day and what I believe is your every fantasy by night—his words not mine—Kent is also a busy philanthropist! Our audience picked one of three dates proposed by Kent. Spending the day at his literal pet project won by a landslide! You'll be enjoying a picnic at the park while the pups from Kent's animal rescue organization play at the lake's dog beach!"

Esme raised a hand to shield her eyes from the sun and looked across the street at a sedate building bearing the name *Blackstone Animal Sanctuary*. She glanced over to see Joy melt a little.

"You save puppies?" Joy's face lit up.

Esme had never heard Joy squeal until that moment. Within

seconds, Joy threw her arms around Kent, who laughed and hugged her back.

"Yeah, I do!" Kent turned to Esme and Joel with an arm still around Joy. "That's my nonprofit I helped launch a few years ago. I love dogs, and cats, and rabbits, and pretty much any animal."

"Dude," was the only word Joel could muster.

"I love animals too!" Esme's heart tripped with glee, unsure of whether it was from the anticipation of getting to hold puppies or because she was positive another match had just been born. Zack had added Kent and Joy as a match to her prediction of Joel and Madison, and her tingling nose was telling her that match was the source of the second heart light.

Kent shifted his weight from one foot to another. "I can't believe you guys thought I was taking you to a strip club today. Now, if it were just Joel and me on a boring night—"

Joy punched him in the shoulder. "You should quit while you're ahead. Can we go see puppies now?"

"After you." Kent swept an arm toward the crosswalk and escorted Joy across.

Joel held out his arm to Esme. "Uh, shall we?"

Laughing, Esme tucked her hand through the crook of his elbow. "We shall. Sorry your date has run off with another man. Let's go play with some dogs and let Ferris figure out how to wrap up his backfired intro segment."

As the rest of the group picnicked in the park, Esme sat backward on the picnic table bench and watched the show going down. Joy shimmied up the legs of a swing set and used the top as a makeshift pull-up bar. She and Kent were neck and neck in a contest of strength and will. The two competitors had already completed a long jump on the sandy beach of the dog park, a grueling footrace around the entire five-acre enclosure, and a tree-climbing match.

"Who'd have seen that coming?" Joel leaned back on his elbows and watched the action from behind his artsy, blue-tinted sunglasses.

"Why are you so grumpy? Missing a certain angel?"

Surprised, he looked at her over the top of his sunglasses. "What are you talking about?"

She smiled and twirled a stick an enthusiastic Labrador mix had dropped off in her lap earlier. "Maybe Kent just needed someone willing to kick him in the ass, and you just needed a muse for your new book?"

"Ah. So you know about that, eh?" Sunglasses back in place, he turned back to what was now a contest of balance as the contenders sat straddling the top bar of the swing set and stared out across the lake. "How did they even get up on top of there?"

"Don't change the subject!" Esme poked him in the arm with the stick. "You've been littering the entire house with drawings of Madison all week. The two of you sneak off so you can draw her in various costumes. Where does she get all of those, anyway? Never mind. Not important. You enjoy drawing her, and she enjoys posing; seems like a match made in Heaven."

Sighing, he took the glasses off and faced her again. "Madison's a cool girl. And that angel costume was inspired. You're right, she is a muse. I'm using the drawings in a new series about a fallen angel battling demons to redeem herself. I like her. She's smart and funny, and we have a good time just hanging out and talking. Plus, she lets me draw her, and that rocks too."

"You know what would be amazing?" She poked him with the stick again.

"If you stopped poking me with that damned stick?" Joel quirked an eyebrow. "Or if Kent fell off that bar and landed on his head?"

Esme risked a look at the swings and almost fell off the bench. Kent and Joy were now hanging upside down and swinging from their legs, which were hooked over the top bar. Regaining her balance, she pointed the stick at Joel. "No! I meant that if you and Madison got voted into the Love Shack this week! We could get a confirmed match. That would be helpful."

Joel nodded, a thoughtful look in his eye. A rambunctious black-and-white dog came bounding up with a ball in her mouth. Joel grabbed it and gave Esme a wink. "Yeah, that would be cool. You really think we're a match?" He let out a wistful sigh.

She smiled as he bounded off with the dog. Turning her attention back to Kent and Joy, she watched as they both grabbed the top bar, flipped down to hang by their hands, and dropped to the ground with ease. "I think so."

Her thoughts swung back to Zack. He was probably watching the live feed, and she couldn't wait to get home—well, back to Heart House—and talk through the day's adventures with him. The butterflies in her stomach had eased into a slow and silky churn at the thought of sharing ideas and stories about the matches with him, and a happy warmth twirled its way up through her chest to glow on her cheeks. She hoped he had been able to see all the ridiculous contests Joy and Kent had challenged each other with all day, and that he'd gotten a good laugh at the beginning of the date. She wouldn't say no to some rest, relaxation, and serious cuddling tonight. It had been a long time since she'd looked forward to sharing personal space, let alone her thoughts, with a man.

twenty-nine

. . .

Esme

JUST STAY *calm and be cool,* Esme thought as she passed the fountain out front of the house and made her way to the front door. Her arms and legs wanted to run, jump, and throw themselves around Zack, but thank goodness her brain was in charge. The first thing she noticed when walking in the front door was the absolute silence throughout the house. No television was on, nobody joking over the pool table. In the darkness of the night, a dim light glowed from a lamp in the kitchen. Weird. Where was everyone?

Making her way through the giant sitting room, she slid open the patio doors and stepped outside to more eerie silence. Empty hot tub, empty pool, and empty furniture. Things were getting creepy. At this time of night, the house should have been bustling. Kent and Joy had run off as soon as they were out of the car, talking about doing some other challenge, and Joel made a quick exit of his own.

Where was Zack? They hadn't made plans to meet tonight, but normally he hung around after watching the live feed of her dates. Each time he'd been possessive, and while it had been an annoying behavior, she'd come to expect and even appreciate that alpha side of him, especially when they were alone. As a matter of fact, she longed for him to be there waiting.

Not finding him on the beach, his usual moonlit haunt, she paused, knowing the cameras were watching everything, even if nobody was monitoring the footage in real time. Or at all, if she were to put trust in Zack's limited knowledge of reality television production. She sat down in the warm sand and wrapped her arms around her legs, watching the waves lapping gently against the shoreline. The day had been an incredible success, even though her own date was a bust.

Kent and Joy were obviously a match. And she'd already pinned a target on Madison and Joel. Two down, three to go. The odds were in her and Zack's favor, if the two of them could pinpoint the last three couples. The first Love Shack ceremony had ruled Wesley out as a match for herself, which meant her potential matches were limited to Trey and Zack at this point.

"Argh." She rested her head on her knees and gave up on trying to make sense of the matches by herself. She needed to find Zack and tell him about the day so they could put their heads together and figure out the rest. Or kiss more. Who was she kidding? Just thinking of him tightened her chest so much the butterflies fluttering in there must have been crushed.

The only place she hadn't checked was his house. Eyeing the cameras one last time, she set off down the moon-lit beach.

Zack's house was ablaze with lights.

Voices carried down to the bottom of the steps that led to the beach, and she heard his voice along with the tinkling laugh of … Isla? Her butterflies turned to lead and dropped into her stomach, and she heard the thud they made. Her throat tightened, and she found it hard to breathe. He wouldn't.

But he did. She crested the stairs and Isla came into view, sitting on the edge of his hot tub, her auburn hair dripping. She wore the very definition of an itsy-bitsy-teeny-weeny-bikini.

The gate gave a cringeworthy clang as she grasped it for support.

Isla's head popped up. "Oh. Hi, Esme!" Cheerful as always, she beamed up at Zack, who had just stepped out of the house with towels in his hands.

Esme didn't respond with a greeting. Déjà vu. Just mere nights ago, she'd stood by this pool as Zack wrapped her in a warm towel. Her vocal cords were frozen.

Isla looked from one to the other of them. "Uh, thanks again, that was helpful!" Hopping up, she stood on tiptoe. She kissed Zack on the cheek, grabbed one of the towels, and with a wave, eased past Esme and headed down the stairs to the beach.

While she had been out on a not-date with Kent, Zack was frolicking with Isla at his house? She should have known. How could she have been so stupid? Once a playboy, always a playboy. How many other women in the house had he been taking for moonlit walks on the beach or kissing against his stupid wall?

Zack stood right outside the door. Shirtless, board shorts slung teasingly low as usual. After running a hand through his damp hair, his face lit with a smile. "Hey, Es. You're back! How'd the date go?" Zack took a step toward her, and she took a step back.

"You didn't watch?"

"Uh." Zack's arm dropped, and he watched her, wary now. "No. Isla asked if I'd mind giving her a surf lesson, help her with some technique she's been working on improving. I thought it would be more fun to get the scoop from you when you got home. Was that a bad idea? Did something happen with Kent?"

Thoughts churned and burned in her mind. A surf lesson? Seriously? Thank God there were no cameras to catch this debacle. Matchmaking was her legacy. A talent passed down almost from generation to generation. Or maybe it was a curse, brought on by her mother breaking the chain of arranged marriages. After all this was over, she needed to go home and allow her grandmother to do all the marriage arranging for Esme her heart desired. Because Esme clearly shouldn't be trusted. How could she have been so stupid to think she shared something special with Zack MacKenzie?

He reached for her and enfolded her in for a hug, and she stiffened, feeling hot waves building behind her eyes. She wanted to believe he was sincere, but every fiber of her being twitched to run. Zack's arms tightened around her, and he pressed his lips to her hair.

"Don't do a runner on me, Es. Tell me what's wrong. What happened?"

Shaking her head to clear her thoughts or possibly to dissuade her traitorous inclination to melt into his hug, she stepped back. One of the cast members would have had to be in danger of disembowelment or loss of a limb for her to miss the live stream of Zack's date. What was it Molly was always going on and on about? Zombies and an apocalypse? Even that wouldn't have dissuaded Esme from the footage. He should have watched her date.

Her error in judgment felt like a brick around her neck, and she was drowning in regret. But he smelled so good: a mix of salt water, sunshine, and something uniquely Zack.

"Huh." She swallowed hard. "So, how many of the other girls have you brought here, Zack?"

Backing away another step, she shook her head and didn't let him respond. "I'm tired; it was a long day. I'm sure if you go hunt down Kent and Joy, they'll tell you all about it. I am going to bed."

She spun on her heel to head back to the house but stopped and turned. "And Zack? I think it's best if we just play the game on our own. You work your matches, and I'll work mine for the ceremony. See you tomorrow at the Love Shack announcement."

thirty

. . .

Zack

ZACK PULLED ON A HENLEY, shoving the sleeves up his arms. The cool consideration Esme had given him last night was nothing compared to the arctic freeze-out he'd been subjected to all day. Behind his eyes, a slow ache had grown, and he pinched the bridge of his nose. Attending the Love Shack ceremony sounded about as awesome as being disemboweled by rabid chipmunks. No, disembowelment sounded better.

After a quick glance in the mirror, he fixed his hair and strode out to the large living room used for filming these segments.

Ferris was on him as soon as he walked in. "Zack Attack, my man! Good to see you looking well rested today. Early night last night?"

"Uh, yeah?" A swipe of his eyes across the room verified Esme wasn't in attendance yet.

"Hmmm." Ferris tapped a finger to his lips. "Esme is missing, isn't she? I wonder why she's late."

Probably another ploy to avoid me, Zack thought. Sullen, he took his assigned seat to the right of the host chair. Last night, he'd rushed as fast as he could through Isla's surf lesson so he could get up to the house and meet Esme. Why was she so upset he hadn't watched the live feed? She didn't like being filmed and was so self-conscious about attention on her; he thought she'd be relieved that he waited for her firsthand account. But no, he'd fucked up somewhere in that logic.

"Here she is, looking lovely as always! Welcome, Esme. Now it is time to get this Love Shack ceremony rockin'!" Taking his seat, Ferris smiled at the assembled cast, beam turned on high.

Zack risked a glance across Ferris at Esme, who sat ramrod straight and kept her gaze pointed ahead.

With a signal from Ben, the host sprang to life. "Welcome back, lovebirds, to this week's Love Shack ceremony. Whew! How time flies here on *Perfectly Matched*! Am I right?"

"Hell yeah!" Kent helpfully supplied.

"That's right! And what an interesting week. I have to say, Zack and Trey, you do put the play in cos. Cosplay that is. Those costumes! What a treat! What did you think, ladies?" Ferris fanned himself with his note cards and shot a conspiratorial smile at the women seated on one of the couches. "And then Esme, Joy, Kent, and Joel shared a sweet picnic with cute, adorable pups. Which, by the way, Los Angeles, are available for adoption from the Blackstone Rescue."

"Hell yeah!" Again, from Kent, who drew Ferris's attention.

"Kent, you were technically on a date with Esme, but from what we saw, you spent a lot of time with Joy. I'd say you two actually turned love into a battlefield. The pull-ups and foot racing! What was that all about, hmm? Maybe you also had a little love connection on the side? And Esme, you and Joel were conspiratorially close at that picnic table. Any sparks there, you two?"

Esme jumped to attention at her name. "Oh, we may have been discussing some sparks."

"Ooh, that sounds deliciously secretive." Ferris rubbed his hands together. "And speaking of secrets, we've had a lot of sneaky, sneaky behavior happening around Heart House in the last week, and the audience just may have noticed, if this week's Love Shack vote is any indication."

Zack heard Esme's sharp intake of breath and saw her knuckles turn white as she gripped the sides of her chair. The guilt pooling in his stomach snaked its way up his spine and caught in his throat. He'd promised her they wouldn't be caught, that nobody would watch the footage of their night in his room. Had he been sure? No, it was just a guess. What a dumbass move. Esme was already apprehensive about the attention from cameras and of being humiliated on this reality show, and he might have just ruined everything for her.

"Stay tuned to find out who America may have busted, after these messages!"

"I don't feel very well. I need some air." Esme jumped up from her seat and made a dash for the back door, and Zack followed on her heels.

Standing with her arms wrapped around herself, back to him, she shook.

"Es, you okay?"

Rounding on him, she hissed under her breath. "You said nobody would watch any of the late-night footage!" With a shake of her head, she laughed but her eyes remained flat. "I should have never listened to you."

"I know, I know, and I'm sorry. If that is the big reveal coming up, I'll fix it. I'll call Olivia and figure it out."

"What? You're going to charm your way out of it, as usual?"

Surprise choked him. "Is that what you think I do? Charm my way out of problems?"

She just raised her eyebrow and stared at him coolly.

"Wow… It sucks if that's what you think."

Ben whistled from inside, and Esme headed back to the seating area. Shoulders slumped, he followed her and they took their seats again.

Wesley stopped at Zack's chair on his way back from the kitchen with Ferris and the crew. "Uh, everything all right with you, Zoom?"

Straightening, Zack held up a hand, and Wesley slapped it. "Yeah, man, everything's great."

With a nod, Wesley sat on the couch, and Ferris plopped back down in the host chair.

"Welcome back! You all know the drill. America had the chance to catch up with our couples on this week's dates and vote on whether to send a lucky couple into our very own Love

Shack tonight to see if there is a confirmed match from any of the dates. Of course, things don't always go as planned around the Heart House! Especially with this crazy group!"

Ferris turned to Esme, and Zack hated seeing the dread in her eyes.

"Esme!" said Ferris. "How do you think America voted?"

Her face was pale, and he imagined she was trying to regroup. Before she could answer, Zack jumped in, turning the spotlight on himself—waters he was very comfortable swimming in. "If I were voting, Ferris, I'd definitely vote for Captain America. I mean, that shield was pretty badass, and well, my mermaid date—need I say more?" He waggled his eyebrows at Molly, who giggled from her seat between Madison and Joy.

"Interesting! Thanks for that insight, Zack. Well, America voted, but not for any of our couples that went on dates this week. Episode after episode they've watched a romance blossoming, and their voices have been heard. This week, going to the Love Shack—"

What Zack had come to think of as suspense torture music was piped in through speakers during Ferris's dramatic pause, which only seemed to add to Esme's anxiety. She sat twisting her hands and bunching her skirt, knuckles white with the grip.

"Joel and Madison!"

Esme gasped, sitting up straighter. "Oh my God. I mean, wow!"

"Yes!" Ferris nodded happily along. "Let's take a look at what these two have been up to behind the scenes, shall we?"

Zack repressed both a groan and a sigh of relief as film clips of Joel and Madison's antics played on the big screen behind Ferris. His palms broke out in a sweat. Would it only be a matter of time or the need for a ratings boost before he and Esme found themselves up on that screen? Not that he would mind, but she would not be happy.

Ferris turned back to the group as the montage reel wrapped up. "So, if the happy couple would make their way to the—"

Madison jumped up with a squeal. "Yay! Let's go!" She grabbed Joel's hand, and they headed out the back door and down the path of flagstones.

The large television in the living room flickered back to life, showing the two entering the small room. Their headshots were displayed on the shack's wall monitors. Music kicked up, and the lights dimmed. Joel and Madison held hands, barely moving, the funky lights swinging around and around. A green bar flashed up on the monitors with the words *Perfect Match*. The cast exploded from the couches with cheers. Zack released a sigh of relief when Esme joined the celebration. He followed her out the front door when she fled the scene.

"Es, wait up." She rounded the firepit in front of the house and headed toward the beach. He jogged to catch up.

"Zack, please. I just want to be alone so I can process everything."

"Process what? What is going on? Ever since you got home last night you've been distant, and I need some help here, Esme." With a burst of speed, he managed to get in front of her. "I thought things with us were going well. Amazing, as a matter of fact. I think you're amazing."

"You know who I think is amazing?"

Instinct and the tone of her voice made him freeze. She asked one of those questions—not quite rhetorical but close enough that any guy would be answering at his own risk.

Carefully, he took a step back. "No, who?"

"Isla. I think she may be your match. And I can't stand in the way, Zack."

He considered her and carefully chose his next words. "Okay. I think this whole game may be wearing on you, Es. I don't give a fuck about the matches. And I don't want to spend time with Isla. I want to spend time with you."

She gave him a half-hearted smile. Cold fingers of dread curled around his heart. "Did you ever stop to consider that I don't want to spend any more time with you, Zack?"

Shocked, he stood there, hands on his head, as she walked back into the house. What the hell had happened? Shit. She walked away. No girl had ever walked away from him. He was fucking Zack "Zoom" MacKenzie, pickup artist extraordinaire. She wanted to walk away? Fine. He'd show her what she was missing.

thirty-one

· · ·

Esme

ESME GLARED at the costume hanging on the back of her bedroom door. What was with the producers and their theme parties? Tonight's genius theme was Arabian Nights, which came with the obligatory belly-dancer-meets-Princess-Jasmine costumes for the women. Vaguely Eastern-themed pop music floated up to her window from behind the house, where a giant Arabian-style tent had been erected.

She fell back on the bed with a sigh and threw an arm over her eyes, shutting out the world for a few minutes. Her stomach still churned every time she thought of the horrifying and public split from Clayton.

The morning it happened, he'd sat across from her at their favorite brunch spot, calmly eating his eggs Benedict while she ran down their wedding planning itinerary for the day.

"Clay, we need to make a decision on the song for our first dance. What do you think: 'Perfect' by Ed Sheeran or 'How Long Will I Love You' by Ellie Goulding?"

Clayton took a sip from his coffee mug, watching her over the rim. He set it down, a smile tugging up the corners of his lips. "What if we go a bit country? I'm partial to 'God Gave Me You' by Blake Shelton."

She held up a finger as her phone vibrated on the table. "Hold that thought."

Frowning at the unknown number, she answered, assuming it was one of the vendors.

"Ms. Adams, Elijah Wilcox from the *Post*. I was wondering if you had any comment about the photo on Page Six this morning."

"I'm sorry? What photo?" Her phone buzzed with another incoming call, this time from Alex. Hanging up on the reporter, she answered that call. "Hey Alex, no rehearsal this morning?"

Clayton's phone buzzed on the table, and he picked it up without looking. "Hello? Yes, this is he." He paused, then said, "No comment."

"Esme, have you looked at your Tik-Tok feed this morning?" Alex asked.

Esme glanced at Clayton, who was now very focused on his plate of food. "No, Alex, we're at breakfast and I haven't looked at anything yet this morning. Can I call you back?"

Hanging up the phone, she set her eyes on Clay. "Was that a reporter calling you too?" Annoyed when he ignored her question, she slid his plate toward her. "Clayton? What's going on? Why are reporters calling us?"

When he didn't answer, she grabbed her phone and tapped the music note icon. "Oh—" Scrolling through the feed, she lost count of the posts and stitches, but the one thing she couldn't lose track of and unsee? The photo. Of Clayton kissing Luke outside of a popular restaurant the night before.

How could she, a so-called relationship expert, have missed something like this brewing? And he did it with her assistant, a person she trusted more than anyone in the world with the personal details of her life and career. Was Clayton gay? Was he bisexual? How could she not know? Worse, the entire world knew before anyone had let her in on the secret. She was stunned. "Wow."

Clayton winced and leaned forward, trying to take her hand. She yanked it from his grasp.

He clutched his napkin instead, eyes focused on her. "We were going to tell you when the time was right."

"Don't you think the time was right before you both ended up on the city's largest gossip site? Look!" She shoved her phone in his face and waved it, her voice climbing in pitch and volume. "Everyone on social media is talking about it, and it's already a publicity nightmare! Look what they're saying about us, Clay!"

"Let me call Luke. He can get hold of your agent, and we'll clean this up."

"Oh, no. You've both done enough already. I don't need your help. I don't even want to look at your face right now." Throwing her napkin down, she grabbed her handbag and ran from the restaurant, calling Alex on the way out. "Can I come over to your place?" Not only had her future marriage just crumbled all around her, but her reputation and business were already being slammed on social media. She had lost everything in the span of five minutes.

She sighed and shoved the memory away. Cutting Zack loose was the right thing, especially since they were surrounded by cameras on all sides. She rolled her eyes at the memory of him laughing with Isla last night. How could she even have thought they could be together when he was nothing but a player? The way he taught men to manipulate women in order to woo them was embarrassing. And she needed another public disaster as much as she needed a third eye. She would rather cut out her own heart and stomp on it than experience another humiliation while the whole world watched and gobbled popcorn.

"What are you doing, Esme? This farce of a dating show is supposed to be your chance to reinvent yourself and your career, and instead you've spent the whole time chasing after another loser."

Addressing the room did nothing to improve her mood or lessen the impending doom she felt brewing from her relationship with Zack.

As the universe kept demonstrating, she was much better at picking matches for other people than she was for herself. Her focus needed to be on the cast, her clients. She was saving the world, one relationship at a time.

A knock at the door interrupted the thoughts rolling through her mind.

"Esme? It's Joy and Molly; we're coming in."

Esme fought the urge to cover her eyes at the bright jewel-toned clothes the girls wore. "Wow, you two look colorful. We're all going to look like veiled Skittles."

Both women were decked out in outfits bedazzled with cut-glass gems and accompanied by shimmering veils. Joy's was gold and Molly's red. Glancing at her own purple costume, she couldn't help but giggle.

Joy laughed. "No shit, right? I think the producers robbed Aladdin's closet."

Molly twirled, holding her veil out at arm's length, then brought it in to cover her face as she batted her eyes. She dropped it and waved a hand at the door. "We were sent to summon you to the party, by order of Ferris and Ben." She took the deep purple and lavender costume off the back of the door and shoved it at Esme. "So, get your cute butt in the bathroom and change."

"Wow, bossy much?" Taking the costume, Esme hesitated. "I don't think it's a great idea for me to go down there. I'm not very good company tonight."

Another knock at the door was followed by Isla poking her head into the room. "Everyone's getting antsy downstairs. Kent and Zack have been throwing back so many tequila shots I'm going to start calling them Jose and Cuervo."

A pointed look from Joy had Esme in the bathroom, stripped down, and changed into the Harem-Girls-R-Us outfit within a few minutes. She followed the others down the stairs and out to the back patio, where Isla grabbed her hand and tugged her down into a corner onto a pile of satin pillows. "I wanted to talk to you alone."

"About?"

"Zack. I mean, I was wondering if you two were like a secret thing or something? Because if you are, I'll back off. The other night when you found us at Zack's pool, I felt like there was some vibe going on between you two."

"No." She forced herself to smile while trying to keep her hands from shaking. "No vibe. He's all yours."

Joy stomped over, glared at Isla, and clutched Esme's arm. "Come with me. Let's go inside."

She let Joy drag her through the living room to the still camera-less closet, which had become the cast's hideout when they wanted to talk strategy or have a minute alone.

"What the hell?" Joy stood in front of the closet door she'd thrown open, frowning at what was inside. "Oh my God, scoot over and let us in."

Joy shoved Esme into the closet, where she fell into a very surprised and rumpled Ferris and Wesley. Joy squeezed in and shut the door. "Uh, does anyone have a light?"

"I do." Ferris rummaged around, and the soft, white light of his cell phone lit up the cramped space.

"Esme, what are you doing?" Joy demanded. "You can't let Isla have Zack!"

Esme looked from Ferris to Wesley to Joy and back again to Ferris and Wesley. "I knew there was something between you two."

Joy rolled her eyes. "Duh, who didn't? The way they make eyes at each other every time Ferris comes on set…"

"Wait, you all knew?" Wesley's voice came out in a squeak.

"What brings you two to the camera-dead space?" Ferris's brow quirked from behind his thick-framed glasses.

"Isla is moving in on Esme's territory, and she needs to stand up and fight for her man."

"Zack is not my man." Esme leaned her head back against the wall. "Obviously, Isla is his match. Now I know the one thing that's been throwing my radar off." She looked pointedly at Ferris and Wesley. "Is this why there still isn't a camera in this closet? Because it's your secret make-out spot?"

Joy tapped her foot. "Right. Forget them for now. So, all those moonlit walks on the beach and sneaking away with each other, plus the complete jealous breakdowns on the earlier dates all meant nothing?"

"How do you know about—"

"Oh wow, this is good stuff. Can we get out of this closet and turn our mic packs back on so we can repeat this for the cameras?" Ferris reached for the door handle and Joy slapped his hand. "Ow." He shook it out. "Esme's right, you know. Zack's not into her. Look, Esme, I like you and I don't really want to see you hurt, no matter what Olivia wants for the ratings."

"What?" Joy and Esme's exclamation echoed in unison.

Ferris nodded. "He made a bet with Olivia to win the show. He bet her he could seduce the matchmaker. If he does, he'll automatically win. If he fails, well, then Olivia can cast him in any reality show she wishes for the next ten years."

"Oh no." Esme held a hand to her stomach, where an ocean of regret was roiling around. "I think I'm going to be sick." She pushed out of the closet, ran out the back door, and sank to her knees a few feet away from the festive décor. Joy held Esme's hair back from her face as her whole body heaved.

A Zack-shaped shadow fell over them. "Hello, ladies. Whoa, Esme, are you okay?"

Esme nodded, refusing to look at him.

Joy growled at him, hugging Esme defensively. "Actually, I think Isla was getting ready to come over and ask if you wanted to go walk on the beach. Isla, come here!" Joy waved the other woman over.

Zack's eyebrows drew down, and a little muscle started twitching in his jaw. "Ladies, will you please excuse us for a minute?" he said to Joy and Isla. "I'll take care of Esme. I need to talk with her in private. About our strategy."

Isla looked between the three of them and stepped away in one graceful motion. "Sure. I'm just going to get a drink and see what the others are doing."

Esme stood glaring at him and crossed her arms. "Joy and I were having a conversation. Thanks for interrupting."

"Yeah, you moron." Joy scowled at him. "What kind of person wants to talk strategy with someone who is obviously feeling under the weather?"

"I said I'd take care of her." Zack threw his hands in the air, then pointed at Esme. "You didn't leave me much choice, since you avoided me at every turn today. And I'd like to go for a walk on the beach with you, so what do you say?" He held out his hand.

Esme studied his eyes, trained on her own, and his outstretched hand. How easy it would be to take his hand, walk past everyone, and stroll along the beach with him. That was the problem. Zack made her forget everything important. Every time she was around him, he wound her up, and she did things very un-Esme-like. All eyes would be on them, and she couldn't let it happen.

Biting her lip, she shook her head. "I can't, Zack. You need to focus on who is the best match for you, and it's not me. You live your life out loud and should be with someone who shares the same vibe with you. Maybe someone who likes to gamble a bit more than I do."

"Gamble? What do you mean? I don't even like to go to casinos."

Joy snickered and grasped Esme's hand. "Come on, let's go."

Esme stood her ground and squared her shoulders. "I know about your bet with Olivia. That's really low, Zack. Even for you."

Muscles danced along both sides of Zack's jaw as he stared back at her. "Seriously? You're upset about a joke I made before I even met you. You really think I'm that much of a dick?" He dropped his voice and took a step toward her. "Everything I've said and done has been one hundred percent from the heart."

"Well, there lies the problem. Right, Zack? Your heart doesn't seem to work like a normal person's heart. You think it's okay to manipulate women into liking you, and you've taught your philosophy to all these other guys at one point or another. It's just wrong, and I can't support it or you." She bolted for the door before the tears burning behind her eyes managed to escape.

"Oh my God." Zack ran his hand through his hair. "I teach guys who are otherwise shy how to talk to women. What, so it's wrong for men to flirt with women? It's wrong for men to act in ways that make them attractive to women? It's not my fault women eat the stuff up. Why do you spend your whole life matching people together if you don't think men and women should try to attract each other? I don't get it, Esme.

"No. You know what? I think this is really about the fact you like me and you don't want to, and it bugs the crap out of you. Well, guess what, Esme? Just because you're not the only woman who ever liked me or was attracted to me does not make me an asshole. And you know what else? Maybe it's time for you to start gambling. You've never taken a risk in your life. Esme, just let loose. Nobody here is judging you. As a matter of fact, they'd all probably fucking applaud if they saw you take a damn chance for once instead of hiding away in the background, thinking love is only meant for everyone else. You deserve to live your life out loud too."

She winced as his voice rose and realized the music had stopped. Everyone was staring, Ben and the camera crew included. Hot tears burned behind her eyes.

Nobody was applauding.

Zack sighed and threw his hands up in the air. "Who wants to do more shots? Let's get this party started! Isla, get over here and let's do body shots. Too bad Madison isn't here; she'd love this fucking party."

Esme felt a tear slide down her face as Zack walked away. Ferris looked at Ben, who whispered under his breath, "Ferris, that right there is your ticket back to *Forever After*."

"No, it's not. Just delete the footage, Ben. Nobody needs to see it, trust me. Call the control crew and have them take the other cameras down for the next ten minutes."

Ben coughed. "Are you sure? Olivia—"

"I'll take care of Olivia."

Ben nodded and called the directions in over his radio.

Holding a hand down to Esme, Ferris helped her to her feet and gave her a neatly pressed handkerchief. "Come on, Esme, let's get you inside and cleaned up before those cameras come back on."

thirty-two

· · ·

Zack

GRAVEL CRUNCHED under the tires of the car, and Zack thought the production assistant who was driving could lay off the lead foot. They'd get to Isla's family home all too soon as it was. It didn't help that with every bump they hit, guilt punched Zack in the stomach. Over and over.

The look on Esme's face as he had torn her apart at the party last night horrified him. Ferris had spilled the beans about his deal with Olivia, and he'd watched his budding relationship with Esme go down in flames. But even that wasn't enough to curb his need to be the center of attention. Esme thought they weren't a good match because he was outgoing and loud, but the idea of living a quiet life under the radar scared the hell out of him. Being invisible meant all he'd have was Esme, and she could leave him there alone anytime she wanted. Just like his parents and everyone else in his life. Hell, she already had left him.

"You know, scowling at the camera won't change anything." Isla placed a hand on his shoulder.

Running a hand down his face, Zack nodded and unfastened his seat belt as the car slowed to a stop. "Sorry, I guess I haven't been very good company so far on this trip."

Isla's sunny smile didn't help his disposition any. "No worries! I am just really excited to introduce you to my mom and dad and brothers." She hopped out of the car on her side and closed the door.

Just how many brothers did she have? He put on his game

face and exited the car only for Ferris to grab him by the elbow and yank him closer. "Smile pretty for the cameras, Romeo." Ferris let go of his arm as Ben counted down and gave the host his cue.

"Welcome back, America! I'm standing here outside the childhood home of the lovely Isla, for her and Zack's first *Perfectly Matched* solo date! Tell me, Zack, are you ready to meet the family of the girl who our other resident love expert has dubbed the one and only for you?"

Zack choked when Ferris slapped him on the back a little too hard. Straightening, he gave the camera a tight grin. "Well, Ferris, I've always been a hit with parents, so I don't foresee any issues."

"Oh Zack, surely a charmer like you has given a parent or a big brother—or six—something to be anxious about before." Ferris smirked.

Six older brothers? Zack groaned inwardly. The day was not looking good at all.

Isla smiled at him around Ferris. "I'm not worried. I think my family is going to love Zack. How could they not?" Batting her eyes at him and then winking for the camera, she stepped forward and waved him along. "We'd better get in there; I'm sure they're all piled up at the front windows trying to get a glimpse."

"We'll let you two get to it then." Ferris swiveled back to the camera. "Remember, America, you'll have the chance to participate in voting for the final Love Shack ceremony following this date. I can't wait to see who you choose! Ferris out!"

Zack stood patiently while the crew fit him with a mic pack, since Isla's house wasn't wired for sound. He pegged Ferris with a glare. "What the hell was that? Were you trying to bait me into a fight with Isla's brothers? And 'Ferris out?' Seriously?"

Ferris shoved his glasses up on his nose and scoffed. "Maybe I'd like to see you get your ass kicked. Would serve you right.

You made the nicest woman in the world cry on national television. And I don't have to explain my art to you." He huffed and stomped off to his waiting car.

Ouch. But Ferris was right. He had made her cry, and he felt like crap for doing so. And now he was stuck here and could do nothing about it until they got back to the set.

Isla grabbed his hand. "Come on, Zack. Let's go inside and say hi. I promise the rest of the evening will be a good time. My parents said it was okay for us to stay the night here, since it's a long drive back to the beach house."

Would it be okay? Because the self-loathing churning in his gut indicated otherwise, and the last thing he wanted to do was stay the night with Isla. Sighing, he stood up straighter and tried not to glare at the camera Ben held as he prepared to follow the crew up the walkway to the house. For once in his life, he wished all eyes were not on him. He'd break every camera he could find if it would give him the chance to do last night over again.

The front door opened, and an explosion of people poured out of the house and swarmed him to give him hugs. Isla favored her mother, but the whole family was picture-perfect.

Isla's mother squished him in a hug and pulled him along into the house. "Come on in, Zack. We're so glad you're able to spend a couple of days with us! We've all been watching the show, and it sure seems as though you all have been having a lot of fun. Maybe you can tell us all about what it's like behind the scenes? You all are just in time for supper."

"Sounds great."

He doubted the behind-the-scenes dirt would be appropriate dinner conversation and winced at the memories of Esme, her hair spread out, on his bed. Why was he such an asshole? After years and countless women, he had finally found the perfect one, and he fucked it up. Big time. And now he had to eat pot roast and potatoes with Isla and her family before he could even consider a plan to fix what he had broken. If it was even able to be fixed.

THREE SERVINGS OF ROAST, two hundred stories, and an actual family sing-along later, Isla led Zack out the back door and down a flagstone path. "Mom put us out in the guest house for some privacy." She looked at him when he stopped suddenly. "Wow, you look miserable."

"I do?" Zack cleared his throat. "I'm sorry. I'd be lying if I said I wasn't slightly intimidated by your pack of older brothers. Maybe we can keep this date PG?"

Isla laughed and tilted her head with compassion. "Oh, Zack. You poor thing. Look, I'm going to let you off the hook, okay?"

Zack stared at her. Let him off the hook? And why was his gentlemanly behavior so funny?

"Look, I have a fiancé. The thing is, as you've seen, my family is pretty traditional and what I'd call conservative. Right?"

Zack nodded. "Wait, you're engaged?"

"Mm-hmm. He's the lead singer of a rock band in LA that's really going places right now. The dating show was just a rebel move to annoy my parents. After I saw the cast though, I figured if I brought a womanizer like you home, he'd look like an angel when I bring him around." Isla snorted and laughed harder. "Only thing is, you've gone all gooey and soft and un-douchey lately, so it's kind of a bust. I should have targeted Kent."

Zack ran through a mental list of the matches in the house. Last night they'd outed Ferris and Wesley, and now Isla had a secret fiancé. Madison and Joel, Kent and Joy, Molly and Trey—if he took Wesley and Isla out of the picture, that left—him and Esme. His heart raced, and his pulse throbbed with the realization. She was his match. Flooded with relief, he laughed. He felt so completely wrong without her, and the whole time it was because it was right for them to be together.

"Isla? Can you help me find a phone? I need to make some calls."

The first one was going to be to Olivia, to figure out how he could get off this damn show.

thirty-three

. . .

Zack

THE ROOM HUMMED. The whole hospital hummed with machines that breathed for patients and performed other life-saving feats. Zack sat in the uncomfortable plastic chair, watching his father sleep.

The journal lay open on the bedside table, Dad's handwriting shaky on the most recent entry:

'25: Z. showed up for chemo #12. Brought terrible coffee. ROI: Everything.

Zack's throat tightened. He'd been so focused on winning the show, on getting that talk show deal to prove he was more than a washed-up surfer, that he'd missed what mattered. His dad didn't need him to win. He just needed him to show up.

His father's eyes opened. "How's the show going, hotshot?"

"I quit."

Dad's eyebrows rose. "The talk show deal, I know that was important to you."

"Doesn't matter." Zack leaned forward. "I met someone, Dad. And I screwed it up. But I'm going to fix it."

A slow smile spread across his father's face. "Now that sounds like a good investment. What's the ROI on love?"

Zack laughed, tears burning behind his eyes. "I'm hoping infinite."

"This journal was never a bill, kiddo." His dad tapped the worn cover. "It's how I remember you."

"I'm supposed to ask you about the BMW."

Dad smiled. "You always drove like a promise. Promise to what, I'm not sure... My wallet maybe."

Zack laughed, then stopped. "I want to pay you back. I want to pay you back for everything."

"You already are, Zack. You're here." Dad picked up the pencil with trembling fingers, reopened the journal to a blank page and wrote slowly:

25: Z. finally found the one investment worth making. ROI: TBD, but I'm betting on infinite.

The breath Zack had been holding his whole life could be released.

"So, tell me about her." Dad set the pencil down, eyes bright with interest.

"Her name's Esme. She's stubborn, brilliant, and way too good for me. But I'm going to try anyway."

"Then what are you doing sitting here with me? Go get your girl, son. That's a better investment than a talk show."

Zack stood, then hesitated. "You sure? I was supposed to win. I was supposed to—"

"You already won." Dad squeezed his hand. "Now get out of here before I change my mind and make you stick around for Jell-O."

"WHAT DO YOU MEAN, you aren't going back?" Olivia paced the conference room, the very room where his ego had gotten the better of him and set him on this insane journey of self-discovery. Her fingernails were sculpted to points, a style that fit her dragon-lady persona.

"I'm not going back to the show. I understand it is a breach of contract, but something more important has come up. I've already asked my attorney to reach out to you."

"Breach of contract?" Olivia slammed her fists down on the table. "Yes, it is a breach of contract. And you lose our bet. You lose your half of a *million* dollars, you get to pay me for breaking your contract, and I own your ass for the next ten years."

Wincing as each bullet point hit home, he nodded. But losing the money didn't matter as long as he got his girl. He had friends who could help him get a foot in the door somewhere in broadcasting. It would just take him longer. And if none of it worked out, well, there was always the bar.

"Olivia... Wouldn't it be even better for your ratings if I won the bet because I am actually in love with the woman? It would be way better for ratings than if the pickup artist just triumphed over the matchmaker. You could help make it happen. I can win her back with your help."

"Excuse me?" Olivia snarled and laughed at the same time. "I will do no such thing."

"You need *Perfectly Matched* and the happenings at Heart House to be a success, right? And you need high ratings on the *Forever After* finale? Why not combine the two and help me win Esme back? If I do, I win the bet, but you give the winnings to her. If I don't, then we can discuss the ten-year casting." Before she could interrupt, he held up a hand. "But I have a suggestion for that as well. Have I told you about my buddy, Jake? Single dad? He takes his daughters to this dance studio every week, and let me tell you, the drama among the dance moms is insane. And he's a good-looking guy. I think it would be a smash hit."

Olivia narrowed her eyes. "So, you're basically getting every-thing you want, and I get my ratings and a new hunky show star?"

Zack grinned, finally sure of himself.

thirty-four

. . .

Esme

OLIVIA PROWLED around the living room. Esme sank down as far as possible in the armchair of doom. The rest of the cast huddled on the couches, waiting to hear whatever it was the producer was going to dump on them this time.

She stopped her pacing and faced the cast. "I'd like to thank you all for your time. Without our other love expert finishing the show, we have no show. I'm canceling the production. Your per diem payments will be deposited into your accounts within the next five business days. The crew will start removing our equipment, and you are all welcome to spend the rest of the evening packing. We've already made travel arrangements for all of you and will be sending cars in the morning." Olivia left without another word.

Esme's heart pounded and her vision blurred. Zack wasn't coming back. Isla was gone too, which drew a scowl from her. The competition was a draw, her career was still dead, and she had no money. What was she going to do? And why did she miss him so much?

Wesley knelt in front of her. "Esme, are you okay? Can I get you something to drink? I think you may be in shock."

She shook her head and choked back the tears burning behind her eyes. "What am I going to do? I have no life since everything blew up in New York. I live with my mother and my grandmother. My bleak job prospects fall somewhere between screening applicants at my grandmother's outdated dating service and working at a doggy playdate matchmaking service."

Wesley patted her hand. "Well, dog owners are kind of crazy —they spend a ton of money, so you might be okay."

A sob broke through and his eyebrows flew up. "Um, I mean that doesn't sound bad though. At least it's something, right? And you have a life; you have all of us. We're your friends and we love you."

She nodded, swallowed her tears, and gave him a watery smile. "Thanks, Wesley. If you'll excuse me, I think I need to go pack." Her failure too raw to process, she ran for her room.

AFTER PACKING, she decided to visit the patio one last time. Esme flipped another page in the worn paperback copy of *Fifty Shades of Grey* Kent had loaned her to read. She was still shocked by the hidden depths running through the doofus Kent, and had never expected him to be a steamy romance fan. But the sexcapades of Christian Grey and Anastasia weren't holding her attention, and she set the book down as Ferris plopped onto the seat across from her at the table.

"How's my favorite matchmaker today?" He beamed, as usual.

She shrugged noncommittally and picked up the book again so her hands had something to do.

"Are you all packed up?" Ferris poked at her again with another question.

She slid a glance over to the host. She realized the show being over also meant Ferris was out of the job that was supposed to be his big comeback.

"I'm sorry the show didn't work out, Ferris. What will you do now?" She reached over and squeezed his hand.

Ferris leaned back, and she followed his gaze to the hot tub where Wesley, Joy, and Molly were engaged in lively discussion.

His lips curved into a smile. "Oh, I wouldn't be too sorry. I'm not."

"Ah, right." Her heart skipped a beat at the twinkle in his eye as he continued to watch Wesley. At least something good had come from the show. A few things really—a few of the matches did seem to be working out.

Ferris pulled a file folder from his satchel and slid it across the table. "Olivia asked me to talk to you."

She picked up the folder and opened it, and actor headshots slid out across the table. Confusion, curiosity, and utter anger at Olivia strangled her voice. "What are these for?"

Ferris cleared his throat and tugged at his shirt collar, then pushed his glasses up on his nose. "Olivia is considering a new show using some of the footage we captured the last few weeks. Those are actors we could use to film some shots that could be substituted in for Zack, including a show finale. I thought maybe you could help me choose someone you felt chemistry with—"

"You want to replace Zack with an actor? You're crazy, Ferris." She shook her head. "No, I'm not doing that. It's dishonest and doesn't feel right."

"Hmm. I told her you wouldn't be on board." Ferris tapped his lips with a finger. "Doesn't feel right because you think it's more unethical reality-show bull honkey, or doesn't feel right because it's not him?"

She averted her eyes so he wouldn't see the tears threatening to fall. Why was he so nosey and also so right? Ferris had an uncanny ability to ferret out information with just a glance.

"Did Olivia tell you all why Zack left and production shut down?" he asked.

Another shake of her head had him sighing. "I'd love to show you the footage, but I can't make you suffer that long." He beamed another smile at her.

She rolled her eyes and stood up to leave, because now he was teasing her and she wasn't in the mood to hang around and let him practice his reality show host schtick at her expense.

Ferris grabbed her arm and tugged her back down into her seat. "Wait a minute; I'm serious."

Esme studied his face, his earnest posture.

"Because Zack and Isla decided not to return?" Her voice came out in a whisper.

"Well, yeah, they both decided not to come back. But they're not together. Isla ran off to elope with her super-secret rock-and-roll fiancé."

"Wait, what? She had a secret fiancé?"

"Mm-hmm." Ferris leaned forward, way too into dishing the scoop. "She planned the entire time to find a way to take Zack home as an in-your-face attempt to sway her family's opinion of the real guy in her life. Batshit crazy, am I right?"

Esme drummed her fingers on the table. She couldn't decide if she was relieved at the news or offended on behalf of Zack. Huh. She examined the thought for a moment, let it roll around in her mind. When she started this journey, there was no way she'd have taken Zack MacKenzie home to introduce to her family. But now? Maybe she would, because she had caught a glimpse of the real man behind the player.

A wistful longing curled through her belly. The house had been quiet without him. Why couldn't he have returned and told her this himself? Because he didn't want her. Chewing on her lip, she looked at the headshots staring up at her from the table. If she had talked to him about Isla instead of distancing herself from him, would he still have left?

"Zack's right. I spend too much time in my head."

"Um, okay." Ferris quirked a brow at her. "Everyone does that sometimes, no?"

"Not like me. I find it easier to disappear and not stand out. You know?"

"Well, I'm not sure that's a bad thing. I mean, it's probably what makes you so intuitive and good at your job, right? Analyzing and figuring out peoples' quirks and likes."

Esme scoffed and waved him off, feeling her cheeks burn.

"No, for real, Esme. You are good at what you do. For the most part, anyway."

Startled, she frowned at him. "What do you mean, for the most part?"

"Math isn't your strong suit, eh?"

"What does math have to do with anything?" She shook her head at him.

"Well, you technically have three couples in this house and a fourth out at the honeymoon site."

Puzzled, she stared at him. Three couples? But none of the people in the house were her match.

"Me and Wesley, Molly and Trey, Joy and Kent…"

"And Madison and Joel! But that would mean—"

"That the person for you has been Zack all along? Perhaps."

"Ferris! I'm a terrible matchmaker. Was Zack meant for me the whole time? I mean, he's pushy and obnoxious and very full of himself and—"

"And pulls you out of your head where you like to hide? Yep. I agree."

She punched Ferris in the arm. "I was going to say loud. But you're right." She sat back. "And I really screwed it all up. I'm great at arranging other peoples' love lives, but when it comes to my own, wow, I suck. I have to find a phone; I need to talk to him." Jumping up, she yelped when Ferris yanked her back down and tapped the pile of headshots.

"Ferris! I am not picking a random guy from a pile of head-shots. I need to find Zack and tell him he's the one. I want him."

"You can call him after we wrap everything up. Look, if you are so opposed to picking an actor, which I told Olivia you would be, there is another option."

Suspicion wound its way up her spine, warring for her attention with the aggravation burning through her chest. She growled at the host in frustration. "What other option?"

"Whoa there, girl. Calm down. Olivia wants the cast to be at the filming for *Forever After's* finale. That way, the audience gets an additional glimpse of you all this week while she figures out what to do about wrapping up *Perfectly Matched* and saving some face." Ferris patted her on the shoulder. "Plus, the Zack replacement actors will be there to fill out the crowd; maybe you'll feel different when you meet them in person. I've gotta jet, need to figure out my next steps."

Kissing her on the head, he skipped over to the hot tub and laid one on Wesley before heading out.

Maybe she hadn't gotten her happy ending, but four other—no, five other couples counting Isla and her renegade fiancé—were getting theirs, and that had been her mission after all. Saving the world, one relationship at a time. Someday, she'd manage to save one of her own. All she had to do was film one more scene, and she would be free. She was not going to pick a random actor and pretend to be a match. She would get through filming, go back to LA, and put all of this behind her. Maybe it was time to find a new career. Something that let her live a bit more out loud, as Zack would say. Just not on television.

thirty-five

. . .

Zack

ZACK TUGGED at the collar of the button-up shirt that was insistently strangling him. Was it hot, or just him? Had Ferris been successful in getting Esme to the set? A clap on his back turned him in anticipation of catching hold of the pipsqueak host and interrogating him about Esme's arrival. Instead, *Forever After's* bachelor, Chance Wilkins, stood in front of him with a high-beam smile.

"Zoom! Man, I've read all of your books." Chance pumped his hand up and down enthusiastically. "I always wanted to sign up for a seminar. The way you and your friends can land any chicks you want, well, it's impressive. I studied your books and methods, and here I am! I've already got the network lining up follow-up shows, and sponsors are clamoring at my door, ready to throw money at me. And I've got this entire houseful of hot ladies at my beck and call."

Zack winced at the pride in Chance's voice and guilt churned in his stomach over how much he had enjoyed being the leader of his movement with all eyes on him. Esme was right. He was unleashing monsters onto womankind. He was ashamed of the man he used to be and the things he found important. Only, in the end, it had brought him to her, so he couldn't regret it all. He reached into his pocket, the round-edged box calming him. If he could pull this off, he could redeem himself and maybe change the minds of some of his followers.

"Hi, Chance. You can call me Zack. I hope you'll give the new books I'm about to write a look too. You could say I've had an eye-opening experience, and maybe my prior approaches weren't the most appropriate, especially when it's time to grow up and get serious."

Chance shook his head and laughed. "Whatever you say, but as long as I'm landing the finest ass out there, I'll keep playing. It's almost showtime; I gotta go warm up. Nice to meet you, Zoom."

A slight touch on his elbow turned him around again, but still no Ferris in sight. A small woman with almond-shaped eyes, a generous nose, and graying hair piled on her head in an elegant updo stood smiling at him. She looked familiar, but he couldn't place her.

"Hi, I'm Zack MacKenzie." He grasped her hand gently. "Do I know you?"

A wide smile spread across her face, and she patted his hand. "Oh, you might say I know you, Mr. MacKenzie. We met in a coffee shop a few months back while standing in line."

"Ah! Yes!" Zack snapped the fingers of his free hand in recognition. "I gave you my business card because you insisted I should meet your granddaughter, as she was relocating back home after several years." He angled his head and aimed a stern yet playful look her way. "You never called."

"Mmm." She nodded and withdrew her hand. "Not personally, no. But I believe a business acquaintance of mine did. Olivia Marcum?"

Zack stepped back. Narrowing his eyes at her, he wondered what her game was. Nothing good could come of it if she was in business with Olivia.

"Oh goodness. You didn't have a good experience on your show? Olivia hired me to help with casting the matches. I was hoping maybe you found yours?"

"Wait. You're the consultant matchmaker?" Zack took a closer look at her now, because there was something more familiar about her than just a run-in at a coffee shop.

She offered her hand again. "Miselda Lovesmith. It's a pleasure to make your acquaintance again. Now that introductions are out of the way, can we talk about what you're about to walk out on that stage and do?" She nodded at his pocket. "My grand-daughter is stubborn, and as you've learned has a mind all her own. I think you may need backup."

Zack's jaw dropped, and his mind raced. Matchmaker. Granddaughter. Esmeralda. Miselda. And family resemblance in more than just name. "Mimsy?"

Her laugh tinkled, and she patted him on the arm. "It's about time you figured it out. Now come along, let's go find our marks and get this show on the road."

Our marks? Zack followed her in awe, and they walked behind the facades set up in the courtyard as a backdrop for the *Forever After* finale set. Mimsy was a force to be reckoned with, and he could see where Esme got her determination.

Chance was out on the set now, facing off with two lovely and very anxious ladies awaiting their proposal. Zack mused how cutthroat this show was; there could be only one woman in the end. In another time, he'd have been stoked to get the bach-elor spot on *Forever After*. But fate, fortune, and a tiny woman named Mimsy had led him to Heart House and his real future. Well, maybe. If she was agreeable.

He swallowed hard, pulse racing. She had to be agreeable because he couldn't imagine his life without Esme.

Clapping and cheering from the *Forever After* live audience commenced after Chance's big finale reveal, and he came running offstage, pulling a screeching and cheering blonde along with him. "You're up next, Romeo. Good luck!"

Zack scowled as Ferris strolled onto the stage from another entrance across the set. Where had he been hiding? The host held one hand behind his back and gave a thumbs-up with the other. Zack took a deep breath, trying to slow his heart rate. She had come. Ferris had gotten her to their secret finale.

After the cheers and gasps at the ex-host's surprise appear-ance settled down, Ferris beamed at the audience. "Hello, every-one! I hope you are enjoying this gorgeous evening under the setting sun. How about that proposal by Chance? What a way to woo a lady... Or several ladies in his case."

Ferris cleared his throat. "As you may know, I've been spending my summer hosting a new show called *Perfectly Matched*." Waving his hands to quiet the clapping, he bounced on his heels. "Yes, thank you! It's been quite a show, especially thanks to your help, America!" Applause erupted again, and Ferris waited, soaking it in.

Zack growled. Since he was not a patient person, he stalked out onto the stage, and the crowd grew quiet. Ferris jumped when he realized he wasn't alone.

"Zack, so good of you to join me onstage after you went missing last week, you scoundrel! Want to give us a clue where you snuck off to when Isla revealed her fiancé? What do you think, everyone? Zack left us all hanging. Sadly, America, *Perfectly Matched* has been canceled and the Heart House closed for good. So Zack, what are you doing here at the finale of *Forever After*?"

Ferris pulled an extra microphone out of his back pocket and handed it to Zack.

"Well, I'm glad you asked me that question, Ferris. Good evening, America. And hi to my fellow cast members I see out here in the crowd tonight." Zack gave a wave to the crowd seated at tables on the patio as if they were attending a dinner party.

"Zoom rules!" someone yelled.

"Thanks, Kent, back at you, man."

He had to stifle a laugh when he saw Joy punch Kent in the arm. His girl Esme knew what she was doing when it came to matching couples. His. Girl. He saw her in the audience, a vision in a peacock-print dress, her gorgeous hair flowing around her shoulders. Zack choked back tears burning behind his eyes. He'd missed everything about her. He frowned at the stressed look on her face; he just wanted to see her smile again. He caught Esme's gaze and saw her try to shrink back into the crowd.

"Ferris, it's like this. I screwed up. Majorly. And I owe Esme an apology for my behavior the other night because I was the one in the wrong, not her. I've spent so much of my life chasing after other people, trying to be noticed... I never took the time to slow down and look at what I had right in front of me. And then a chance encounter in a coffee shop led me to this reality television show and the girl of my dreams."

"I see." Ferris watched him so long Zack shifted nervously where he stood. "The girl of your dreams? Does that mean you've figured out the final matches?"

"Well, I hope I have, for sure. If she'll have me."

Ferris looked out at the crowd and back at Zack with a grin. "You know, we're kind of hijacking another show here, and Chance's bride hasn't even had the opportunity to let us know if she accepts his proposal. Maybe we should take a vote. What do you think, audience? Do you want to continue to the end of the bachelor ceremony, or do you want to see Zack and Esme's final matches and what woman has stolen the legendary Zoom's heart after all this time?"

The crowd roared and began chanting, "Matches. Matches."

"Well, Zack, I think it's time to reveal your matches. Even if I do get fired. Again." Ferris turned back to the cheering crowd. "Should we get the cast up here and see how the final match ceremony ends?" More cheering erupted from the crowd.

Zack saw Esme hiding between Molly and Joy. He strode off the stage area toward her.

"What do you think?" He held out a hand to her.

She shifted her gaze around and squirmed. "What are you doing, Zack?" she asked in a quiet voice.

"Winning." Zack grabbed her hand and pulled her to the stage, and the other couples followed.

The façade behind Ferris lit up like a giant monitor, and on the left side were Madison's and Joel's headshots. The word *Matched* glowed in pulsing green letters above the photos. Ferris looked up as headshots of the other cast members appeared on the screen.

"All right, to refresh everyone's memory, we had ten individuals move into our beach house. A sly and talented love specialist helped us choose people who matched perfectly with another member of the cast. We may or may not have thrown in a surprise or two. Let's welcome our seasoned expert onstage, shall we?"

Esme gasped when Mimsy walked onstage and Zack felt her hand stiffen in his, then relax.

"Miselda Lovesmith, welcome to the final match ceremony of Heart House. Have you been keeping tabs on the cast as they've played the game this summer?" Ferris grasped Mimy's hand and brought her over to his side.

"Oh, I've watched every week. It has been entertaining, that's for sure."

"I understand you have a special connection to one of our cast members. Would you care to let everyone in on the secret?"

Mimsy elbowed the host. "Maybe we should let Zack and Esme put up their final matches, and then we can talk about secrets. What do you think?"

Ferris grinned at her and slung an arm around her shoulders. "I like the way you think, Ms. Lovesmith. Esme, would you like to go first?"

Zack felt her trembling beside him as she shook her head no.

"I'll go," he blurted. Before walking up to the console that had floated down from the scaffolding above, he turned to Esme, who was chewing her bottom lip. "Es." He squeezed her hand. "I need you to not only trust in me but trust in us. Can you do that? Trust us, baby?"

Esme hesitated and his heart thunked to his stomach. She bit her lip again. "I don't know, Zack. Is there an us?"

Zack smiled. "I'd like for there to be. Are you willing to give me another chance to show you?"

She nodded. That was good enough for him. He strode forward and punched his matches into the console.

thirty-six

. . .

Esme

MIMSY WAS ON SET? Confusion threatened to kick the kung-fu stomach butterflies' butts. Jitters were no joke. Esme's whole body shook while she watched Zack quickly punch in his matches. He'd come back, and she suspected he was partially responsible for this hijacking of *Forever After's* finale. She couldn't help the genuine smile that found its way to her mouth; it was such a Zack thing to do. And damn if he didn't look good in a button-up shirt and dark blue jeans, and his signature casually messy hair, which her hands constantly wanted to run through.

Old Esme would have been backstage and heading out the back door by now, but she was ready to stand up and take a chance. But she needed to stop and think. Mimsy was here. Mimsy had been watching the show and stood hand in hand with Ferris. The two of them beamed so hard the audience must have been blinded by the glare.

"All right, Zack has punched in his final matches. Esme, are you ready?"

Everyone stared at her. No, she wasn't ready, but there was no time like the present to embrace her new place in the spotlight. *Trust in us.* She looked up and caught Zack's eyes, as blue as the sea tonight, watching her with an unspoken plea. Her gaze roamed over the other couples onstage. Madison bounced up and down.

With a deep breath and a hand to her stomach to quiet the battle raging inside, Esme stepped up to the console, where eight names waited for her decision. Wesley and Isla's names were out of the running, due to having pulled out of the competition. One had run off with her secret fiancé and the other disqualified for an affair with the host. Joy and Kent... Those two as a match was a no-brainer. Madison and Joel were already confirmed by the Love Shack ceremony. Her hand hesitated over the console. Molly and Trey—a total surprise, but they worked.

Her heart raced. It was true. Zack had been meant for her. Elation released the butterfly battle from her stomach.

She tapped her and Zack's names and stepped back. Zack's hand found hers and squeezed.

"Wow, this is all so exciting," said Ferris. "As you all can see, we've got our unlit hearts up on the screen! If all the hearts light up, then you've all just won the two million dollars! If none of the hearts light up... But let's be honest, something will, right?" He waggled his eyebrows and Mimsy giggled. "If none of the hearts light up, then that's the end of the road. But I've got a feeling we're going to see some lights."

The stage lights dimmed and the candlelight from the audience tables danced. Esme stood as still as possible, trying not to breathe. Music swelled through hidden speakers, and a set of hearts lit up. And then a second set. A third set.

"Oh my God, you're killing us! C'mon!" Kent's voice boomed over the music.

A fourth set of hearts lit up, and the world exploded in a series of flashing lights, confetti, and cheering cast members. Ferris worked to get the cast and crowd under control.

"You all did it! Four perfect matches! Well done. What do you think, Miselda?"

"I couldn't be more pleased. Especially for my granddaughter, who is a brilliant matchmaker but has a difficult time following her own heart."

Esme swallowed hard, one hand clutching Zack's and the other over her chest. Her grandmother had chosen Zack for her. How many times had Mimsy told her the best thing to do was trust herself? And she'd never listened. They would share teatime, Mimsy swirling her cup after she'd finished drinking. One of her favorite pastimes was reading the leaves. Mimsy always said a matchmaker's greatest gift was her intuition. Esme had no problem following her intuition when it came to the love interests of others, but when it came to herself, she was intuition blind.

It was all too overwhelming. Zack tugged her to him, his arms going around her and drawing her in close. His lips brushed against her ear, and his whisper tickled, sending an involuntary shiver down her spine.

"Don't run away ever again. I've got you. Always."

And she realized he did have her, in every way. Body. Heart. Soul. Six weeks ago, she had walked into her worst nightmare— a reality television show—trying to save her career. And instead, Zack had shown her it was okay to let people see her sometimes, and he had saved her heart.

He stepped back, and holding her arms, he bent down to look into her eyes. "You good?"

The celebration around them had quieted, and all eyes were on her and Zack. She swallowed hard and nodded. He grinned and drew her offstage. And then he dropped onto one knee, taking her hands. Her heart beat in her throat. She barely registered Ferris dragging Ben backstage to follow them with the camera.

"Esme. I was a real schmuck when we first met. I'm not going to deny it. I made a bet that I could seduce the matchmaker I was competing against on a reality television show. I was cocky and probably obnoxious. No, I know I was obnoxious, magic tricks at the bar night and all. I never thought in a million years I'd meet a woman and in less than two months fall head over heels for her. And then you came along, with your sassy animal-print clothes, hilarious sense of humor, and innate goodness. You made me want to be a better person. The matchmaker seduced me."

He grinned up at her. "And I promise, I don't have any tricks up my sleeve tonight and no wacky props, except this one."

Letting her hands go, he produced a rounded velvet box from his pocket. "Esmeralda Adams, will you marry me?"

Silence fell over the set. Adrenaline tingled through her body and the fluttery feeling in her belly intensified. She was drowning in Zack's gaze, barely aware of what was happening around her. Mimsy's voice over her shoulder tore her back into reality.

"I think this is the part where you say yes, dear."

With a laugh, Esme lured Zack back onstage and fell to her knees in front of him, towing him down with her. "Zack, never in my wildest dreams did I expect to find the person for me on a reality television show. Oh my God, my heart is pounding in my chest so hard." She clutched his hand harder. "Yes! I will marry you."

He put his arms around her, and they tumbled over onto the floor. In one smooth move, he slid the ring onto her finger and kissed her knuckles.

"Thank you for giving this lost pickup artist a chance."

A chance at love with her perfect match. That was way better than revenge sex.

epilogue

. . .

Esme

ESME SHIFTED from foot to foot, clutching her bright-green skirt. A hand on her back and familiar warmth had her settling, and she leaned back into Zack. His breath tickled her ear as he wrapped his arms around her from behind. She caught his eye in the dressing room mirror. Her kung-fu butterflies danced every time she looked at her husband.

"The zebras on your skirt are growing on me, Mrs. MacKenzie."

Twisting her head to find his mouth for a brief kiss, her lips curved up into a smile. "Why thank you, Mr. MacKenzie."

"Maybe later we can lose the skirt and send them back to the jungle?"

With an exaggerated gasp, she turned and playfully slugged him in the shoulder. "Zack! We're about to go on camera, and who knows if these mics are on or off. I still can't tell, even after months of wearing them half the time."

Molly appeared out of nowhere in the sneaky way production assistants had of popping in and out of rooms unnoticed. She cleared her throat in apology for interrupting. "Hey, guys! You're up. Go ahead to the stage and have a seat on the couch."

Esme's heart flipped around and did the dance-of-the-butterflies in her chest when Zack grabbed her hand and squeezed, then led her out onto the set. So much had changed in a year. Zack's father was in remission, their book was climbing the bestseller lists, and she was married to the man she'd once thought was her complete opposite. He pulled her down on the couch next to him and slung an arm around her shoulders. He sat back, relaxed and open, inviting her to loosen up with him. With a chuckle, she settled back. Both looked at Ferris expectantly.

Ferris gave a nod to his camera operator and turned on the charm. "Welcome, everyone, to my weekly videocast, Friday with Ferris. I'm Ferris Jenkins, and today I'm sitting here with two very special people who are amazing friends of mine. They've some exciting news to share with us, and I hope you are as excited as I am to hear what they have to say! Esme and Zack MacKenzie, a lot has happened since you left Heart House and *Perfectly Matched* wrapped a year ago. Want to fill us in?"

Zack nudged her shoulder as a signal she should speak first. "Thanks for inviting us over, Ferris. It's been a while since we've seen you. Things have been so busy. I've missed you and our chats! But it thrills Zack and me to be here today to announce we have a new book coming out this week called *Opposites Attract*."

"Wow, sounds interesting, and the topic sounds like something I think the two of you have some experience with, if I do say so myself." Ferris leaned forward with a pointed look for the two of them.

Zack laughed. "I guess you could say that, Ferris. I'm just glad Esme agreed to give me a chance because I don't know what I'd do without her. And that's what the book is really about —looking for the person who completes you and not judging too quickly if they seem to be the complete opposite of what you think you want."

"And in addition to the book, I think you have some other news?"

Esme ignored the cameras and concentrated on her hand in Zack's. "We've launched our new dating app and have been working with Mimsy on growing the matchmaking agency. It's really taken off, and Zack, being the charmer he is, talked me into agreeing to a new reality show where we try new things together that take us out of our comfort zones. We've been filming for a few months now, and it's going to premiere next week. You may see some familiar faces, right, Ferris?"

Ferris slapped his knee and leaned back with a laugh. "Yes. Wesley and I may or may not make an appearance, along with some other former *Perfectly Matched* cast members. What's it like having your day-to-day lives filmed, now that you are together?"

Esme turned to Zack, getting lost in his eyes for what felt like eternity. "Easy. This man distracts me from everything and makes it all okay."

Zack hugged her closer and placed a kiss on the top of her head. "I enjoy every minute I spend with my wife and have no issue sharing with the world that I am the luckiest guy on the planet. I'm so glad she gave me a chance and agreed to marry me."

"Awesome. I can't wait to see what adventures happen to you as well as how things go with your clients as your business grows. I love you both. Thanks for joining me today. And everyone, go out and buy the book, *Opposites Attract*, which is available Tuesday."

Esme looked at her husband, and a thrill shot through her. Zack gave her a wink. He was perfect. Perfect for her. Real perfect.

Dear Reader,

I hope you enjoyed *Real Perfect*! Because I enjoyed this zany cast of characters so much, I wrote some bonus behind the scenes confessionals. If you want to read them, all you have to do is scan the QR code with your phone, sign up for my news letter, and you'll get an email giving you access!

Lyr Gray

about the author

Lyr Gray writes contemporary romance because she's a sucker for witty banter and second chances. A romance author and actor, she lives in Oklahoma with three dogs who think—no, know—they run the house, eleven axolotls with permanent smiles, and one skeptical lizard. All are spoiled rotten by this devoted pet mom. She's a fitness enthusiast, rom-com devotee, and firm believer in happily-ever-afters. *Real Perfect* is her debut novel.

Follow her online at the following social media sites:

instagram.com/lyrgraywrites
facebook.com/authorlyrgray
tiktok.com/@lyrgray